BEAT THE KETTLEDRUM

(A BABYLON/PERSIA NOVEL)

KRISTIN SWENSON

PG
B

First published in the United States in 2025 by Pretty Good Books,
Charlottesville, Virginia

Identifiers: ISBN 979-8-9989339-4-3 (ebook); 979-8-9989339-5-0 (trade paper)

PART I

(CA. 560 – 550 BCE)

CHAPTER 1 (MEDIA)

*T*he wind off the mountains was buffered with warmth. Another summer. The stream rushed with thirst-drenching snow-melt and flashed with sleek trout. Amytis's mount snorted at the splash as they plowed through. Water drenched her mid-calf boots, but Amytis hardly noticed. It struck her every time: this was the stream where she'd spent her last afternoon with Mandane. Never could she have suspected that it would also be Amytis's last day in Media for years, decades of confusion, pain... love and life. Babylon.

Who could have imagined – Amytis least of all – that she, the bastard daughter of King Astyages would become not only wife of Nebuchadnezzar but Babylonia's queen mother? When her son Bushu, as Amel-Marduk, took the throne just over two years earlier, Amytis had finally left Babylon and returned home to Media. She had hoped that her absence – a glaring reminder that her son's veins ran with foreign blood – might help traditionalists accept that he had pledged himself wholly to Babylonia, even called himself "Servant of Marduk."

Nebuchadnezzar, in his final year, had promoted the worse of those, his ambitious son-in-law Igliss (Neriglissar) to qipu of the temple in Sippar, giving the man even more power and credibility. At the time, Amytis had hoped that that would satisfy Igliss's ambitions. At least Igliss was still in Sippar, some distance from her son in Babylon. She tried not to worry about it, now, to have confidence in the strength of the throne, the elders of Babylon, and in Bushu's wise leadership. Amel-Marduk, she reminded herself. That was his name now.

Amytis retraced the path she and Mandane had taken that fateful day, through the woods to a clearing. It was a tangle of vines and undergrowth now. The fruit trees old, leggy – unpruned for years. Amytis pulled her mount to stop. Here, the shepherd slaves she'd known as a girl had finally gotten a baby – Cyrus, Mandane's son. The house was a heap of charred rubble – thanks and punishment for raising him as their own. Despite neglect, the peach trees were in bloom.

And that boy was grown, a young man, from what she'd heard, king of the modest land he'd inherited. As soon as she learned that the child was not dead as rumor had it but found, Amytis had been eager to meet Cyrus, whether in Media or in Parsa. But her father King Astyages refused it absolutely. His explanations kept changing, each as unsatisfying as the last – how Cyrus needed to focus on his own nation, attend to his Parsa without their meddling; that her presence there would make him look weak, needy; or how Media was her home now and deserved the allegiance of her presence. Ironic, that one, Amytis thought. Truth was, she didn't want to leave, wanted never again to leave this wild land. She needed Media, and Media needed her.

Amytis's legs had dried and her feet were warm again, if wet. She rode into a small village. Midafternoon, and the market was busy. A woman in the colorful weave of her tribe, felt cap flopped over one ear, looked up from the heaps of vegetables she was selling, one hand extended with an eggplant for a boy. She waved with the other. Amytis waved back. A young man carrying loaves of bread ducked his head in respectful recognition as Amytis passed, before he trotted along his way. She liked to visit, and she liked to come alone. The people trusted her more easily that way, and their trust made her safe.

Amytis reined in in front of a round building, the skin flap of its door fixed open. An elderly man appeared at the entrance. He nodded to Amytis and leaned on a worn cane, waiting as she dismounted. He followed her inside. There, three other elders greeted Amytis warmly and ushered her toward a neat pile of goods laid out on wool rugs. Bridle pieces wrought of strong iron in intricate patterns – vines and stags and sunburst circles – lay displayed with pride next to shields pounded thin and embossed with stylized images of forest and mountain.

"It's fine work," Amytis said, "such as only your people can do. The king will be grateful. A good year." She accepted a cup of steaming tea from a shy girl who darted back out as quickly as she'd come. "And have things improved with the Busae after my last visit – you've each got satisfactory grazing ground?" Amytis sat, listened, and talked with the men until the sun moved past the door. They rose when she stood, each nodding as she left.

Amytis remounted. She waved a goodbye and cantered out of the village. Things had improved within Media since her return. She knew it, even if her father wouldn't admit it, and was pleased. Amytis patted the horse's neck. They followed a winding goat path, criss-crossed with the hooves and padded feet of others unseen. Through branches black in the shadow of a blazing sun, she watched an eagle circle, lazy rings belying the swift death its talons could bring. Amytis closed her eyes and inhaled the smell of rotting leaves and new pine; of sweet blooming things; and musky hides, watching still in the darkness all around.

At the lake, clear as glass, Amytis dismounted long enough to skip a few stones across its surface. It was a bittersweet ritual, bringing to mind the man – like her, a nobody at birth – who still dwelt in her heart. Khai had grown his business of goods and services into such a broad-reaching family affair that she'd heard of the Egibi corporation even here, within Media's circles of influence and trade. But true to his word, Khai himself never came. Amytis watched the stone skitter the surface, hopping once, twice, three times before it sank out of sight. Ripples from each step spread out, collided, and moved on. For years to come, Amytis, upon whom the terrible grief of surviving a child was thrust, would replay that afternoon, wondering what she could have done differently. Had Anahita had been offended by the stones infused with illicit longing, absent a pure heart? Should Amytis have stopped to make a sacrifice or oblation to Mithra on a high peak or prostrated herself in a desolate valley? Finally, though, Amytis knew that one way or other, if not that day then another, if not Nathan then a different scribe would tell her, "They have killed Amel-Marduk! Your son is dead."

* * *

As it happened, with Amytis's son, the half-Mede on the throne, Igliss had gathered about him a party of traditionalists, elite Babylonians like him. Nurturing some "pure Babylonia" ideal, all the foreign influence in Babylon troubled them. They didn't blame Nebuchadnezzar, of course, not publicly. That would have been dangerous. But when he was dead... Well, they hated Amel-Marduk. The hostility grew easier to cultivate among others as Medes continued to emigrate from Astyages's incompetent rule to Babylon. There, they found themselves competing with Babylonians for less and less work.

Meanwhile, Igliss continued to feed his own ambition for the throne. His wife Cassiya, Amytis's first friend, couldn't control him. She had her hands full with their son. That boy was just as mean and disrespectful toward Cassiya as his father was. Cassiya was never a bold woman, but this undid her.

At around the same time that Cyrus took the throne in

Anshan, Igliss and his cronies began to challenge Amel-Marduk's throne. First it was simply a matter of contested rule: Igliss had solicited such a strong following that he began to claim to be king, even while he was still in Sippar and Amel-Marduk was in Babylon. It was untenable, of course. Only one can be king.

In August, unnamed assassins, never caught, slew the young king in his rooms. He left no heirs.

So it was that Igliss, son-in-law of the former king Nebuchadnezzar and father of Nebuchadnezzar's grandson, ascended the Babylonian throne. The degree of his pleasure was matched only by Amytis's grief.

It was indeed the Jewish scribe Nathan who delivered this terrible news alone. In the face of the storm of her grief, Nathan offered the only acceptable balm: silence. And remained with Amytis until she bade him to leave. Even then, he hesitated.

"There is more," Nathan said gently. But when Amytis raised her face to him, her eyes haunted, her expression ravaged by grief, he doubted the wisdom, the kindness of telling her this other truth. Then, no. It was better she hear it from him.

"The Egibi, Khai," Nathan began. He hated the hope that flashed across Amytis's face. He knew his next words would crush it. "He works for the new king now, Igliss."

CHAPTER 2 (BABYLONIA)

"*M*edia?" You want to go to Media?!" Khai said. "No."
He laughed at the absurdity.

Ever since Iddina had returned from Parsa, he'd been itching
to get back on the road.

"Ecbatana is *the* center of trade," Iddina said. "You know that."

"I also know that that's the home of our former queen...
whose son we killed."

"*We* Egibis didn't kill Amel-Marduk."

"Fine. Babylonia. But –"

"Besides, I though you and Queen Amytis were friends."

Khai coughed into his shoulder, buying time to collect
himself. When Khai spoke again, his voice was soft.

"That was a long time ago," he said.

The distinguished entrepreneur looked at his son, his eldest.
He was proud of the young man before him. But they were
different people. No doubt about it. While Khai had built the
family business – and name – from nothing, into a vast corporation spanning finance, real estate, trade, and more through savvy,
skill, and a lot of hard work... Iddina had grown up knowing
nothing other than wealth and admiration. Khai turned back to

his desk on which several clay tablets lay waiting his review. "We have plenty to do here."

"It's drying up, though. You've said so yourself. Ever since Nebuchadnezzar died and all that construction and renovation tapered off, skilled exiles competing for jobs..."

"Some work is harder to get, yes. But for us... besides the other matter, I can't let you go. We've finally got some real land – that new date orchard." Khai paused, scratching his chin. "I don't yet know what we'll do with the salty section."

"What if I took a team northwest, instead?"

Khai looked at his son, grudgingly pleased to recognize the same eager ambition, after all. From a no-name farmer on the fringe of Babylon, Khai had worked for the king himself – and for queen Amytis, too. Until... Khai shook away the memory. In a way, he still worked for her, though Amytis had long ago moved back the long miles to Media. That he now managed the assets of Babylon's most elite citizenry was good work, yes; but it also enabled him to protect – indirectly, anyway – the land she loved.

"I could intersect with the same trade route but stay out of Ecbatana, well west of it."

"Hmm. Maybe," Khai said. "That new Lydian king... what's his name?"

"Croesus?"

"Yes, Croesus, " Khai said. "Word has it that he's been snatching up Greek settlements along the coast and making the most of lucrative trade across the sea. I think Sardis is nearly on the coast, just across from the sea from mainland Greece. Still, I'm not sure that Croesus and Astyages aren't friends, maybe even related. Didn't Astyages's sister marry Croesus? Or maybe it was the other way around..."

"I don't know. You taught me to stay out of such things," Iddina said, scowling. "I'd be fine. It's just trade, after all."

"I'll think about it. And stop pouting. You're too old for that." Khai waved his son away and returned to his bookkeeping.

A servant knocked at the open door. "Sir?"

Khai looked up.

"The king would see you."

"Now?"

"I believe so. Yes."

Khai sighed. He put down his stylus, slipped on the stiff outer robe that his daughter had left hanging from a hook that morning, and set out for the palace.

* * *

IGLISS SAT in Babylon's throne as if it grew out of his ass, Khai thought. He crossed the same stones he had first crossed, a poorer man but with huge ambitions, to consult with the late, great Nebuchadnezzar. Like then, behind the throne stood the king's favorite courtier -- Belshazzar, in this case -- just as Igliss had once stood. Khai felt a sudden tug in his chest at the absence of Amytis's vivacious face. These days, Queen Cassiya hardly ever appeared outside of her quarters.

The crown prince Labashi-Marduk, on the other hand, came and went exactly as he pleased. Slaves and servants were obliged to satisfy the child's every wish. Sometimes he sat in the throne room with his father, on a diminutive throne made just for him. He would appear occasionally, bedecked in flamboyant robes strung with golden bracteates, wearing his own crown. The boy, about seven years old now, expected every homage. He even carried a miniature version of Igliss's scepter. And when the prince got tired of hearing complaints from shepherds about the price of wool, widows cheated out of dowry earnings, and priests about the constantly necessary temple repairs, he simply got up and left, stirring a bevy of anxious and obsequious servants to followed in his wake.

Khai was relieved, as he crossed the hall, to see the child prince's throne empty. "My lord," Khai said, bowing to the king.

Though they had had a long business relationship, Khai learned that Igliss as king hungered for all exhibitions of deference and constant recognition of his lofty position and was quick to anger, if denied them.

Igliss sat back, deep in the throne. "It has come to my attention that there's trouble up north. They say a renegade king – Appuašu – has expanded into Syria, Babylonian territory. Nabonidus advises me to take an army and put it down immediately."

Nabonidus. The king had been smart to keep him on, not that he posed any threat to Igliss's position or reputation. On the contrary. Nabonidus worked for Babylonia as if he had been born here, Khai thought. Through a succession of kings, he had accommodated himself to the court like an intelligent beast to its task – without ambition but with an honest dedication and abilities that inevitably propelled him into positions of greater and greater responsibility. It helped that his mother, transplanted from Harran was so well liked. She had leveraged her popularity in Nabonidus's best interest, that and in the interest of their native god, Nanna-Suen. If there was anything "off" about Nabonidus it was his devotion to the moon god – a minor thing, given the circumstances.

Igliss shifted on throne. He leaned forward and gripped his fingers, tugging the long digits. His eyes darted about. "I suppose I have to go." He knit his fingers tightly together.

"At least we have a military unrivaled in the world, my lord."

Igliss sat back a little. "Yes. Yes, we do."

Khai waited.

"I want you to procure supplies necessary for the campaign."

"As you wish, of course." Khai nodded. "But can you tell me, my lord, do you mean armaments? Food? Means of transport? Bandages and medicine for the wounded?" It was dangerous to goad the man, poke at his insecurities. Sometimes Khai couldn't help it. Everyone knew it was Neriglissar who had killed

Amytis's son – not with his own hands. But it wasn't much different.

Igliss flushed. "Nabonidus will tell you what we need." Igliss brushed his hands over the throne's arms as if to polish it yet further. Then, having regained full confidence, he leaned forward. "We've known each other a long time," he said.

Unbidden, to Khai's mind leapt images of their journey, decades ago to Media to the palace at Ecbatana to fetch the princess who would become Nebuchadnezzar's wife. He remembered how hungrily Igliss had watched the lush landscape – all those trees, seeming endless miles of them (and lumber so scarce in Babylon). Igliss knew they could pressure King Astyages to give in, give it all up. It was all within grasp. The treaty granting equal status between the empires had never been ratified. They hadn't reckoned on the girl – no princess but a fierce bastard. Khai grinned to recall how she thrust herself forward, demanding answers. Amytis. His heart hurt. The smile fell away. Igliss had never lost his desire for wild Media's riches – the timber and what lay beneath those wild mountains and streams.

"Under the previous administration and Nebuchadnezzar's too, you managed some of the palace affairs..."

"Yes," Khai said, only that. Though the memories were vivid. It had started with those gardens – monumental, like everything Nebuchadnezzar did, and controversial like everything connected to Amytis. Khai noticed that Igliss hadn't used Amel-Marduk's name, "previous administration," indeed.

"You even managed to continue to grow your own holdings at the same time. Impressive." Igliss looked down his long nose and fixed Khai with narrow eyes. "I'd like you to handle the business of my... business."

Khai stepped back in surprise. Igliss obviously didn't know the antipathy Khai had for him. His first reaction was No. He didn't relish the idea of working closely with this man. Yet to manage the king's finances – investments and so on – was not only prestigious but could enable Khai to control the king's interests elsewhere. He could try to protect Media. Khai stepped forward again.

"I will do so. Sir," and nodded deeply.

* * *

A SMALL FORM some yards ahead caught Khai's eye as he walked out of the audience hall. Adad-guppi. He trotted to catch up. The old woman didn't hear as well and moved less quickly than before; but even now, nearly 90 years old, she was energetic and sharp. Khai put a hand gently on her shoulder and was rewarded with a wide grin and a dry kiss on each cheek.

"Sit down, boy," she said to him, signaling to a bench in the hallway. "Tell me, how is your family? your beautiful wife, and children -- how many now?"

"We've got three boys and a little girl for whom I'd trade in all the others." Khai's eyes danced thinking of his daughter, unapologetically his favorite.

"No weddings, yet?"

Khai shook his head. "Iddina is old enough – twenty-three years old, he is." Khai snorted. Time went so fast. "Loves the travel part of our business... And the profit."

"You're continuing as Igliss's business agent, too?"

"You knew before I, old mother," he said, using the Babylonian endearment of respect for an elderly woman.

"Congratulations."

Pursed lips qualified Khai's smile. "And how are things here?"

"Some the same, some different. To be expected," she said. "We adapt."

"I saw your grandson Belshazzar. He seems comfortably established with the new king."

"Palace life suits him. Nabonidus, on the other hand," Adad-guppi raised her hands, palms out. "Well, you know my son."

"People like Nabonidus. They trust him."

"The gods have been good to us here. Still, Nanna-Suen, *my* god, remains silent. If only the king would fix his temple in Harran. I've tried to get Nabonidus or Belshazzar to convince him to get started, but they say that Igliss is too touchy to take suggestions just yet. Truth is, Belshazzar is too caught up in Igliss's traditionalism, too worried about fitting in with the conservative elite to embrace my beliefs, his silly old grandmother. If you could find a way --"

"Medes control the area, though, don't they?"

"Yes, with occupying forces in Harran to prove it. Things between us were much better when Queen Amytis was here." She fixed bright eyes on the trim man before her, even more handsome with age, it seemed.

"Yes." Khai glanced at the ground. "Yes, they were." He stood and took her gnarled hands gently between his own. The tattoo of Nanna-Suen's crescent moon that she had etched on the back of her right hand was fading but still visible. He returned Adad-guppi's kisses, her wrinkled cheeks soft against his and walked on.

Adad-guppi remained on the bench. The air around was warm, heavy. It made her melancholy and nostalgic. She had always liked the entrepreneurial merchant scribe and was sorry that things went as they had with the former queen. Adad-guppi had guessed what transpired between Amytis and Khai but never said a word. Long ago, the old woman had determined that for all the gossip that she loved to share, some things shouldn't be said.

CHAPTER 3 (PARSA)

"*G*o ahead, tell him yourself," Nahhunte said to the little girl standing before Cyrus and Cassandane. The young king and queen had been lingering over their afternoon meal and sat, arms entwined, looking out over the kitchen garden and past Anshan's palace walls, rosy in the late day sun. Baby Cambyses slept in a cradle just out of the sun. Evenings such as this had become especially precious to the couple – something to do with how knowing that a thing will end sweetens it beyond imagining. Anshan had been the capital, site of Parsa's palace for generations. Recently restored – small and simple, but healthy – it was again the place Mandane had come to love – the place and its late king Cambyses. It would always be important to their son Cyrus but more important still was the woman beside him and her Parsa home. Cyrus loved Pasargad as his own and wanted nothing more than to settle his family – and Parsa's throne – there forever.

Cook swung through the kitchen doors behind them, took in the adults, the child nervously clutching and unclutching the fabric at her sides. "What's this?" Cook asked.

"Nahhunte reports that the girl, a shepherd, found something in the hills beyond," Cyrus said. "She is about to tell us what it is. When she gets the nerve."

Cook considered the tongue-tied child. "Well, give her something to eat," Cook said as she herself reached across the table. She handed the girl a pastry square dotted with red compote, huffed, and disappeared back into the kitchen.

Cassandane smiled at Cyrus, who observed with satisfaction the child's plump cheeks and bright eyes. It seemed a hundred years ago that Cyrus had arrived in Anshan, the poor capital city of his father's small kingdom, then in the grip of the tyrannous Sadeghi whose opium production had left so many people starving. It seemed a lifetime ago that desperately impoverished families had sent children away to face fates they'd hoped would be less cruel, but seldom were. Yet here stood a girl of his people, healthy and engaged in the enterprise that benefited people and the land itself.

Nevertheless, despite the obvious improvements, questions about what had been Sadeghi's long-term plan and how far he had effected it remained, nagging around the edges of the kingdom's peace. They were about to learn more.

"Go on," Nahhunte prompted the shepherd. "What did you find?"

The little girl swallowed and shyly brushed crumbs from her mouth. "A lot of things, sir," she said.

Cyrus sat forward. "Things?" he asked gently.

"In a cave, sir. Shiny and expensive, I think. I came across them with my goats." She started then, nervous, remembering the responsibility.

"The groom's boy is looking after your animals," Nahhunte said. "Tell the king where the things are."

"Better, show me," Cyrus said. He pushed his chair back. To Cassandane he smiled. "Come along?"

Cassandane looked at their baby son. Cambyses, named for

Cyrus's late father, continued to suffer fits that came without warning and raged through his body like a storm before they left him again – shattered and shaken but alive. She shook her head. "Tell me what treasure you find."

"Get Prexaspes," Cyrus directed Nahhunte. "He'll want to be in on this." Indeed, whether Cyrus wanted it or not, the son of Parsa's most noble tribe, who once bore Cyrus peculiar contempt had become his closest friend. Prexaspes now insisted he accompany the young king wherever he went.

* * *

THEY RODE, Cyrus and Prexaspes (with the girl atop his saddle, pointing the way) across the plateau and into the hills. When boulders made the way too rugged even for the sure-footed horses, they dismounted and scrambled up the last stretch on foot. The girl disappeared, wriggling into a small opening in the brush-covered boulders. Cyrus looked at his friend, shrugged, and to Prexaspes's dismay followed. The men inched their way through a dark and narrow passage. They had to bend to fit through the last stretch which finally opened into a large space. The girl was there, waiting.

Finally, standing again, they let their eyes adjust. They were in a wide room, faintly lit by a small opening to the sky. The girl swung her hand all around. Cyrus whistled low. Inside were piles of the finest weapons – iron swords with the etched blades of Luristan craftsmen, shields, staves, huge bows with a graceful turn in glistening wood, even equipment for a small cavalry. Cyrus and Prexaspes turned around slowly, looking at the well-ordered heaps of a substantial armory. The girl clasped her hands behind her back and watched them take it all in. Prexaspes picked up and replaced sword after bow after breastplate after axe.

Finally, Cyrus found his voice. "You're right," he said to the shepherd girl. "A lot of things – shiny and expensive, indeed."

Prexaspes returned a heavy stave to its place. "Sadeghi promised the people that he would give them a strong defense." He grimaced. "Looks like he planned for war."

CHAPTER 4 (BABYLONIA)

"*N*o travel for you – not for a while, anyway," Khai said to his son.

"But I –"

"We need you here," Khai said. "The king requires more of me. Indefinitely. I'm to be his business agent."

Iddina nodded and grinned, "Nice," he said, clearly impressed.

"You'll need to run more of our own affairs."

Iddina's grin widened.

Khai looked at his son, trying to reconcile the little boy he remembered with this young man. "And we should think about a wife for you."

"I already have. A Nur-Sin girl."

Khai raised his eyebrows. "Prestigious family."

Iddina nodded. "Same as the king's," he said.

Khai suspected his reaction to that bit of information – distaste – was the opposite of what Iddina expected. He kept it to himself. Khai pulled up a chair at the big table. "In the meantime, you need to learn the books, the details of borrowing and lending, how to manage rentals... The business will be yours one day, and it doesn't run itself." Iddina sat, too.

"Now," Khai said. "There's a big plot of land, an estate actually, four brothers in debt to the temple..."

Iddina proved to be a good partner. By early February, the Egibis possessed the deed to 24 kor of land straddling the New Canal across from the Enlil Gate. Some of the property was already planted with date palms. Bright green shoots of barley and wheat blanketed several acres, and still more of the land was freshly broken and ready for planting.

* * *

THE WEDDING WAS the most ostentatious and expensive affair that Khai had ever seen. Iddina loved every minute of it. Khai hoped that his son might learn to love his new bride, Nupta, at least a fraction as much as the dowry that came with her.

Despite the economic downturn, complicated by the burgeoning population of skilled exiles, descendants of those whom Nebuchadnezzar had used to advantage, the Egibi family firm expanded. In addition to the debt credit service that had earned them considerable financial wealth over the years, Egibi holdings increased to include docks on the river and an impressive home in Babylon's inner city.

Meanwhile, King Igliss sought, in good Babylonian tradition, to portray himself as a faithful servant of Marduk. With Khai's capable leadership, he concentrated Babylonian resources on the restoration of Marduk's Esagil temple in Babylon and the Ezida in Borsippa, which pleased the elite priesthood and the powerful, conservative Babylonian citizenry. He also saw to it that the canals in Babylon received attention that he claimed his predecessor the half-Mede had neglected, and he made a show of refurbishing the Chapel of Destiny used in the annual New Year *akitu* celebration.

Igliss also channeled national funds into the purchase, renovation, and luxurious furnishing of a palace on the banks of the Euphrates.

Igliss made a show of saying it was "For your queen Cassiya, daughter of the great Nebuchadnezzar." Few were fooled. It was easy to see that Igliss liked fine things at least as well.

Still, the work that Igliss commissioned didn't come close to the pace of Nebuchadnezzar's building projects. In fairness, no one's could have. Nebuchadnezzar would become legendary for his construction... and infamous, too – that "tower that reached to heavens," navel of the universe, the Entemenanki alone took the work of people from all over the world and still it was not done. So, when Nebuchadnezzar died so too did the number and scope of Babylonian projects. So it happened that the restlessness of unemployment and (hand-in-hand with that) resentment for people of foreign descent (especially with respectable occupations) that had plagued Amel-Marduk's brief monarchy continued to simmer just below the surface. Despite it all, Igliss didn't pay any attention to Nanna-Suen's sanctuary in Harran. Not even when he planned his first military expedition to the region.

CHAPTER 5 (BABYLONIA)

"*T*alk to him, Nabonidus," Adad-guppi pleaded with her son, when she learned of the king's plans to head north to confront the Cilician king Appuašu.

Nabonidus said, "It's not for me to decide, Mother. We'll be in the area but only because Syria is under attack. The whole region is in upheaval. Croesus is growing to the northwest, and word has it that Astyages is massing his Median troops to the east. We can't afford to lose Cilicia, the only buffer between those two."

"But Cilicia, Nabo. It's so close to Harran. And you know as well as I that if the king were to make Nanna-Suen's temple strong and beautiful again, reinstate the old rituals and sacrifices with respectable and pious staff, then the god himself would come to our aid."

"But Median forces now occupy the area. Besides, Igliss doesn't care for Nanna-Suen. Our god gets him nothing."

"Just because all these rich Babylonians love Marduk --"

"Yes, just because. That's all he needs, gods be damned."

"Watch your mouth!"

"You know what I mean. Igliss's piety is only a show. But it works. As long as he throws money at the Esagil, prays fervently and publicly, and stands in for the pageantry, he gets patronage and political support from the citizens who can give it most."

"It isn't right."

"Yet it's the way things are. Listen, I'm sorry, Mother. But think of it this way." He lowered his voice. "Perhaps Nanna-Suen will see to it that Igliss's reign is brief and a better man takes the throne."

Adad-guppi quickly glanced around. Seeing noone, "You Nabo," she said. "It's you who should be king."

Nabonidus shot her a stern look.

"I'm serious. Maybe you could do something on the campaign. War is a dangerous business. Accidents happen."

"Stop. Besides, if something *were* to happen to Igliss -- if he were to die tomorrow, his son would take the throne. And no one wants that."

"You're right." Adad-guppi shook her gray head. "Still, you --"

Nabonidus put up his hands. "I have to go. Keep an eye on Belshazzar. I convinced the king that leave him here. Besides, he knows the empire's management as well as anyone."

"He'll be thrilled to have more authority."

"Just don't let him get too sure. Igliss's ego is as big as a bloated horse and just as foul if popped."

The army tracked north, following the Euphrates, a constant and familiar presence all the way. The Babylonians defeated the rebel king in Syria, and chased him back to his capital in Cilicia. But they failed to capture the renegade king himself. Igliss didn't see the point of pursuing the wily man and his dangerous troops when they had such spoil already. So they returned to Babylon, floating their gain down the Euphrates.

* * *

WITHIN DAYS OF RETURNING, King Igliss became feverish and

distracted. After he collapsed on his throne, unconscious, he took
to his bed.

While doctors dressed in the fish robes of the original sages
came and went from the king's quarters, Nabonidus sorted
through the aftermath of the military campaign and quietly
distributed its spoil among Babylon's population as he deemed
fair. Apart from items of particular historical or cultural interest,
Nabonidus saw no reason to keep money or other valuables for
the palace. Commanders and soldiers received the most. The
temples and temple staff after that. And still there were goods to
share with the citizens of Babylon and to put toward public
works.

Belshazzar learned too late of Nabonidus's intentions for the
war's winnings.

"You did what?!" Belshazzar exclaimed. "Do you have any idea
the favor we could have curried…?"

But the plans were already public. So, publicly Belshazzar
smiled and cheered his father's decision. But his loyalties lay with
the power of the throne, a power for which he'd hungered all his
life. And this charitable distribution would not help things.

* * *

"BE A FRIEND TO THE PRINCE, until I'm well," King Igliss wheezed
to Belshazzar from the eiderdown pillows of his bed.

"You know that I will support him always," Belshazzar said.
He passed the king's wife on his way out the door.

Cassiya slipped into a chair next to Igliss's bed. He gestured to
bring her head close to his mouth. "Witch," he hissed. "You should
be here, worthless woman, not me."

Cassiya stood up in alarm.

"She cursed me!" Igliss yelled. "Curse her!"

A doctor hurried forward and laid his hand on the king's arm
as an attendant led the horrified queen out.

"The gods will lift any curse," the doctor said. "Priests and magicians are praying for you, our lord and king, right now, even as we speak."

Indeed the sacred precinct was abuzz with activity. The courtyard rang with the bleats and cries of animals sacrificed in the king's name. Priests poured in and out of the Esagil. It was a lucrative time for the temple as citizens who depended on Igliss's favor dumped money into its coffers in an effort to appease the gods. And Belshazzar tried to demonstrate that he was in support of it all, honoring the well-bred king and high god Marduk most of all.

CHAPTER 6 (BABYLONIA)

*D*espite the effort, Igliss never recovered. Within only about two months of the king's return from Syria and the Taurus Mountains, he died. Labashi-Marduk, an only child, became king. Although it was a rightful succession, some said it was against the will of the gods. For Labashi-Marduk was a still just a child and "had not yet learned proper behavior." To say the least.

Within only a few months, the boy-king's wickedness became apparent in many ways. Labashi-Marduk had no interest in the maintenance of river quays, roads, or even temples and wouldn't hear any advice to channel resources to them. The priests quickly grew disgruntled, and merchants complained that their business was compromised. Yet no one dared speak a word to the boy, as he had met the first attempts with a brutal hand, laughing as he watched the executioner cut off their ears or tongues.

In short, Labashi-Marduk proceeded to rule the kingdom exactly as he had ruled the nursery: with obnoxious entitlement and random terror. In public he called his mother a "stupid woman" and would have nothing to do with her. Few knew that the little king still summoned Cassiya to sing him to sleep nearly every night.

"Can't you control him, press upon him your role as his father's choice of a ward?" a beleaguered scribe asked Belshazzar one day. The scribe had just left Labashi-Marduk having agreed to compose a poetic ode, entirely fictitious, of the boy's great achievements as king. He was to read it for Labashi-Marduk while the king sat on his toilet.

Belshazzar shook his head vigorously, his cheeks jiggling. The smooth confidence with which he had presumed to manage the kingdom was gone. He had watched Labashi-Marduk cut out the first complainer's tongue with manic amusement. After the boy-king had demanded a whip for play and then used it against the man who had brought it to him, Belshazzar had kept as far from the king as possible. His eyes were wild with anxiety at the thought of approaching Labashi-Marduk with anything at all.

"Are you not a 'friend of the king'?," the man asked.

"Oh, yes," Belshazzar said, trying to steady the twitch in his right eye, "But to 'control' the king, well that's not my place."

Others, too, came to Belshazzar... at first. But as he consistently deflected their efforts, people took to asking his father Nabonidus to intervene. Nabonidus alone dared stand up to little monarch. With egoless diplomacy Nabonidus could sometimes sway Labashi-Marduk away from the boy's more egregious and sadistic notions. The old man also managed to persuade Labashi-Marduk to "assign some of the onerous and dull work of monarchal tasks to a person less important, less busy than yourself, great lord." And the boy king agreed.

So Belshazzar reassumed some responsibilities. He also began to formulate a plan.

* * *

EVER SO CAUTIOUSLY, Belshazzar sounded out the thoughts and feelings of well-placed persons. Carefully, privately, he sought out one by one disgruntled courtiers and court officials.

"The king is an only child and with no heir of his own. If something were to happen to him..." Belshazzar said to the chief steward, a man who Belshazzar knew was terrified of the capricious boy now on the throne.

"What, you? Do you mean to be king?"

"Me?" Belshazzar said. "Gods, no. I'm just a simple courtier."

"You were at King Igliss's right hand. And he appointed you as friend to his son."

"I've had some experience, it's true. But I depend on the wise counsel of others. My father especially."

"Nabonidus. Of course."

Belshazzar would let them think for a moment or two before offering, "My father is a man of experience -- from court to battlefield, temple to tower -- decent and just. But I know you're aware of that."

More often than not, they'd say, "Now there's a man who would be a fine king."

Belshazzar would nod, the corners of his lips turned down as if contemplating the idea for the first time.

"But he's an elderly man, is he not?"

"What is age in a man like my father!" Belshazzar would say. "And just look at his mother," a comment that inevitably brought a chuckle from his audience. Adad-guppi was still a lively presence in the palace. Then, Belshazzar would direct the conversation to some detail about the court or temple concern.

As it was, Belshazzar thought a lot about his father's age. At seventy, Nabonidus was indeed an old man. If he were to take the throne, it would be only a matter of time, and not long at that... Belshazzar could almost feel the weight of the crown on his head.

He let the idea run its course. Sure enough, within the month, a group of over fifteen court insiders and high-placed citizens approached him in his quarters

"We've been thinking... should Labashi-Marduk die without an heir... might your father be willing to assume control?"

"To be king?"

The men nodded.

Belshazzar stroked his chin. "I can ask him."

"Soon?" the head groom asked.

Belshazzar nodded slowly.

"You'll be sure to tell him that this is not something only those of us present feel. Each of us has talked with many others, all of whom are in favor of your father acting as king."

"Of course."

* * *

"No," Nabonidus said. "I have absolutely no desire to be king."

Belshazzar had anticipated this response and had prepared. Belshazzar appealed to Nabonidus's sense of duty to the nation that had adopted him and to the people who depended on its smooth operation for their livelihoods, for justice, and for peace. He stressed the fact that many people wanted Nabonidus to govern.

But it was Nabonidus's own private piety -- a desire to elevate his native god, Nanna-Suen, beginning with reparations to the god's temple in Harran -- that finally convinced Nabonidus to agree.

"But I will have no part in hastening the process, Shazzi."

"No one would want you to, Father. Absolutely not. Besides, it's only if something were to happen, only so that the nation wouldn't dissolve into chaos."

Nabonidus sighed deeply.

"Oh, thank you," Belshazzar said, "thank you, Father. This is the right choice and will be a great relief to others."

The very next day, the men planned how they might get rid of Labashi-Marduk. Once they had gotten the king's night guard on their side, the rest was easy. What they hadn't counted on was the fact that as tyrannous as Labashi-Marduk could be, he was still only a ten-year-old boy.

So it was that Cassiya was singing to the drowsy boy when the assassins, scarves around their heads and dark robes hiding both weapons and identities burst into his room. There was no time to reconsider, no time to hesitate. When Cassiya threw herself over the slight body of her son, hers was the first to take a sword. It ran through her back, through her heart, and into the chest of Labashi-Marduk before either had a chance even to scream. Labashi-Marduk had ruled for only three months. And Cassiya, the last of Nebuchadnezzar's legitimate children, died with the honor of a brave and noble mother and queen.

CHAPTER 7 (BABYLONIA)

*N*abonidus took the throne with the very public backing of not only Babylon's formidable military but also the city's most prominent power brokers -- the entire administrative board of Marduk's temple (the royal representative, the qipu head of the administrative council, the shatammu who managed the temple estates, and the tupsharru or chief scribe), elders of the powerful Nur-Sin family and other highborn citizenry.

He got off on a good foot. When Nabonidus took the throne, he had agreed to his estranged wife Nitocris' demand that he reinstate the goddess tradition and appoint their daughter to that lofty post – to serve Ishtar at her temple in Uruk. The girl had been raised there, after all. And there was solid historical precedent for it. He didn't mention that there was even greater historical precedent to install her in service of Nanna-Suen. For that, he'd have to find the right occasion.

Indeed, in decades of research, stolen hours spent entranced by ancient times, Nabonidus recalled once reading of a tradition of the king's own daughter serving none other than the moon god's high priestess, specifically in Ur. But when Marduk became the high god of Babylon, the king's daughter had been removed from Nanna-Suen's Ur and sent instead to Uruk to serve the goddess Ishtar. Recent kings had abandoned even that tradition. Even more popular was Nabonidus's decision to go back to Cilicia and put an end to King Appuašu, who had eluded Igliss even as the Cilician kept pushing into Babylonian territory. Nabonidus saw no need to remind how near that was to Harran, and how neglected was the temple there, the other temple of the moon-god Nanna-Suen. It was there that his mother had served, a priestess herself when Nabonidus was just a boy. The great god would show him when it was time. No, for now he would focus on the practical details of battle.

Besides magicians and diviners, Nabonidus gathered an elite band of less than 500 troops. It was a diverse group, composed of soldiers from points throughout the empire. They were men that Nabonidus had trained, if not personally, then by training their teachers and commanders. He would leave the remaining army of Akkad in Babylon. Some people asked about Croesus – would Nabonidus continue west – control the Lydians' expansion. Nabonidus would not. As far as he could tell, it wasn't the business of Babylonia. Let the Lydian have what he had. Nabonidus was no Nebuchadnezzar.

CHAPTER 8 (MEDIA)

*A*mytis stood on the palace wall and looked up at a sky thick with stars broken only by the dark peaks of jagged mountains otherwise invisible in the night. Amytis never did learn to read the constellations like the Babylonian sages. They were mad about the stars.

Who knows, she thought, maybe if she had, maybe if she had been more humble before the gods, more penitent and generous... maybe if she had commissioned or even herself woven a goddess's blue *pishannu* scarf, traded in her hanging gardens for yet another temple complex... Maybe then her son would still be alive, reigning in a Babylon of peace. After all, look at Adadguppi, more devoted to her god than to the succession of Babylonian kings that she served so well. And now it was that woman's son, and him grown to old age, who sat on the Babylonian throne. Nabonidus wasn't even of royal blood or Babylonian, for that matter. Not that she begrudged either one. She always liked the old woman and respected Nabonidus. Maybe, if Amytis could have mustered such piety... "Who knows?" Amytis whispered and leaned out over the parapet, casting a moon shadow down its wall.

A bustle of activity at the gate -- a man on a horse, the guards' low voices, their seizing the reins -- caught her eye. The man dismounted. She strained to hear. A guard removed a sack from the man's travel bags. Amytis leaned farther, listening hard.

"My lady?"

Amytis drew back, surprised. "Nathan, what are you doing here?"

"Same as you, I suppose, enjoying the full moon on a clear night. My father used to say, 'The heavens declare the glory of God.'" The scribe walked up beside her and put his hands on the top of a crenellation. "I couldn't sleep," he admitted.

"I forgot. You're staying up here for…"

"Sukkot, yes."

She shook her head. "I can't keep track of your festivals."

"As long as you let me observe them."

Amytis looked behind him to a crude structure, so frail it was barely visible. "No wonder you can't sleep."

Then Amytis looked back over the wall. The men were gone.

By the time Amytis and Nathan had arrived at Ecbatana almost five years ago, each had found ways to set weariness and grief aside to make a new life in Media and in its court at Ecbatana. Nathan's facility with Akkadian was useful, and the scribe fit in, finding people who shared his Israelite background.

They stood, Amytis and Nathan, in companionable silence for a time until Amytis said, "Do you miss Nippur and your family there?"

"I hear from them every now and then, as you know. But God, has taken me here. 'A wandering Aramean was my father,' we say -- 'my father' being our ancestor Abraham, or maybe all our ancestors put together."

Amytis smiled at the garrulous scribe, her only friend from days in Babylon. All his stories, his "traditions." She envied them sometimes. Amytis glanced over the wall again. Nothing.

"The singers tell that when Abraham was a boy, his family left home in Ur and traveled to Harran to settle there."

"Nanna-Suen's cities," Amytis observed.

Nathan nodded. "And like the crescent that evokes the moon-god's image for his devotees, there's controversy over whether or not our god has horns. Well, after Abraham settled in Harran, God called him to up and go again. This went on for generations, this wandering. Jacob even went back to Harran, where he married the women who with him became the mothers of the tribes of Israel. I come from a people of walkers."

"For my part," Amytis said, "I'm glad of it. I'm glad you're here."

* * *

FOR AMYTIS, it had been a bittersweet homecoming. Even though Amytis had longed for her wild homeland every moment of every year that she'd been gone, it had been her concern for Media that drove her to Babylon in the first place. And her determination to protect Media's wild integrity that kept her there. Indeed, it was ironic. Her love for home had dictated that she remain far from it, to serve instead as the linchpin of an alliance that protected the land that she so loved.

Her father was a lousy king, though, and even with the Babylonian alliance, in her absence relations within the sprawling empire of Media had deteriorated. When she returned, Amytis found her homeland weak inside and out. Quietly, Amytis had begun the long slow work of repairing relations between the capital and the disparate peoples of the empire – cajoling, threatening, encouraging, and gifting as she saw fit. Her father King Astyages hardly noticed.

Astyages did put her widowhood to good use, though, marrying her to one of his most decorated military generals. The king was happy to have a way to reward Spitamas that didn't cost Astyages anything -- honor enough to be the king's son-in-law.

True, Amytis was past child-bearing and no maiden, but that was that. And Spitamas was grateful.

Suddenly, the silvery light dimmed. "Nathan, look," Amytis pointed up.

A shadow, narrow but sure, crept across the face of the moon. For a moment, the night grew decidedly darker, until it cleared again.

Amytis shuddered.

"Do you think of Babylon?" Nathan asked.

"Every day," she said softly.

Neither one needed to say that an event such as this would be cause for consternation. In truth, it was for Amytis's Media as well. They stood watching the sky, each walking their own paths of memory.

Nathan said, "I've heard rumors that King Nabonidus is promoting his god, Nanna-Suen, even in Marduk's city. That can't be easy."

"You never accepted the Babylonian ways, did you?"

"Their gods and goddesses, no. Some of our people have, though, believing Marduk defeated Yahweh. I believe that our God doesn't change. So, our stories must. It's a big debate. Even the prophets don't all agree." Nathan smiled and turned away. "Well, I'm going to try to get a little sleep before my demanding mistress calls me for scribal duty."

Amytis waved him off with a smile. "

* * *

AMYTIS REMAINED at the wall a while longer. Finally, a horn marking the end of the night watch blew its low moan from the city's walls. Amytis walked back to her quarters. Spitamas was just leaving.

Spitamas the Mede was a gruff, war-weathered man, riddled with pits and scars from years of battle. Had she been a younger bride, Amytis might have been scared of him. But when she first saw Spitamas's nakedness, it was envy she felt. If only her own body wore its badges of survival so transparently.

"Your father said something about a visitor who arrived last night, a merchant or something from Parsa," Spitamas said. "You didn't happen to see him come, did you?"

"No," Amytis said.

"I just wondered, since I figured you were at the wall."

"I was. But not in the middle of the night."

"Your father said that he arrived during the second watch."

"Strange to come at such a time," Amytis mused. "Wait. I did see someone, but I couldn't make out any details. Are you going to meet him?"

"I think so. Astyages sent eunuchs. Said it was urgent. They got me up early enough."

"You're always up early."

Spitamas nodded. "A soldier's curse."

Over the years, Amytis had grown fond of Spitamas and he of her. Neither pretended other than the crude practicality that had thrown the together. Consequently, neither expected anything of the other. That the two veterans -- one of the Babylonian court, the other of Median battlefields -- got along as well as they did was a surprise to both.

"You know that your father wants you there, too," Spitamas said as he fastened his boots.

"I suppose he does."

King Astyages never admitted it, but he valued Amytis's experience in Babylon as Nebuchadnezzar's wife and then queen mother. Astyages solicited her opinions on matters of Median state, especially international affairs. Amytis obliged but didn't regard her father's administration with much respect -- a sensibility she kept to herself.

"Tell him I'll be there in a little while."

"I'll tell him you were out," Spitamas said.

She rolled her eyes.

"Well, it's true. And I'm not up for another lecture from him about forcing you to do this or that."

Amytis laughed. "Suit yourself. I'm just going to freshen up."

It was Spitamas's turn to roll his eyes. They both knew: Amytis didn't "freshen up" to see the king. But if Astyages waited, he'd remember how much he needed her.

Amytis reached for a plum from the ceramic bowl and bit into its sweet fruit.

CHAPTER 9 (MEDIA)

*A*mytis saw the king's steward just outside the audience hall. "Harpagus," she smiled. She thrust her chin toward the door. "A visitor, I hear. Do you know from where or why?"

"It's hard to tell." Harpagus frowned.

Amytis had known Harpagus all her life. He was a young man when she was born but already steward to the king. So he seemed terribly old and dignified when she was a girl. Her own father was unpredictable -- the combination of insecurity and power a volatile mix. Harpagus was a steady and unflappable presence whenever some outburst or another of the king's sent the palace spinning in frenetic anxiety. In such circumstances, Amytis longed simply to be near Harpagus. When she was very little, she would take hold of his hand. And he let her. As she got older, it was enough simply to be near him.

And when she had returned to Media, he was the first to greet her. He had been stiff and his voice gruff, when he saw her -- the hard-headed girl return as a woman chastised by life and grief. Later, she attributed his extraordinary protocol to the off-putting nature of her bitterness, the toll that mourning took on her face, the cloud it threw over her hazel eyes. But he had been changed, too, she could see it -- by something terrible.

Astyages acknowledged Amytis's entrance with barely a nod in her direction. Nathan was already there, busily scribbling as the king listened to the palace astronomer and a priest. Their voices loud with passion. Nathan looked up, his eyebrows high, as Amytis took her seat.

"But it is the gods that determine events in the heavens," the priest was saying.

"I'm not saying that that's untrue," the astronomer replied. "I'm just saying that the heavens define the actions of the gods."

Amytis looked over at Nathan, but he was intent on his writing.

The priest bit his lip, clenched and unclenched his hands at his sides. "So you're saying that the gods are helpless in the face of the stars and constellations."

"I'm not a priest. I don't know how it works, but I do know that the stars are predictable."

The priest threw up his hands, "If they are, it's because the gods made them so."

The astronomer emitted an exasperated huff.

"Gentlemen," Astyages interrupted. "I summoned you here to discuss the eclipse. Can we get on with it?"

"It was a significant event," the astronomer said.

"We agree on that," the priest muttered.

"At its greatest, it lasted one hour and twenty-two minutes."

"My associates are running tests to discern the wishes of the gods," the priest said, glancing at the astronomer, "which will help the king decide what to do."

"Good luck," the astronomer said, "figuring out the details. I suppose some animal will give its life to the process."

A man coughed from the doorway of the room.

"Come in," Astyages said, and the door guards stepped away.

* * *

THE MAN, dressed in clothes so clean they must be new, bowed to each person, beginning with and most deeply for King Astyages. He barely nodded to Amytis, which gave her a chance to study his face.

His skin was pock-marked, his nose fleshy and red. Most striking, a white scar ran from the corner of one eye to the ear of the same side. He caught her gaze and grimaced an exaggerated smile.

Amytis looked at her father.

"My lord, king of the great lands of Media, powerful and wise ruler of countries far and wide..." the man began.

Amytis groaned while Astyages sat back, his lips turned down, head nodding in stern approval.

If I may," the visitor said.

"Go on."

"I believe I can help."

Astyages sat forward. "Help?"

"Make sense of the eclipse."

"Partial," Amytis said. The man was shifty, clearly bore a motive he wasn't keen to reveal. "It was over almost as soon as it began. Our magi have things in hand."

The visitor ignored her. He looked around at the men. "Ah, but perhaps I presume. We tradesmen often hear things before others do." He bowed as if to go.

"Wait," Astyages said, adjusting himself on the throne. "What is your sense?"

"I am just an itinerant merchant, a poor traveler who trades in small things but so necessary that I rarely take the price my goods are worth. But I come from a cruel land growing more terrible by the day. One of your vassal kingdoms, my lord." He bowed again to Astyages.

Amytis leaned forward. "You speak in riddles," she said. "Tell it plain."

The man blinked hard and gave his head a quick shake, as if to loose a fly from his nose. He looked at King Astyages, who nodded.

Amytis jerked her chin up. "Starting with who you are."

Again the man looked at Astyages.

Again, the king nodded for him to go on.

The man raised his eyebrows and inhaled deeply. "Long ago, I was the groundsman for a distant king who desperately needed my help. I gave it willingly, thinking nothing of my own sacrifice or suffering. Over the years, I improved his earnings and eased the pains that troubled his soul." The man clasped his hands together and lifted his eyes to the ceiling like some adoring supplicant. "But then, one day, the king's son appeared." He dropped his hands and looked back at Astyages. "-- a child, really. But the boy was hard-headed and set on seizing control; and my work took me farther and farther away. I couldn't watch him all the time. I tried to counsel the king to be wary; but when the boy became a young man, he pushed his father aside and forced his own dangerous and irresponsible ways on the country."

"And forced you out?" Amytis asked.

The groundsman glanced briefly at Amytis. "I would have stayed if my help were welcome, but the youth is arrogant and scheming. Besides, now the old king is dead, from what I hear." He looked down and shook his head. "For all I know, his son killed him."

"Where is the place, and who is the youth, the king?" Amytis asked.

"His father called him Cyrus. The place is Anshan."

Astyages started. "In Parsa?"

"That's the place. Vassals of yours, yes?" The man tilted his head and raised his eyebrows.

Astyages stammered, "The king, Cam... years ago... I, my dau-
-"

"Perhaps I was mistaken. Are they not subject to you?"

Astyages got hold of himself. "They're a poor kingdom and didn't seem worth the attention."

Amytis narrowed her eyes. "You said that you can help make sense of the eclipse," she said. "What is your sense?"

The man took his eyes reluctantly from Astyages. Avoiding Amytis, he addressed the group with increasing fervor. "Just as a weird darkness blotted out the moon's light last night, that young man is a black spot gradually covering the land. If unstopped, vassal or no, he will obliterate the brightness of Media and indeed the world."

Astyages's eyes were wide. His mouth dropped open. Amytis huffed, and he shut it.

Amytis said, "I thought you said that his country is small and diminished even further by your departure. How is it that this boy became such a, a black spot, as you put it and powerful enough to frighten you, such a capable man? As my father said, they're a poor country, no longer really even vassals of ours." Amytis laid her hand on Astyages's. " Why trouble the king of Media about it? As a matter of fact," she leaned forward. "Why should we pay attention to you at all, when we've got perfectly good, well-trained men to interpret signs?" Amytis gestured to the astronomer and priest, who looked at each other, nodded, and sat up taller.

"I've seen things. I've heard things."

"So you said."

"The youth has taken Elam."

Astyages inhaled sharply.

"How do you know?" Amytis asked.

"I learned from Babylonian merchants," the groundsman explained, "Men with a reputation for honesty and fair dealings - - of the Egibi corporation, if you know them."

Nathan glanced at Amytis. Her face was stone.

"They told me that the Babylonians are pulling out all civic association. Only tradesmen now go to Susa from Babylon. Cyrus has made an alliance with Elam. He has integrated their archers into his force and has provided funds from Anshan to shore up Susa's defenses. It's only a matter of time before he expands again, probably into more of your territories, regions north and east of Susa, I suspect. I am telling you -- this Cyrus is bad. I knew him for many years, from when he was just a boy. I tried to teach him sense and his place. But he's foolish and stubborn. He certainly couldn't succeed against you, but he could rally those ignorant peasants in Elam to cause a lot of trouble."

Astyages said dazed as if in sleep, "The young man is my grandson."

Amytis looked at the groundsman but spoke to her father. "You don't have to explain. He knows."

The groundsman feigned surprise.

"You've known all along," Amytis said. "And that he came from Media as a ten-year-old returned to the only parent alive -- his father, King Cam of Anshan." And Amytis suspected she knew this man – of him, anyway – as the cause of a misery that landed a young woman in Babylon... and in her son's heart. "But so what. What do you want?" Whatever the case, anyone could see this man could not be trusted. Anyone except Amytis's father.

"Only to alert your lordship," the man bowed to Astyages. "I'm sure it's nothing you cannot handle, King Astyages, but perhaps your lordship agrees that it's better to cut such things off early."

Astyages nodded slowly. "Thank you for making the effort to get such news to me."

"It is my pleasure and duty as a man of greater Media to serve, your lordship," the groundsman said with a sweeping bow. Whether the smile he gave to Amytis before bowing was crooked from the scar on his cheek or from some twisted humor, it was hard to tell.

When the man had left, Astyages said, "Damn that boy."

"That boy is your grandson," Amytis said. "As you just observed."

"And what of it?!"

"He is my sister's son."

Amytis watched her father stoke his anger and felt like a little girl again, anxious and wary. She had seen this too many times: something poked at the king's insecurity and he became unpredictable, volatile. Instinctively, she looked to Harpagus. His face was white.

Amytis longed for her sister. Sweet Mandane. She would calm the king, reveal and explain away the falseness of this ugly visitor. But Mandane was dead, at her own hand; and it was Mandane's own son, whom Astyages now hated. Feared? Amytis twisted on her chair.

Harpagus caught her eye and said, "My lady."

Amytis took a deep breath. "I suggest that we learn the truth of it for ourselves – of Cyrus's actions in Susa and greater Elam."

"Spitamas," Astyages said, "I want you to go to Susa." He continued as though Amytis were no more than a mote in the beam of sunshine from window to floor. "Take twenty men, lightly armed, nimble. Remind them of our strength. Remind Cyrus, too, if he's in the area. If it means that someone dies, so be it."

Amytis stood. "We don't know their intentions. Maybe they're peaceful. So many men and armed too will only unsettle them."

Astyages scowled.

"I'll go with Spitamas," Amytis said, "Just us."

Astyages glared at his daughter. "Fine. Take her," he said.

They left. Amytis went one way, Spitamas another. Harpagus, steward of the king, remained with Astyages. Of course.

"Cyrus," Astyages stood. He paced across the cold floor. "He should be dead."

Harpagus said nothing.

CHAPTER 10 (MEDIA)

The king sat back down and pursed his lips. "I knew it. The gods warned me. It was those magi – those supposed seers who led me to believe the prophecies had been fulfilled, the child would be no threat to me. Now this." He fumed.

Harpagus stood still as stone.

"Well, get them!" Astyages barked.

"Only the younger is with us now," Harpagus said. "I'll bring him straight away."

* * *

THE MAN, who had rushed to meet the king's summons, froze, letting his fur-lined cape slip off his shoulder. His face was as pale as the flesh of a freshly plucked chicken. He wished his cousin were still alive to absorb at least some of this blame.

"You told me that the dream had been fulfilled," Astyages said, his voice grating and shrill. He tipped his face down and looked over thin eyebrows, his chin doubling under. "You did not tell me the truth of the gods' warning!"

"I, I, your lordship, I --"

"Sew his lips," Astyages said.

"No!" the magi sputtered.

Harpagus rooted his feet, and fixed his hands to his sides as if it were they that had been sewn. Memories of the punishing horror he had endured at this king's command rushed in. He could only hope that as in that night, they would lift him from this body, from all feeling. And so it was that Harpagus observed the man's terror, witnessed his screams as if from far above, a hovering specter.

"That'll teach you to think before you speak the gods' will."

The guards took the magi by his arms, and his mouth dripping blood dragged him from the room as the poor man barely conscious cried incoherent supplications and apologies to the gods and king.

Before his cries had died out down the hall, Astyages said, "Damn that boy, and damn him again. I should have killed him when I could."

* * *

AMYTIS REGAINED her composure and calm as soon they had left the hall. She and Spitamas walked the long corridor flanking the audience hall, through courtyard and halls. With ease, Amytis matched her stride to Spitamas's. Only when they neared their own rooms did the man finally slow.

"What were you thinking?!" Spitamas said, without looking at Amytis.

"About my sister and the son she grieved unto death."

"That son is a danger and a menace."

"You don't know that."

Spitamas spun on her. "I do know that, and so should you!"

"Because of what some smooth-tongued wastrel said?"

Spitamas shook his head as he opened the door to their front room. "Women," he muttered. "War is much easier. And now you're coming with me?"

"And we'll need a scribe," Amytis said, crossing the room to a window overlooking another courtyard.

"See? Already with the ideas."

"If there are indeed Babylonians -- merchants or otherwise..."

Spitamas sat with a grunt. He put his feet up on a wooden stool. "Tell him to keep his mouth shut and his head down."

"For certain," Amytis said, removing her earrings, a pair of tiny, flashing silver trout. She laid them on a table and ran a finger over their smooth surfaces.

"Did you notice anything odd about Harpagus in there?"

"Odd? How?"

"He looked, I don't know, stricken. Shocked or upset or something."

"Looked the same to me -- dour and tight."

Probably no time, Amytis thought, to ask Harpagus before they leave for Susa. Funny, she had never actually asked him what he thought or felt about anything.

CHAPTER 11 (PARSA)

*A*s had been the case some years ago, Cyrus sat with the note, a mere memo, and let his mind wander. A few years ago, Cyrus had folded that same scrap of parchment along old creases and looked up...

But his eyes weren't on the gleaming woodwork of this palace addition, neither the tidy courtyard below nor the fields beyond, where grain waved green in the spring's mid-morning. He didn't see the flocks that freckled the surrounding hills, not even his wife -- so tall, her hair the color of burnished mahogany pulled loosely, here and there, into the tiny clasps of a dozen golden hair rings from the crown of her head halfway down her back -- standing in the doorway.

He saw instead the face of an old friend, the guide who had escorted him years earlier from the snowy mountains of elegant Ecbatana south to this rude plateau. Cyrus ran a finger over the parchment's ragged edge, bowed his head, and groaned, recalling how that very face was shredded and the man killed for Cyrus's own ten-year-old folly.

Cyrus flinched at the hand laid gently on his shoulder, then looked up, clasped it with his own, and smiled apologetically into Sanda's face, straight with concern.

"Our son?" Sanda asked, her forehead drawn tight. "I worry, too – and how it comes on without warning! But –" her face relaxed, clear and smooth. Her eye caught the parchment between Cyrus's fingers. "Something else, then."

Cyrus drew Sanda around to stand in front of him. "I've told you about Zubaba, who brought me a Median slave boy here, the long-lost prince of Parsa. Before he left, he gave me this note." Cyrus extended his hand. "A contact in the town of Shugalli. In Elam."

Sanda opened the parchment. She read its few words, looked at Cyrus, and shrugged.

"He said that if I were ever there... The man is, or was, one of the elite elders."

Sanda shook her head. She handed the worn scrap back to Cyrus. "Maybe my father knows him, or the town, at least."

"Elam in the old days was glorious, Zubaba said. And we were the closest of allies, Anshan and Susa."

Sanda watched the lines in Cyrus's face drop away. His mouth pursed, giving the swoop of his lower lip even more fullness. "I may have cousins just over those hills and all the way to Susa."

Sanda smiled. "Maybe you do."

Cyrus drew her, laughing, down to his lap. "But why should I care, when you have given me all the family I could ever want?"

He buried his head in her neck, hiding the ambivalence he felt about the shepherds who had raised him, the first and only family he had known until he was ten. Lies stirred that fiery anger – how they had never told Cyrus that he was really the son of a Median princess and King Cam of Anshan. When he had confronted them after a happy reunion, they'd said only that there was more to it than Cyrus knew. He never saw them now.

Cyrus put his hands at Sanda's waist and eased her back up to standing. "There's something else."

Sanda straightened. "What is it?"

"I know that Anshan has always been the site of Parsa's palace." He looked up into her face.

"But?" she gently prompted.

"I'm thinking of moving it. To Pasargad."

Cassandane's eyes opened wide. She clapped her hands over her mouth, then with a happy squeal, took his head in her hands and buried her face in his curly hair. She shut her eyes and kissed the top of his head. "Don't make this move for me," she said, leaning over, her brown eyes finding his. "Don't do it for my father or for my brother."

"It's for me," Cyrus said. "Pasargad is the first place I have ever felt at home since leaving the cottage in Media." He took her hands and, squeezing them, smiled into her eyes. "Pasargad -- you, your family -- is the only true home I could ever have. Besides, it's not so far and still within greater Parsa. I could renew our ties with Elam. Peace and strength. We'd never have to leave."

The sun itself couldn't have been brighter than Sanda's smile. "Promise? Our home forever?" she asked.

"I promise," Cyrus said. "Forever."

That was years ago. Since that moment, the young king and queen of Parsa had talked often of their dreams for the palace, their dreams for the country as a whole. Nominally a vassal of Astyages's Median empire, it was too far south, too poor and uninteresting to gain his attention. There was no reason to imagine that their dreams and ambition, simply contentment within its borders would be difficult to achieve. Since that moment, they'd been thinking how Pasargad – the palace complex they'd build there – might reflect their dreams.

Cassandane squeezed Cyrus's hand to get his attention. When he looked at her, she nodded to the scrap of paper. "Tell me?" she asked.

And so he did. He had always told her everything.

* * *

A SOUND at the doorway made them both turn.

"Pharnaspes!" Cyrus said. "We were just talking about you."

"I don't want to interrupt," the man said, nodding to his daughter. To the young royals' great pleasure, Pharnaspes had relocated himself and Otanes, Cassandane's brother, to the palace at Anshan. They fit into the community immediately and were soon indispensable to its workings.

"You're not interrupting," Cyrus said. "What is it?"

"Trouble among the tribes."

Sanda brushed her hand along Cyrus's cheek, then set it lightly on her father's shoulder. As she left, Cyrus called after her, "Pasargad." She threw a smile over her shoulder.

Cyrus turned back to Pharnaspes. His father-in-law's expression stole the smile from Cyrus's face.

"A Mardian killed a Dropici shepherd... with a sword from the cache. Confronted, the man proudly displayed the weapon and the flock. Admitted everything. Chiefs from the neighboring tribes convinced the Mardians that the man should be punished. It's resolved... for the time being, anyway."

Cyrus shook his head. "Call a meeting of the chiefs."

Pharnaspes nodded and left.

Cyrus looked at the parchment in his hand and jumped up. "Pharn?" he called. But the man was gone.

"Want me to get him?"

"Otanes!" Cyrus greeted the lanky youth who stood in the doorway. "I'll talk to him later. Come in. You just missed your father."

"So I gathered. I can still get him back, if you'd like. I just wanted to tell you that we're out of the big bows."

CHAPTER 12 (PARSA)

*Y*ears before, when Cyrus, no prince by the looks of it then, had first ridden into the territory of the noble Pasargad tribe bearing the gruesome evidence of terror in the kingdom, Otanes was just a boy. And when Cyrus finally ridded the area of its tyrannous groundsman only to learn later that the man had been secretly amassing an armory of weapons, Otanes was the youngest to stand in line willing to master a means of defense.

Cyrus recalled the youth, long-limbed and graceful even at eleven years old, reaching for a simple longbow, while others seized magnificent swords, spears, and decorative shields. Some men – who Cyrus knew had no horses – even took bridles, attracted by the fantastic handiwork on cheek pieces and studded brow straps. Although Otanes wasn't strong enough to draw the bow, he never wavered in his choice. Its weight was light but the wood, from yew trees that grew far to the north, in Media, was hard.

Otanes carried the bow with him everywhere, nonplussed by the amusement he caused, and set it up near him when he practiced on the common, smaller, and more pliant models. Eventually, people accepted the oversized arc of the longbow as simply another limb of the quiet boy's body. While stocky men thrust and feinted with throaty grunts among the shouts and guffaws of their peers, Otanes quietly drew his bowstrings over and over.

Day after day, Otanes sought his targets with feathered arrows that he multiplied in the evenings from wood trained straight and down-the-line true. His obsession never let up despite the arrows that dropped far short or swung so wide he might as well have been turning in circles when he drew. Neither did he lose his temper, but steadily practiced. Over and over Otanes shot for the mark. More and more frequently, he made it. He tightened the strings and increased his distance.

Soon, Otanes's chest broadened, and his shoulders thickened, and though Otanes remained slender, his arms developed muscles that seemed to grow straight out of the yew of his bow – iron hard and fluid as a summer stream. No one noticed when he swapped out the common hunting bow for the long one. No one was there when with a great breath, he called on every fiber, muscles trembling, pulled it taut, and exhaled. Only he heard its wood whisper the memory of northern forests and felt it yield, matching his body, strength for strength like a true companion. When the arrow that he loosed sped out of sight, no one saw him smile.

Young women were the first to notice that Otanes's arrows outstripped the distance that even the strongest man of Parsa could throw a spear or shoot with a common bow. And Otanes's aim was far more accurate. He would slip away in an afternoon and return with game, hides intact.

Other such bows had been collecting dust in the old makeshift armory. Every so often, Cyrus had tried to interest a man, volunteering for service, in adopting the weapon. But the bows were unwieldy, tiring to draw (if a man could do so at all), and frustratingly inaccurate by comparison with the more familiar hunting bows. There seemed no sense in it, so the weapons languished... until Otanes demonstrated their capacity. It didn't hurt that he had attracted the attention of the prettiest girls in Parsa.

After that, every young man wanted to learn; but few had the diligence required. These Otanes trained patiently. When after many months, they showed progress, it became obvious that in the right hands – warrior-strong but sensitive and steady – such bows far surpassed any other weapon in accuracy and distance. To be an archer in Parsa became every boy's dream. Now, Otanes was sixteen, and the store was empty.

* * *

THE ATMOSPHERE in the meeting tent was tense. The chiefs of each Parsan tribe were there – the Pasargad, noblest and most powerful; the Maraphii and Maspii, the next most well respected; as well as the agricultural Pantheialaei, Drusaiaei, and Germanii; and nomadic Dai, Dropici, Sagartii, and Mardi, fiercest of all. They sat around a circle on the plush carpet of a broad palace tent. The day was warm. The door was open, and flaps near the tent's roofline allowed a constant breeze through the shady space.

The Mardian chief was quick to say that they'd cut off the offender's hand. He glared at the others as if to dare them to demand more. No one did.

Instead, the talk came around to something Cyrus knew they had discussed among themselves – expansion.

"There are villages to the west, just beyond the hills, rich in orchards and fields. They could just as easily be ours as Elamite," one chief offered.

Cyrus bit his tongue. If he shut the discussion down now, they'd only carry it on without him. Better he should know...

"But stir up Elam, and you'll have the Medes breathing down our necks," another said.

"Or Babylon."

"Babylon pulled out of Elam a long time ago."

"Still, they've been interested."

"The villages I'm talking about are on the periphery. Media wouldn't notice."

"Babylon would."

The talk continued, some men advocating attack; others to desist. That Elam was nominally a Median territory seemed to some chiefs reason enough to leave it alone. Others observed that King Astyages of Media was far away and their own Parsa was stronger than ever.

Cyrus listened to all of it, and when they were done, when they seemed to have exhausted ideas and the pros and cons of each, he circled back to the issue that had first brought them together. "We are all one people," Cyrus said. "Attacks against each other will not be tolerated. As for Elam, time was when they were allies, 'our people,' too. Remember that."

"Give men weapons and training, and they're going to want to use them," Pharnaspes said, when the others had left.

"I suppose you're right." Cyrus leaned back against a cushion roll and retrieved the old note from a pouch at his belt. "Does this mean anything to you?" He handed it Pharnaspes.

Pharnaspes read it slowly, then shook his head. "Where did you get it?" He handed the parchment back to Cyrus.

"An old friend with ties to Elam gave it to me years ago. Said the man might be of help some time."

Pharnaspes turned down the corners of his mouth. "Will you go?"

Cyrus grinned. "They make good bows there."

CHAPTER 13 (PARSA)

*C*yrus found Sanda in the kitchen garden where she was walking around with four-year-old Cambyses, picking fruit and herbs for their dinner.

"Cook has assistants," Cyrus said.

"I know. I just thought we'd help. Cambyses wanted to check on the ants."

Cyrus put his arm around Sanda and took the basket from her hand.

The parents watched their little boy, oblivious to the attention. Cambyses crouched low, hands gripping his knees, and stared at the ground.

"He saw one of those orderly lines they make yesterday and would only leave if I promised we'd come back. *And* I promised him we'd go to the market tomorrow. I hope that's all right."

When Cyrus didn't answer, Sanda leaned out and looked hard at Cyrus's face.

"Yes, sorry," Cyrus said. "The market tomorrow."

Sanda tilted her head. "You said that you'd never keep anything from me."

Cyrus gripped her more tightly and then released her. He

shifted the basket to the other hand and reached up for an apricot. They'd spoken often of Pasargad, their plans and hopes for life there – their home forever. It was Sanda who counseled patience – to prioritize the kingdom's immediate needs, get things among the tribes back on steady footing here before making such a change.

"You know how it is that people unite against a common enemy?"

"Should I be worried?" Sanda asked.

Cyrus shook his head. "I want to start on Pasargad right away... All I want is to be there with you..."

Sanda's worry deepened. "But...?" she prompted.

"There something to the west." Cyrus told Cassandane of his thinking to go to Elam, evan Susa – nothing dramatic, merely the acquaintance of neighbors with a shared history. "Maybe a common ally..."

Sanda heard him out, then smiled.

"Don't you see?" she asked tenderly. "Everything you've said fits with our vision for the Parsa of the future. We've talked about designing the capital at Pasargadae as a model of openness and beauty – no palace wall to impose outside-and-in, but instead orderly gardens and boundless flowing water available to resident and visitor alike. Resolving conflict by finding common friends reflects just that," she said.

Cyrus swept her up, hiding his face in her hair, wondering how did he ever get so lucky? She was not only partner to his dreams but wove them even more perfectly than he ever could. Together, forever together in Pasargad.

With Parsa so small, and their desire for peace so great, neither Cassandane nor Cyrus stopped to consider than an ally here could make an enemy there.

* * *

"I'M COMING WITH YOU," Prexaspes said.

"I don't need a bodyguard, if that's what you have in mind." Cyrus said, noting the firm set of his friend's heavy jaw.

"You'd be surprised." Prexaspes shifted his weight from one foot to the other.

"This is a social visit. There's someone I want to see --"

"Have you ever seen him before?"

"No --"

"Then it's dangerous. A foreign place, people who might make assumptions..."

"Listen. I want to reestablish good relations between Elam and Parsa, like in the old days of Susa-and-Anshan. Cyrus's hand went to the tiny stone cylinder, once his grandfather's, that hung from his neck. "This is merely an investigative visit, investigating friendship. Besides, they know how to make Otanes's bow and have the wood to do it, I suspect." Seeing that Prexaspes was about to protest again, Cyrus added, "I don't want to arrive carrying a lot of weapons."

"Then you need someone to carry them for you." Prexaspes thumped his chest. "Me."

Cyrus shook his head in resignation. "Fine. Come." He put his hand on Prexaspes's shoulder. "I'd welcome your company. But no weapons."

"When do we leave?"

"Wait," Cyrus said. "What about your girl? What's her name – Zarin? I don't know how long we'll be gone."

Prexaspes's smile disappeared. "She's not my girl. And I don't know where that rumor started."

"She's the prettiest. That's for sure. Sanda excepted, of course. And from one of the highest-born families. That should suit you, heir to the chief of Parsa's noblest."

"I know, I know. Don't you start in on me, too. It's just --" Prexaspes looked at Cyrus.

"I *have* heard that she can be a bit, well, high born." Cyrus shrugged. "No worries. There are others."

"So everyone says," Prexaspes muttered.

They rode out the following day. The homely horse that Cyrus had brought from Media had become not only a nimble and intelligent partner for him, but to the surprise of his populace, it had also over the years become white. It also had become the mother of several fine foals.

Not everyone was fortunate enough to have a horse in Anshan, but for those who did, Cyrus commissioned Iranian metalsmiths to work with Elamite craftsmen in fashioning equestrian weaponry. His favorite – a sword that could hang comfortably and safely from the belt of a rider, with a handsome crossways handle that made it easy to retrieve in battle. The scabbard of this *akinakes*, as it came to be called, was decorated in fine detail with the winged lions and stocky heroes of legend and song.

That was the only weapon Cyrus took when he and his best friend left Anshan for Elam. Prexaspes wore the same and carried a small bow and quiver of arrows off his saddle. As concerned as Prexaspes was with Cyrus's welfare, he didn't protest when Cyrus told him that it would be just the two of them – an exploratory visit, nothing more.

CHAPTER 14 (BABYLONIA)

*I*n Babylon, the partial eclipse had indeed caused a great deal of consternation. The king watched it with particular horror – not only because of how it seemed to threaten Nanna-Suen but also because of the interpretations Babylon's priesthood might propose, interpretations that could compromise his plans. That the shadow passed so quickly was a relief. As it turns out, Nabonidus own interpretation – that the moon god had vanquished the threat – was already gaining traction among the religious authorities. Meanwhile, King Nabonidus continued to do for all of Babylonia's gods what was expected of its king. Genuine piety came naturally to him. The same could not be said of his son.

* * *

WITH THE KINGSHIP in his elderly father's control, crown prince Belshazzar swiftly confiscated the former king's sizable estate and kept it for his own. He also retained the business agent who had served Igliss so well -- the Egibi, Nabu-ahhe-iddin, who went simply by Khai.

Belshazzar called Khai into the palace. They sipped a honeyed mint tea, too sweet for Khai's taste, but he'd had no time yet that day to eat, and it stilled his grumbling stomach. The slave Bel-ritsua, whom Belshazzar had appropriated along with all the other of Igliss's property, was a silent presence.

After Khai exchanged the requisite pleasantries -- asking after Belshazzar's mother, yes still in Uruk; Qudashu is fine, thank you -- Belshazzar asked Khai to join him at a broad table. "You know better than anyone these properties," Belshazzar said, lining up documents detailing the late Igliss's holdings, recorded on both parchment and clay, some composed in Khai's own hand, across the cedar table. "Would you continue to manage the estate?"

"If you want me to," Khai replied.

"The first thing I'd like to do is purchase the house that presently lies between yours and mine on Arahtum Canal." Belshazzar waved the slave forward. "I believe that you know Bel-ritsua. He has begun the negotiations.",

Khai nodded to the slave, whose auburn eyes gazed impassively back. Khai knew Bel-ritsua as a shrewd and capable manager who more than any other had enabled Igliss's prosperity. Khai also knew that as intimately as the Syrian knew his owner's business, both personal and professional, the slave kept clear of family drama and kept his mouth shut about what he saw and heard. Belshazzar had made Bel-ritsua his majordomo.

Belshazzar adjusted his blue robe, realigning with thick fingers the golden bracteates that hung in double rows down the front. "Direct any questions to Bel-ritsua. He can handle them or will contact me, if not. So," Belshazzar brought his hands together with a clap. "I'll leave you two to such business. I have a few temples to visit."

Khai and Bel-ritsua bowed to Belshazzar as he swept his robes around him and left.

Bel-ritsua pulled the relevant document out from underneath a stack and slid it in front of Khai. "The former owner and his business partner wish to retain the rights to access the canal from the house's property. Prince Belshazzar already owns the dock next door."

"This piece between our houses on the canal," Khai said. "I'd like to keep the exit behind my house. I can draw up the title accordingly, if you have no objections."

"That's fine," Bel-ritsua said.

Khai waited a moment before he realized that the slave meant for Khai to revise the document on the spot. He looked at Bel-ritsua, standing patiently at the table, and realized that they'd both, in their ways, succeeded. Both had weathered this latest coup d'etat and were trying anew to find their bearings in a shifting world. Khai drew a pen from the well and composed an addendum.

Bel-ritsua laid the document at the table's corner, squaring it neatly. "Let's begin the other open cases. When we've finished with those, I'll show you details for the other holdings in order of categories and the dates of acquisition."

Khai bent his head alongside the slave over the books. They were familiar to him, of course, having worked with Igliss to gain and maintain the most recent properties; but there were some surprises, too. For one thing, it appeared that Nabonidus had turned over nearly all of what he owned -- quite a bit, as it turned out -- to Belshazzar, and Belshazzar had borrowed against them, putting the family in debt.

Now that Nabonidus had gained the throne, they had more power of course, but they also had to pay considerably more to the city's temples precisely on account of being the royal family. The challenge of managing these circumstances was sufficiently engrossing to make Khai finally set aside his concerns about their own Egibi fledgling enterprises in order to manage the problems of the estate that Belshazzar now possessed. As always, coloring the background of his thoughts was Amytis, specifically how to keep the crown's business on strong enough footing that no one would be tempted to lean on Median resources, compromise the wild land that Amytis so loved. At least *this* king, Nabonidus, focused far more on spiritual matters and less on material acquisition than Igliss... And at least he – not his son Belshazzar – was king. After all, Nabonidus wouldn't compromise the treaty that Amytis's fierce stubbornness – merely a girl, then – had seen into being.

After they'd worked for over an hour, Khai asked, "Does the king know how bad..."

The slave straightened up from the table.

"Does he know the state of the family's affairs?"

"They are in Belshazzar's control," Bel-ritsua answered.

"I understand that."

"If you're concerned about meeting the requirement of the annual temple tithe..."

"That's exactly what I'm thinking about."

"They'll need a net increase of about eight percent." Bel-ritsua bent over the table again, arranging the documents. "It will be difficult but not impossible to realize from agricultural -- primarily date and barley -- yields, rental income, and the profit from foreign markets." He pointed there, there, and there.

Khai thought of Media, his own experience of the place... its deep ravines, fickle weather and mercurial skies... moonlight on the mountains' snowy peaks, the scream of eagles and the hush of the forest. Streams sparkling with trout and cold enough to numb limbs in mere moments. He remembered a night listening to the lonely howls of a golden jackal met only with silence...

"Sir?" Bel-ritsua said startling Khai.

"Sorry, yes."

"The requisite increase in income..."

"Right. Tell me again exactly what we need to cover expenses, including the annual temple tithe, and I'll talk with the king."

"Belshazzar should be made aware, of course," the slave said sternly, "and present, when you meet with King Nabonidus."

Khai squinted at the slave. "I suppose you're right... unless he has more urgent business, meeting with his tailor or some such pressing obligation, of course." Khai couldn't keep the sarcasm from his voice.

"Of course," Bel-ritsua said, his face straight as a judge's.

* * *

WHEN KHAI PRESENTED to Nabonidus the problems of Belshazzar's estate, Belshazzar had been absent, claiming an earlier commitment with a Babylonian socialite. The prince had explained that such connections were invaluable, given the unorthodox manner in which Nabonidus had ascended the throne.

For Khai's part, he was relieved that they could make sense of the finances and chart a course that satisfied... without any talk of "securing resources" from places richer in natural goods.

Nabonidus accepted the disappointment – it was that – with only a sigh. Maybe Belshazzar was right, Nabonidus thought. Maybe all those connections, and his way of making them were more important than... No matter. It was just as well that Belshazzar wasn't privy to Nabonidus's plans to correct the red in their balance sheets. He almost certainly wouldn't approve.

CHAPTER 15 (BABYLONIA)

*S*ure enough, when Nabonidus was just preparing for bed, Belshazzar stormed in, demanding to see him. Nabonidus turned from the table where he'd laid the heavy gold bracelet wound round with Ishtar's stars, the sun of Shamash, and the crescent of Nanna-Suen. He unpinned a silver lozenge from his breast, the spade of Marduk.

"What do you mean by telling the temple you won't tithe as expected?" Belshazzar leaned forward on his toes and waved his arms in front of Nabonidus's face.

"Hello, Shazzi," Nabonidus said.

"Do you want to alienate them before you've even performed your first Akitu?"

"It's not what you think."

"Then what is it? Because what I've heard is that you've refused to pay the temple what every king before you has gladly given to the gods who got you here and whose favor your very life depends upon."

Nabonidus scowled. "You're not threatening me, are you?"

"You won't need me for that, if you carry on with this foolishness," Belshazzar said, his face red with the effort of restraint.

"This foolishness, as you call it, is not a refusal to pay. It's simply a reduction in the exorbitant collections that the priests and their ever-expanding staff demand to keep up a lifestyle that I hardly think the gods demand."

"That lifestyle is our lifestyle, father."

"Speak for yourself, Shazzi. No priest or king, for that matter, requires such gold on his fingers, such delicacies on his plate, or obsequious displays of gift-giving as they've come to expect. Sit down."

Belshazzar halted his pacing to grab hold of the edge of a chair. Nabonidus pulled up another. Nabonidus took a deep, calming breath.

"What I proposed," Nabonidus said, "is simply a system to ensure that the funds that we *and others* submit to the temple goes for the things the gods most require -- well-maintained facilities, an efficient staff, and yes the basic daily and holiday sacrifices. I have not proposed to do away with the royal family's temple tithe, just the amount and the means by which it is delivered. I have installed a cash-box system whereby what we and others submit goes directly to the temple's requirements and not into the pockets of well-placed individual temple staff. Speaking of which, I have also reduced the number of administrators to a practical and efficient size."

"What?!" Belshazzar leapt up again and resumed his pacing.

Nabonidus ignored him. "All of this means a consequent and may I say happy reduction in the necessary tithe. What's more, a portion of that temple income will return to the palace in light of and corresponding to the royal obligations for temple management and maintenance."

"You cannot do this."

"I can, Shazzi. I am king, just as you wished."

"You will make powerful enemies."

"Your friends, I know." Nabonidus sighed.

"These people, the temple administrators and powerful citizenry put you on the throne because they believed that you would serve Babylonia appropriately," Belshazzar said, his voice high and tight.

"Well, then, let me serve," Nabonidus roared, bringing his fist down on the chair's arm. He stood up. "I had no thought of kingship for myself, but they brought me to the palace and all of them prostrated themselves at my feet and kissed them. They kept praising my kingship. And you, Shazzi, were chief among them. Now listen. Understand this: if you are to be king after me, there are places outside of this city and gods besides Marduk that require attention and care from this throne. I have not forgotten my commitments nor where I came from. You would do well to remember, too."

"I come from Babylon," Belshazzar spat, and in a whirl of silken robes and a stomping tread, he left.

Nabonidus ran his hands through his thinning hair. "Nanna-Suen, help me," he said under his breath.

* * *

"WHAT DO you know of professionals in Harran?" Nabonidus asked Adad-guppi. If anyone would know about existing assets finally to advance work on the northern temple of the moon god, it would be his mother.

The old woman's eyes shone. "You'll rebuild the Elhulhul, Nanna-Suen's home?!"

"I want to look into it - to excavate the foundations, at least. If we can."

Adad-guppi vigorously rubbed her bony knees. "I have been praying for this day for decades, ever since the Babylonians captured our city and forced us – me, and you just a boy -- to come here. I have prayed to Nanna-Suen, even as I answered to palace officials and bowed to the royal family, even as I searched for opportunities for you to advance. And advance you did, from service to the court, to courtier, to official, head of the military. And now king." She stood up. "Nanna-Suen has surely heard my prayers. He has given me long life to witness this day for myself, to rebuild the Elhulhul." She shook her head in happy wonderment.

"We can't begin yet. I do want to get the statue of Nanna-Suen one day back into the Elhulhul in Harran; but King Astyages and his Medes still control much of the region.

Adad-guppi sat again. "How can I help?"

"We need engineers and archaeologists, local and discrete. I don't want them to arouse suspicion among the occupying troops from Media."

"I knew exactly who could have done the work decades ago. Still, the Harran families that compose each guild are the same. I'll start there."

"In the meantime, we need to go carefully with the religious establishment here."

"Of course."

CHAPTER 16 (BABYLONIA)

*N*abonidus let his new attendant, a youth orphaned in the Cilician campaign, choose the king's clothes for his daily audience. The boy had a sense of propriety and style that utterly escaped Nabonidus who would just as soon show up in the dirty and often bloodied garments of his military exercises (Nabonidus still insisted on sparring with the best warriors), as oil his hair, pull on clean sandals, and don the regal robes to sit the throne. The youth selected the simplest of crowns from among the king's collection -- a crenellated golden band that Nabonidus had commissioned, finding the heavily jeweled models to be too cumbersome for his taste -- and set it on Nabonidus's head.

It would be a difficult audience to manage, Nabonidus felt certain. He needed to enter it with integrity and clarity of purpose.

"Marduk and Nanna-Suen caused me to see a dream," Nabonidus said.

The priests, merchants, and military commanders whom Nabonidus had invited looked at one another.

"In the dream, as vivid as any waking moment," Nabonidus

said, "Marduk commanded me 'to rebuild the Nanna-Suen's temple in Harran.'

The priests murmured.

"He said I was to carry the bricks myself."

"You are sure it was Marduk?" the temple shatammu asked.

"Without a doubt. The snake-dragon on which he stood glared at me with knife-sharp eyes and hissed when I pointed out the obvious problem. Reverently I said, 'that temple which you told me to build, Medes surround it with great strength."

"Indeed," a grizzled army general said. "And we haven't fought the Medes since..."

"Never, as Babylonians, anyway. Not since the empire was established. And you'll recall our alliance realized in the marriage of Nebuchadnezzar to Amytis of Media."

"Quite the historian," a merchant said quietly to his neighbor, who nodded knowingly.

"But their son was assassinated, and Amytis is back in Media. We certainly aren't allies anymore."

"We're better off without that half-Mede on the throne, if you ask me," a priest said. "Babylon should be Babylonian."

"But if *Marduk* wishes that Nanna-Suen's temple be rebuilt..." another priest said.

"I'm still not convinced," the shatammu interrupted, "that Marduk would really want Nanna-Suen's temple to be rebuilt – in Harran, no less."

"Yet the king says it was Marduk himself," the army general said, "who commanded it."

"But didn't say how?" a diviner asked.

Nabonidus cleared his throat. "It's up to us -- to me, first of all as king -- to see that it's done. You are the gods' own representatives," he nodded to the religious personnel, "the bravest and most accomplished military, and men familiar with the territories that greater Media claims to control..."

"'Claims,' is right," a merchant said. "I don't know how you others feel," he looked around at the other tradesmen, "but from what I've seen, King Astyages thinks his reach extends a whole lot farther than it does. Where I do business, just south of greater Ecbatana, no one likes him. They give their tribute grudgingly."

"True too, in the south -- Susa, and east to Parsa, too -- from what I've seen," another merchant said.

"I say we attack," a young cavalry officer said.

The old army officer squinted and shook his head.

"You'll have troops up that way soon, anyway, won't you, sir?" the youth asked.

"Only to subdue the rebels in Cilicia," Nabonidus said. "And remember, the sacred treaty that Amytis finalized protects Media from Babylonian acquisition."

"But rebuilding the Elhulhul does not require defeating the Medes, does it?" a priest asked.

"Nah," the shatammu snorted. Then, his voice laced with sarcasm, "... just inviting them to leave Harran," he said.

Nabonidus ignored the shatammu's tone. He nodded. "Precisely," he said. "Our purpose there would be to improve not destroy a Median territory." He was serious about that. He hadn't known Nebuchadnezzar's wife well – she'd kept to herself – but he respected her. And he respected the treaty between their nations. "But if Astyages would draw off his troops, we could move in to rebuild."

The army officer said, "If it happened he could redirect them..."

The shatammu smirked at the priest. "Yeah, right."

A small voice piped up. "It wouldn't take much," the youngest merchant offered. "There's a new king in Parsa, Cyrus I think he's called, already more friendly with Susa than Ecbatana."

The military men exchanged a look. "I can't imagine the Medes are happy about that," the general said.

*A*mytis forgot about Harpagus in her excitement to visit Susa, secretly hoping to find Egibi merchants from Babylon there, one in particular.

The Median party, ostensibly led by Spitamas, rode west across the mountains, then turned south along the Tigris River. The lowlands made for easier travel, something that Nathan noted with appreciation. He'd never warmed to traveling on horseback. For her part, Amytis welcomed the adventure. Their route traveled through Median territories she'd been meaning to revisit. And she had never seen Susa, the famous capital of old Elam.

After several days' hard riding they passed into territories of the former Elamite state. They skirted cities, taking note of the quality of defensive walls and the size of cultivated land around. In most cases, there were signs of some decay, but not as bad as Amytis expected from the Assyrian records of assault. Most striking, they found no evidence of foreign military occupation.

"Susa will tell," Spitamas said.

But when they arrived in Susa, they still found no signs of recent struggle or foreign occupation. They rode directly to the palace. Guards admitted them promptly, took the horses, and ushered Spitamas, Amytis, and Nathan into the audience room.

There, the old king was seated on a heavy wooden throne. He wore the traditional Elamite headress of a monarch -- a soft cap with a long bill in front and his hair gathered and covered by fabric in the back. A wide green band held the cap in place around which ran a row of many-petaled flowers embroidered in golden thread. Next to him stood a man every bit his younger image. The visitors hardly needed to see the green band to know that this was the crown prince, Tepti.

"Greetings from our father, the great king Astyages," Spitamas said. He extended a mahogany box with ivory and gold inlay and drew back its lid to reveal a mound of lapis lazuli, some polished and some left rough cut.

King Šilhak nodded politely and handed the box to his attendant. His smile was for the woman before him.

"So is this the famous Amytis, widow of the great Nebuchadnezzar and queen mother of the deceased Amel-Marduk?"

Amytis returned his smile, in spite of herself. The old man rose slowly from his throne as he spoke. His son helped him down the step off the dais. "Do you know that we still have alabaster vessels from Nebuchadnezzar and Amel-Marduk here?" He called in a wavering voice to the guard at the door, "Fetch those, would you? Oh, the things they would send of the glories of Babylon."

The prince said, "I suspect you're here for more than greetings."

Spitamas said, "The great king does wish to remind you of his gracious patronage and support."

"How thoughtful," Tepti said.

Undeterred, "... that if you face any kind of pressure or trouble," Spitamas continued, "you know you can count on Ecbatana for aid."

"We'll be sure to send you back with gifts befitting for such generosity."

Spitamas sat back. Things were going well.

"Things here are better than ever, actually," the old king said. "There's a new ruler, up in the highlands –"

Both Amytis and Spitamas sat forward. But -

"Look, Father," the prince interrupted, "here they are."

* * *

A MAN WALKED into the hall, holding two objects against his chest. A scowling boy of about five or six limped just behind him. Amytis winced to see the child haul his right foot, bundled in a crude wad of fabric, as though it were a distasteful sack of garbage on the end of his leg. The boy saw her looking and stuck out his tongue. Amytis caught her breath. No one else seemed to notice. They were all looking at the objects.

Bright white rims of alabaster vessels showed over their cloth wrappings. The king gestured to let Amytis pick up the vessels. She lifted one gently. The man held the cloth while she turned it in her hands. Nathan read its inscription aloud.

"3 GAR 1/3 *qa* palace of Amel-Marduk, king of Babylon, son of Nebuchadnezzar, king of Babylon," Nathan read.

Amytis swallowed hard, her eyes shining. Her own son had held this!, had sent this! She returned the vessel reluctantly. Nathan read the other, "Palace of Nebuchadnezzar, king of Babylon, who walks forth with the support of Nabu and Marduk, his lords, son of Nabopolassar, king of Babylon."

Amytis nodded. She glanced down at the boy, watching her. He didn't smile.

"We don't hear much from Babylon these days," the old king said. "You probably remember," he looked at Amytis, "that Nebuchadnezzar had thought about doing some building here."

Amytis nodded.

"But it never came to pass. We still have some bricks with his name on them, but nothing more."

"Nebuchadnezzar wanted to make us Babylonian," the boy said.

The man shushed him.

"What?" the boy snapped back. "That's what everyone says."

"I'm sorry," the man said, glancing from one to another. "My son doesn't know his place."

The boy scuffed his bum foot on the ground, frowning.

Prince Tepti laid his hand on the man's shoulder, "This is Mardonius, one of our most distinguished army captains."

Spitamas looked puzzled. He opened his mouth to speak.

But Amytis said, smiling at the boy, "And who is the young soldier?"

The boy sputtered, "I am not a soldier. If you had eyes, you could --"

"Gobryas!" the man said.

"You're only here, a stupid servant, because of me," the boy shouted, his face red, and wobbled his way out the door his gait made more awkward by haste.

Mardonius grimaced.

"Thank you Mardonius," the prince said. "You may leave."

When he had gone, Tepti explained that Gobryas had been born with a club foot. His mother had died giving birth, and Mardonius was raising the child himself. When it was clear that Gobryas would never be able to walk very well, much less follow his father in military service, the king had given Mardonius a job in the palace archives. There, Gobryas could not only stay with his father but also learn skills for useful service despite his birth defect.

"But the boy is angry, as you can see," Tepti said, "and Mardonius is unhappy." He shook his head as if to dismiss the topic.

The prince helped the old king back to his throne.

"You mentioned something about a king from the highlands," Spitamas said. "Is that Cyrus from Anshan?"

"King, yes," Šilhak said, "though not of much. Still, he came here with herds, wine. Said they were offerings for the old gods. When he saw the state of their temples, especially Humban's, he asked if he could sponsor renovations." The king paused. "Stay as long as you like. Tepti here will be happy to answer any other questions you have. He'll arrange for appropriate gifts to return to Ecbatana, too."

The prince helped the old king down from his throne again and passed him gently to the arm of a waiting attendant.

Šilhak waved Amytis toward him. He released his attendant and took her hand in both of his, spotted with age. He looked kindly into her eyes. "When it is my time," he said to Amytis, "and I stand before the gods, may Inšušinak judge me to be half so good as your son."

"Thank you," Amytis said, her eyes shining. "May it still be years to come."

*A*fter the king had left, Tepti said, "As my father mentioned, Cyrus of Anshan says he wants to help keep the old ways. He brought enough animals to give each of the temples' officiants (about thirty, when you account for other temples) one head of cattle and six head of sheep or goats. Turns out that Cyrus shares my father's and my interest in restoring and reviving the sacred groves."

"Sounds like a friendly visit," Amytis said.

Spitamas said, "Any other interests that brought him here?"

"Renewing old friendships, I guess," Tepti remarked, "like the lady said."

"Oh?" Spitamas asked.

"He came here with a certain Huban-ahpi from the town of Šugalli. Important family down there. They've long had connections with some of Susa's elite. Business or personal, I don't know. I think they stayed with Kurlush, whose own family came from the highlands near Arjan, I think, years ago. Anyway, it's good to know your neighbors."

"Anshan isn't exactly next door," Spitamas said.

"No," Tepti conceded, "but if you start figuring in places such as Šugalli and Arjan, between here and there, it begins to seem quite close."

"I see." Spitamas pursed his lips.

"We can discuss more later. As you wish. The day is young and the nights short this time of year. We have plenty of time. Let me show you all to your rooms. I'll have the staff draw baths for you."

* * *

AMYTIS SLID into the warm water, sending rose petals scurrying across the honey-gold tub. She ran her fingers in languid circles, swirling the petals back and stirring up the faint scent of lemons. Amytis had dismissed the maids preferring rather to be alone, to let the water and her mind in solitude ease away what stress still clung. She didn't mind a little soreness. They were honest aches and reminded her that she was still alive.

Amytis took a square of rose-scented linen from the tub's rim and dipped it in the water. Water slowed everything down. Babylon. She had tried to keep the city and its associations from her mind for so long. But seeing those things from the palace, her palace. Her husband, her son. She slipped low in the water and let her tears run straight in.

How could Khai...? Tomorrow, she would visit the merchants' colony and learn what she could, whatever it was. An image of the first time Amytis had seen Khai came to her mind -- a careless, confident youth sitting at the lowest table of her wedding dinner as relaxed as if it had been a tavern or his own home. If he were here, an extraordinary coincidence. But if he were, oh the things she would ask – how could he have served Igliss? how Belshazzar now? surely there was some explanation... or maybe her anger and hurt were justified. If she could just ask...

* * *

S<small>PITAMAS WAS WAITING</small> for Amytis when she emerged, her cheeks pink, in fresh clothes and lightly perfumed -- a gift from the palace. He, by contrast, wore the same travel clothes he'd been in all day. Streaks of dust and dried sweat criss-crossed his face. "There is more. I am sure of it," Spitamas said, pacing. "I just can't get it out of these royals."

"What do you mean?" Amytis asked, retying her hair into a chignon at the back of her neck.

"Cyrus. Making those connections... and all that ingratiating religious activity."

"Maybe he's genuinely respectful. Maybe he's actually pious," Amytis said, applying kohl to the rims of her eyes.

Spitamas shook his head. "What king is that pious unless it's his own city, his own gods, his own temple duties?"

Amytis shrugged. She peered into the small oval-shaped mirror and pursed her lips, always so dry these days. She scooped the tip of her finger across a tin of minted beeswax and smoothed it over her lips. "Maybe we should go to the *karum*, you know, the Babylonian merchants' colony. Ask there if anyone had any dealings with him." She said it lightly, as if it didn't matter to her one way or other.

Spitamas grinned. "I knew there was a reason I brought you!" He seized her head roughly and kissed her hair. "I'll go first thing tomorrow. With the scribe, of course. He needs to document this."

"... and with me," Amytis said. "As I've proved myself surprisingly useful."

"Suit yourself," Spitamas said. "Almost time for dinner!"

"Is it really?" Amytis said. "You may use my basin there."

CHAPTER 19 (ELAM)

*T*hey found Susa's merchant colony with ease. While Spitamas asked about recent trade from the highlands and Parsa, Amytis learned that the Egibi corporation did indeed have a presence in the colony. Local representatives weren't any people that she knew, though. Khai rarely traveled to Susa, they told her, but sent Iddina instead. Apparently the elder Egibi rarely left Babylon now, they said, as he was completely occupied with managing the royal estate. Iddina liked to make sure that they knew of the family's powerful reach. That was it. No one could tell her more. No one could tell Amytis what she wanted to know.

As they walked away from the center of hawking vendors and colorful tents, retreating to the quieter perimeter with its orchards and fields beyond, Nathan looked at Amytis with concern.

Feeling his eyes on her, Amytis shook her head. "I just suddenly feel so tired," she said.

Years had chiseled the features of youth revealing a finer frame and softer eyes. But it wasn't age the scribe saw now. He didn't have a chance to ask.

"Look, there's Spitamas." Nathan pointed. The Mede charged toward them. He'd taken Astyages's commission seriously and was determined to find evidence.

"Tell me," Spitamas said. "Did you talk to the Babylonians? the Beggie--"

"Egibi," Amytis said. "Yes."

"And?" he prompted. When Amytis didn't answer, "Did they say anything about Cyrus – you know, taking Elam... as that traveler in Ecbatana said?"

Amytis looked at Nathan. "No," they said simultaneously.

"Well, there's another merchant, said he's happy to talk... " Spitamas glanced back at the action.

"Nathan and I will meet you by that arm in the river." Amytis pointed to a point where the Choaspes diverged.

"Fine," Spitamas said, jigging in place. "I'm learning a lot. Meet you there."

Amytis and Nathan sat on soft grass by the bank. The river wound its way into the city, bringing its famously sweet water to the old capital. Nathan sipped from his hands, cupped at the shore. "Some water?" he asked Amytis.

Her gaze was distant. "Why is it that as much as everything changes, some things never seem to?" she asked.

Nathan was quiet.

"I'm devastated that Khai worked for my son's murderer. Still, I'd hoped..." She looked into Nathan's kind eyes, looked down. "I'd hoped to see him here." She waved her hand. "Silly." She took a deep breath, straightened again. "About my nephew, do *you* think he plans to conquer this region?"

"He hasn't," Nathan said. "Not with arms, anyway."

"Shh," Amytis stood. "Here comes Spitamas."

Nathan scrambled up to stand beside her.

Spitamas bent over to catch his breath. When he straightened again, he smiled. "This has been most useful," he said. "But listen.

Sit down. There's one more guy I want to meet -- a metalsmith. He wasn't there when I went by his shop. But the apprentice said he'd be back in a little while." He rubbed his hands together. "Oh, this is good." Amytis listened carefully – first with concern, then simple curiosity while Spitamas, eagerly told them what he'd learned.

"The people that Cyrus had visited, both Huban-ahpi and Kurlush, have lineages back to the former 'elders of Elam.' Those elders were instrumental in the sophisticated political system of old Elam. For one thing, they centralized goods from their loosely confederated regions and used redistribution to satisfy all needs. Also, the leaders and their territories cooperated in military operations. Their real strength," Spitamas said, punching the air for emphasis, "was that the soldiers were all free citizens. They wanted to be there. No one forced them. Each man cared deeply about the welfare of the collective. The Assyrian assault fragmented them. But each polity had survived."

"Cyrus was here, all right," Spitamas said, "and they like him. He brought gifts of bronze, iron, and gold. He traded really fine short swords, akinakes they call them, for fabric and leatherwork. Also, he gave master craftsmen here advances in pay to make bows. And he hired expert archers to accompany him back to Anshan to help train the young men there. Sounds to me like war is coming."

"But –" Amytis said.

Spitamas clapped his hands. "I'm going to talk to that metalsmith. Get ready to return to Media. I have a lot to tell the king." He dashed away again.

* * *

"IS THAT HOW YOU HEARD IT?" Amytis asked Nathan.

On the bank, she sat again. He lowered himself beside her.

"So Cyrus is making alliances and getting weapons..." Amytis said. "I'm still not convinced he plans to attack."

The river burbled companionably in front of them.

Nathan shrugged. Across the river a herd of goats ambled along worn paths. Youngsters bleated. Nannies shuffled, nibbling here and there.

"Do you see that ram?" Nathan pointed.

Amytis followed his finger to where a stout beast with curved horns pushed his way through the herd.

"Yes."

"He's like the kingdom of Media." They watched him butt one of the females heavy with unborn kids, "Like I said," Nathan said. "He -- Media, Astyages -- keeps bullying his way around Elam."

Amytis nodded.

"But," Nathan said, "I believe that another ram bigger and more refined is coming, who will push him out."

"Cyrus?" Amytis asked quietly.

Nathan wrapped his arms around his knees. "Maybe. Maybe some combination of people from highlands and lowlands -- Parsans and Elamites. Yahweh-God has plans...," Nathan said. "You can see it."

"Do you think that would be better, better for Media?" Despite their solitude, Amytis spoke the dangerous idea quietly.

"I do believe that Yahweh-God is preparing the world for change. From here, it looks like Cyrus is at the heart of it. Don't you see how these people have already embraced him?"

"But he hasn't conquered Elam. *That* we've learned. We saw that even on our way here. They've still got their tribal chieftains in place. Pekod controls the marshes abutting Babylonia, and the prince admitted that there are powerful families independent of Susa throughout the highlands, probably the lowlands, too."

"You don't have to conquer to control," Nathan said, nodding thoughtfully. "They're joining together again, cooperating. Cyrus appeals to their common interests. He's like the hub of a wheel, the axle of a chariot."

"Their forces are far fewer and weaker than my father's. Astyages will fight with all he's got to hold onto power."

Nathan sat back on his elbows. "Maybe I have it all wrong. I'm just telling what I see."

CHAPTER 20 (BABYLONIA)

*N*abonidus's troops retraced Igliss's route for the most part, heading up the Euphrates, alongside the river, to catch the rebel king in Cilicia. They traveled slowly. A mild spring had given way to a scorching summer. They rested each day when the sun was hottest and the air still. Further slowing their progress, Nabonidus took regular side-trips to visit outlying Babylonian settlements along the way. There, he took stock of the towns' needs and sent messengers back to the capital with orders to shore up crumbling defensive walls and restore other public buildings. All the while, Nabonidus was keenly aware of Harran to the east. The city, its temple in particular, pulled at him. In time, he thought. In time.

The terrain changed markedly to the north. Rather than enter Cilicia through the easy but heavily guarded pass, "the Syrian Gates," they took a hard and high road over the Amanus Mountains and caught the Cilician king by surprise. From there, it was easy. Nabonidus slew Appuašu in his palace. His troops swiftly neutralized the rogue element. In place of a king, Nabonidus installed a governor, a high-born native who promised loyalty and devotion to Babylon. All in all, it was a success. Not that it

mattered in any logistical way, but Nabonidus hoped that Belshazzar would see it as good Babylonian kingsmanship.

When the troops left Cilicia, the season had turned, hinting of
autumn. Rather than wait to construct the boats that could take
them all with the river's current down the Euphrates to Babylon,
Nabonidus sent only the wounded and weary by boat. He and the
others would return the way that they had come, following the
river where they could. It felt good to be out of the city. Besides,
the moon was waxing, and Nabonidus relished an opportunity to
worship his native god at his brightest without the impediment
of buildings all around.

It was a clear night, the heavens sparkling with language of
the gods when they camped along the river still north of Babylon
by a few days' travel. The moon big and bright – waxing, soon
full. Nabonidus left his tent to stand on the Euphrates' bank.
Nanna-Suen illuminated everything. He watched the moon's
silver light break across the water and mend again on the
rippling surface. He knew they had to return to Babylon, with its
constant crush and palace drama. But Nanna-Suen, high and
serene in the sky, attended by his heavenly host, calmed the old
king. He prayed for direction and discernment, let the silver radiance bathe his weary face.

* * *

THE CAMP BEGAN to disband while it was still dark, an efficient
and nearly silent process. The sky remained perfectly clear, not a
cloud in sight. Ideally, they would be well on their way before
Shamash rode into the sky and threw his cloak of heat over the
travelers. As Nabonidus moved among the troops, he looked up
occasionally to watch Nanna-Suen's dipping form.

Suddenly, a black form covered an edge of the moon.
Nabonidus watched in horror.

"Get the kettledrums!" a priest called.

As the shadow spread, and murmurs turned to shouts. Nabonidus ordered the packing to cease, commanded calm, and called his attendant and the camp's diviner to his tent. The moon continued to disappear. Nabonidus's heart pounded with worry as magicians' drums rolled with the effort of keeping evil forces at bay.

"Fetch the *Enūma Anu Enlil*," Nabonidus said to his attendant. He pointed to a box of tablets. "The compendium of celestial omens. There." Nabonidus selected a chapter. The diviner and a scribe looked over his shoulder.

Scanning the text, the diviner called, "Prepare a lamb!"

His assistant dashed to retrieve, in the crude space of the military camp, a table that could serve. They killed the animal and laid its entrails out on the bloody table. The diviner invoked the gods and went to work examining patterns in the lamb's organs. Nabonidus stood next to him, pointing, peering, and conferring with the diviner until both stepped away.

Nabonidus returned to his tent. While the troops milled about restlessly, Nabonidus's attendant fixed to the king's chest a breastplate of beaten gold bearing the image of Ninurta dispatching the giant Anzu bird-dragon in hand-to-hand combat. A fistfight broke out on the edge of the camp. Nabonidus's attendant draped around the king's neck an amulet bearing the symbol of Nanna-Suen -- a crescent, its ends pointed up like a bull's horns, so that it hung on his chest just above the golden battle. The melee outside increased. Nabonidus stepped in front of the troops. They quieted. He raised his hands. The skirmishing ceased.

In a clear voice, loud enough to reach the farthest men, Nabonidus said, "In this month of the work of the goddesses, the Son of the Prince has shown a sign to the world. The Bright-Light of illumination has revealed his intention. Nanna-Suen, the lord of the crown, who leads all people –"

Murmuring rose and fell.

"-- made known to me, reverent shepherd who takes care of the great gods' holy houses, exactly what the god desires."

He had every ear now. This was it, Nabonidus thought, the opportunity he had known in his zealous heart that Nanna-Suen would make available: finally, it was time.

"Nanna-Suen requests a high priestess."

Finally, the king's daughter would serve again not Ishtar at the goddess's temple in Uruk, but Nanna-Suen in Ur. King Nabonidus would be the one to see it happen. He himself would install his daughter in her proper place: high priestess at the Etemenniguru, Nanna-Suen's "atmosphere-maker" temple in Ur. Nitocris wouldn't be the only he expected would resist. But the eclipse was a sign that things were changing... or should. Nabonidus was sure of it.

"The portent revealed in the liver of the lamb," Nabonidus continued, "has confirmed his divine majesty's sign and decision. When we have returned to Babylon, I will visit the sanctuaries of Shamash and Adad to seek additional counsel from the omen-telling gods."

The soldiers shuffled their feet.

"Finish packing. We leave immediately."

"It's what you've been waiting for, isn't it?" the diviner asked Nabonidus, when the others had left to resume packing.

"What do you mean?"

"To champion your god."

"I am merely interpreting."

The man shrugged. "There are two temples for Nanna-Suen," the diviner narrowed his eyes, "Ur in the south, Harran in the north. You're from Harran, aren't you?"

"Astyages of Media occupies Harran now. Surely, the only sense is that Nanna-Suen intends the priestess for Ur." And with that, King Nabonidus ended the conversation. They left shortly after that.

As they neared Babylon, Nabonidus thought to himself: the

power of the gods was shifting. The king's heart beat quickly – with anticipation and excitement now. Nanna-Suen was waxing indeed.

CHAPTER 21 (MEDIA)

$\mathcal{T}$he Median contingent traveled back to Ecbatana as swiftly as they could, passing straight through the mountains, despite the hard and dangerous road. They, too had seen the eclipse – significant, this one. And Amytis wanted to head off whatever monstrous interpretation Astyages might have courted in the meantime. They had concrete information to information, not vague prophecies, insinuations of rebellion or coup. More than once, Nathan bit his tongue rather than complain. He could see from Amytis's face that her mind was far from the bruising pace of their mounts or Cossean threat.

The afternoon sun glinted off the silver-capped palace walls at Ecbatana as the travelers rode into the city. Amytis had thought a lot about what they had learned on the long ride back to Ecbatana. When they finally arrived, she went not to Astyages but straight to Harpagus. Amytis glanced down the hall, empty, and rapped on the door.

"Come in," a voice called.

Amytis stepped inside a small room, paneled in bare cedar and pine. Amytis had never seen the room before. Now she wanted never to leave. Wooden cubbies filled with rolls of parchment ran floor to ceiling. A woolen tapestry depicting the mountain forests, birds and beasts, hidden in branches and brush hung over another wall. In one corner, under the room's only window was a low leather armchair, its seat deeply indented.

"Hello!" Harpagus said, hurrying out from behind a heavy table. "What brings you here?" He straightened the parchment strewn over the table -- more maps, Amytis could see, and sheets of lists -- numbers and place names.

"To talk with you," Amytis said, folding her hands in front of her and unfolding them again. "If I may."

"Always." Harpagus gestured to the armchair. "For certain."

"I'd rather stand," Amytis said. "I won't keep you from the king's business."

"Such as it is," Harpagus said. He stood quietly waiting. "A little wine?" he asked, lifting a flask.

"Yes, thank you."

Harpagus took a cup hidden in one of the wall cubbies and poured.

"It's about Cyrus."

Amytis watched Harpagus freeze, and then he handed her the cup.

"Do you mind?" Harpagus asked, sitting down.

Amytis shook her head. She sat, too. "Tell me," she said.

Harpagus didn't meet her eye. But he nodded just the same. Amytis waited as he took long draught from his cup.

"Mandane's son," Harpagus began. "Cyrus." He paused, opened, and closed his mouth again.

Amytis took the flask and refilled Harpagus's cup.

Harpagus drank it in one gulp. "Many years ago... twenty-five, to be precise..." Harpagus told Amytis everything that had happened -- how Astyages dreamt that one day his grandson, a child of Mandane's – "The magi were very clear: Mandane's, not yours would claim the throne."

"That's why he sent her to marry so far away," Amytis said. "Queen in a place so insignificant it wouldn't matter."

"And it's why he brought her back," Harpagus said. "A second dream, the same interpretation..." Harpagus told Amytis how the king determined to kill that baby at birth – she gasped – how Astyages had commanded Harpagus to see that it was done. Harpagus looked up at Amytis, his eyes haunted. "I couldn't do it. I had a little boy, too."

Harpagus told Amytis that secretly he gave the baby instead to a man he had known – an honest man, and "I'm sorry, so sorry!" Harpagus cried, "I told him the baby should die. Astyages had made terrible threats to me, if I didn't carry it out. So I told the man, Mithradates, the same." Harpagus hung his head. "I'm so ashamed. I have just always found a way to do what my king asked."

"But you took me to Cyrus – fine, happy – a baby living with those shepherd slaves."

"By the grace of the gods, it happened that Mit and Spaco had been desperate for a child of their own. And Spaco *at that same time* had birthed another infant – dead."

Amytis remembered the couple, both from the brief visit Harpagus had initiated and years before that when as a girl Amytis had accompanied Mandane to their cottage, again to assist with a pregnancy that ended too soon. "So they swapped the babies," Amytis said.

"Yes. But Mandane never knew," he said. "All she knew was that her son was dead. She killed herself for grief." He bent his head. "I hope that one day you'll forgive me," Harpagus said.

Amytis's eyes were dry. She had already wept rivers for the twin whose life had been her sole responsibility, an instinct of protection that had led Amytis to take her sister's place in Babylon. "I am grateful that you spared the boy," Amytis said. "That was the end of it. There is nothing to forgive."

"But that wasn't the end," Harpagus said. "Not for me." He looked at his hands, laid out flat on the table.

"Go on," Amytis said gently.

"You know that Cyrus was discovered. Magi reinterpreted the dream, convinced Astyages that it had been fulfilled... He said he was happy that Cyrus was alive. But between the shepherd slave and myself, your father learned the truth about how the boy came to be alive -- that I had lied."

Amytis caught her breath and nodded.

"So Astyages killed my son," Harpagus said.

"No."

Harpagus nodded. His eyes were hollow, his skin gray. "And fed the boy to me."

Amytis put her hand over her mouth.

"My wife couldn't bear it, all of it -- our son's death, my complicity..."

"Yet you stayed."

Harpagus took a deep breath. "I stayed. Ironically, I was the boy's first teacher – in horsemanship, palace protocol. I felt like two men. I hated the boy, resented him for being alive much less there in palace and doing everything I said, doing everything well – just as I would want from my own son."

Harpagus gagged, recovered again.

"And I grew fond of him for all the same reasons. Still at the thought of Cyrus these senses battle within me."

"And my father?" Amytis asked. "What about my father?"

"I do whatever he asks of me." Again Harpagus hung his head. "I don't have your fire, your fortitude or clarity to rebel." He shook his head, looked at her again. "I have served faithfully, loyally. The gods make a king – my king." Harpagus shrugged. "It's what I've always believed."

"So the only outlet for your anger and hurt is..."

"Cyrus," Harpagus finished for her.

Now Amytis understood the reason for the haggard eyes, the

heavy air that hung around Harpagus like a storm almost, but never breaking.

"But you're back from Susa,' Harpagus said, brisk again. He stood, refilled their cups. "You came to me."

Amytis looked at the old manager, the man who when she was a little girl had somehow both served her tyrannous father and made her – his bastard daughter, disdained with no inherent value – feel seen... and almost safe. He sat before her now, having regained an equanimity she couldn't begin to imagine having after what he'd been through. So she took a deep breath and reported what she'd learned. And what she'd concluded.

Amytis told Harpagus about Cyrus's activities in Susa, his overtures of diplomacy, his giving and commissioning weapons. She told how Susan nobles welcomed the young king, how Parsa had prospered under his leadership. She couldn't help but compare their dynamic peace while Media fractured and struggled under Astyages's rule despite her efforts. And Harpagus let her do it, heard her out. Amytis wrapped her hands around the cup. She looked down at the ripples and realized that she was shaking. "Now you tell me this. This horror that you endured. And it makes me even more certain..." She paused. "I have to make sure – *we* have to make sure that Astyages sees Cyrus for what he is: no threat but on the contrary a capable young ruler interested in the far more difficult task of peace. If Media is to engage Cyrus at all, it must be as friends... family." Amytis stood. She strode across the room and back. "For the welfare of Media, never mind Parsa, Astyages must understand that that alliance is the better way."

"I understand the king is waiting on your report?"

"Yes," Amytis said, momentarily flustered. "I'll see you there."

As Amytis rushed to her father's throne room, she made an effort to calm herself, to pay attention to Astyages's moods and calibrate her contributions accordingly.

"Where have you been?" Spitamas demanded from the doorway of the king's rooms. "Astyages has been waiting for our report."

"Just freshening up," Amytis said.

Spitamas looked at her dusty robe, the trousers still streaked from riding. Amytis brushed her hair away from her face defiantly. He shrugged. "Well, get in here."

Harpagus was already there, dutifully standing off to the side of king's throne, a quiet presence, attentive but expressionless. Amytis caught his eye. He returned her smile with a light nod then fixed his gaze ahead at nothing in particular.

While Astyages leaned forward, devouring every word, Spitamas launched into his report. Amytis heard it, shorn of any nuance or detail. She thought about the elegance of the court at Susa, the happiness with which the prince had shared his enthusiasm about restoring Elam's sacred groves, the bustle of business and excitement among officials and nobles, the optimism in renewing Elam's network of cooperating chieftains. Spitamas communicated none of this.

She recalled her reverie by the city's clear stream and

Nathan's prophetic vision. She thought about the nephew she'd so briefly met -- brutal manipulator of state power, or facilitator of a people's redemption? Amytis had decided. She hoped she was right.

"Well?" Astyages said, staring hard at Amytis.

"Excuse me, Father. Did you say something?"

Astyages leaned forward and spoke slowly, "I said... Do you have anything to add to your husband's report?"

Amytis looked at her father's face, lined by a lifetime of anxious suspicion, not battle, his nose bulbous and red, his eyes small and sharp. As she had predicted, he too had decided. That was clear. Astyages jutted out his chin and squinted as if he to drag the reply he wanted from her lips. Now was not the time, she saw.

"Spitamas covered everything," she said.

"You?" Astyages said to Nathan.

The scribe glanced at Amytis, then said to the king, "I have nothing to add, your majesty. There are my notes, of course."

"Ah, yes. Notes," Astyages said sitting back.

Nathan said, "But I believe your eunuchs have already fetched them from our travel bags. If you have any questions or wish to discuss them...."

Astyages waved his hand dismissively. "I've heard enough."

Amytis's sigh was audible.

Astyages skewered her with his eyes. "Unless there's something else you want to tell me?"

His posture, his tone, the very room itself – suffocating in its effort to exude grandeur – Amytis felt herself again the wounded little girl and felt again the old steely rise of her own disdain. She relished its delicious resistance... and recognized the danger of it, too.

Astyages said, "But did you *see* the moon swallowed up mere nights ago?"

"That doesn't mean that Cyrus will attack you," Amytis fired back and despite herself added, "whatever your lacky of boot-licking magi say." In the corner of her eye, Amytis caught Harpagus – so quiet, so dignified. She tried to channel his control. "Far better to make an ally of Cyrus, share any strengths…"

But the eclipse!" Astyages said, "It is always ominous."

"For others, maybe." The scribe's remark felt like a reset in the atmosphere… for Amytis, at least. It's all she needed.

"Yes," Amytis said. "Ominous for those who stand in the way of such an alliance. Father, if we take any action with respect to Mandane's son, your grandchild for gods' sake, it should be one of friendship. We are family. I've long wished to go to Anshan, to see –"

"No," Astyages said. He held up a hand. "I appreciate your report, the advantages of 'good relations…' . It's been most instructive."

Amytis left the ostentatious throne room with a kernel of hope. She determined to circle back soon – to remind Astyages how beneficial for Media, for the welfare of this empire (and all of the wildness she treasured – not a point of interest for Astyages) to make alliances, do the hard work of peace. If it came up again, she would remind her father that to make Cyrus and his Parsa a respected ally would only benefit Astyages's empire. Yes, the thought itself – the hope in it – eased a chronic under-current of dis-ease.

* * *

NOT BY ACCIDENT, Amytis wasn't there when King Astyages summoned his steward close. Astyages had heard their report. And he had heard Amtyis's plea. But. A woman, what knowledge could she have of these things? Sometimes a person – a king! – had be forceful. And wasn't it true, for as long as he could remember that he'd felt that people – all kinds of people – had been angling for his throne?

"Harpagus," Astyages said, "assemble the army, see to their training, that they're polished ard up to it. I'll call a review of the troops myself before we're ready to move out."

"Sir?" Harpagus said.

"You heard me."

Harpagus nodded. "Yes, sir."

And when the steward had left, King Astyages smacked a fist against his palm and muttered to himself, "It's time to remind that Parsan upstart of the might of Media.",

As he worked out a plant, the king of Media thought to himself, he'd tell this daughter of his who, back from Babylon seemed to think she knew the best way to run an empire... He'd tell her what she wanted to hear. What difference did her opinion make? He was king, and he'd do what was best. For him.

CHAPTER 23 (BABYLONIA)

*a*s soon as Babylon got the news that Nabonidus's party was approaching, the city's most powerful and influential diviners and scholars began to press for an audience. Everyone wanted to talk about the eclipse.

"I will consult the patron gods of omens -- Shamash and Adad -- for details," Nabonidus said. "Only after that, will I discuss it further."

Nabonidus indeed consulted the gods. But he did it himself. Only after that, did he invite input from the divines and scholars. Then, as promised, he convened a group of the most distinguished, most qualified, and sat back to hear what they would say first.

"A bad sign," one of the elder omen-readers offered immediately. "You could hear the copper kettledrums a mile away."

The others nodded their agreement.

"Do you think they worked?" a skinny scholar asked. "My wife has been distraught ever since." He twisted his stylus nervously. "I've hardly slept. Night time is the worst. She hears in every sound the talons or hoofs of the dark-walking demons." The others looked silently back at him. "Sorry. Right." He cleared his throat. "My colleagues dictated the exact time and duration of the event. It's in my report here."

Nabonidus stood. "It was indeed an auspicious sign, this darkening of Nanna-Suen's face. The god is unhappy."

"Or Marduk, maybe Shamash, is displeased with Nanna-Suen and decided to blind him for a time."

Nabonidus recognized the speaker as a high-ranking priest from Marduk's temple.

Another, who Nabonidus knew to be on close terms with Belshazzar said, "Indeed Marduk would countenance no rivalry should Nanna-Suen attempt to usurp the Babylon's divine throne. With finances diminished as they are, perhaps Marduk is angry that Nanna-Suen should request resources from Babylon."

"Or is angry with us," a young magician piped up. "Either way, there could be trouble ahead."

"Mmm, yes," several of the gray heads muttered. Nabonidus let them talk. In the hum of their voices, the name of Marduk was a constant.

"The *Enūma Anu Enlil* has a clear interpretation," Nabonidus said.

They fell silent.

"Nanna-Suen requests a high priestess."

The first diviner spoke up again. "With all respect, your highness, this is not exactly your area."

Nabonidus lifted his palms from the table and then set them down again, very quietly. "Just because I did not attend your schools or apprentice with priests and judges, I am not incapable of observing the evidence and seeking out the truth. The interpretation is there. Written right into those tablets. Frankly, I'm surprised that none of you offered such information."

The older men exchanged uneasy glances. Younger ones examined their robes or shoes.

Nabonidus took a deep breath. "It was the *moon*, men, that stood still. The great Nanna-Suen hid his face from us, his servants on earth, only for a time but long enough to be certain." The muttering began again. Nabonidus spoke over it. "I believe that you know my mother, Adad-guppi." He looked around. Each man acknowledged yes. "Some of you may not know that she, now the estimable queen mother, has been a lifetime devotee of Nanna-Suen while also respecting and fulfilling all of the expectations and requirements of the god Marduk here in Babylon." The men looked up and nodded. "You all know, too, that we have done our best to satisfy the obligations of this office to keep all temples in good working order -- strong foundations, straight walls, plastered neatly."

"Yes," the men answered one after another. "Yes."

"So I have been asking myself how to satisfy this request of Nanna-Suen's. The temple in Harran, neglected though it may be, cannot be a candidate. That region is in the control of the Medes. Years ago, Nanna-Suen left, and left it so. But the other temple, the temple in Ur, is also in need of restoration, and it is staffed by an old team. They are conscientious and diligent, but none has any relation to the crown. Ishtar has had the daughter of the king in such a position for many years. That is the tradition." Nabonidus paused.

The men waited.

"I have taken care to inquire further, to ask the great omen-telling gods, Shamash and Adad. To my first question -- whether our initial interpretation was correct -- they said yes. I then asked if the priestess could be a certain daughter of one of the king's relatives. They said no. I asked the third question with some hesitation. 'Should the priestess be my own daughter, beloved of my heart, who has grown up and served in the temple of Ishtar since a baby?' Their answer..." he looked around at each one, "was Yes. As it was in times long past, Nanna-Suen's temple should have a priestess, the king's own daughter, to serve not in Ishtar's Uruk but rather in Ur."

The men shook their heads. Nabonidus sat down. First one

and then another began to talk. They spoke and argued over each other's voices. Nabonidus remained quiet until the din subsided.

The eldest diviner spoke. "Even if your daughter were to leave the lady of Uruk to take the post for Nanna-Suen in Ur, no one knows the correct protocol, the garments, the jewelry, the rituals of initiation.

Nabonidus said, "I myself will investigate the orthodox traditions. I will make absolutely sure, before my daughter is uprooted from her home and burdened with this new position, that it is conducted in the most proper manner, that every expectation and wish of the god, of the gods, is taken into account, respected, and observed." He stood up. "I thank you for your invaluable contribution to this thorny matter."

Two elders began to speak.

"I wish you well," Nabonidus said, one hand high, "as you return to the work from which I have taken you."

The shatammu of Marduk's temple was the last to leave. He looked at Nabonidus, head to toe, as if seeing this king for the first time. He pursed his lips, clenched his teeth, and walked out.

When Nabonidus was finally alone again, he hung his head and exhaled. His next challenge, he knew, would be more formidable.

Sure enough, when Nitocris learned of his plans, she sent a missive warning that removing their daughter -- the king's daughter -- from the goddess's service would be catastrophic. Maybe not right away, she wrote, but it was an offense against Ishtar and would surely have consequences. Susanni should remain exactly where she was. Couldn't he see that it was destined to be?

Nabonidus laid the message aside. He called his scribe and dictated a simple response noting his resolution to follow through with the moon god's request.

"Add that I, Nabonidus, will travel in person to Uruk within

the next moon cycle, and that I welcome the opportunity to see
Nitocris when I fetch our daughter."

* * *

DOWN THE STREET from the palace, Belshazzar listened to the
leather soles of his sandals slap slap slap against the stone pavers
of the Entemenanki courtyard. He stopped short of the bronze
studded temple doors and took a moment to look up at the
ziggurat Nebuchadnezzar had built – over and over, never satisfied, always reaching higher – for the god. So impressive, his
neck couldn't even take the effort of seeing to the top from so
close. Belshazzar stepped between the recumbent golden dragons
flanking the temple door. Their lapis-blue eyes seemed to follow
him, judging always judging. Belshazzar straightened his richly
adorned robe and checked, yet again, that his belt lay flat, flat
against an impossibly round belly he thought with a grimace. He
tugged the tunic across his chest, ensuring that it remained
unwrinkled, the better to show off the heavy chest piece –
Marduk's space at the center - that he had chosen to wear for the
occasion.

Inside, Belshazzar shook out his arms, letting their ornate
embroidery ripple along the cotton weave. His shoes were the
closed-toed fashion of this season's winter courtiers. As crown
prince, he noticed with pleasure that others now followed him in
the latest styles. He had been popular before; now he
commanded the attention not only of Babylon's up-and-coming
but also of the old stalwarts. He had curried their favor for years,
eager to demonstrate his Babylonian-ness in the face of a
speckled pedigree. But now his father was king. Finally, he
thought, he'd arrived... almost. With any luck, it wouldn't be long
before Belshazzar would wear the crown. His diadem – he could
see it now – would be the heaviest his thick neck could hold. He
had already commissioned it, quietly of course. Belshazzar

walked through the lofted common space to the office of Marduk's high priest.

The shatammu looked up from lists of the temple prebends. "Good, you're here," he said.

"Of course. The greatest god's greatest servant calls. Any would answer."

"I'm not so sure." The shatammu stepped around the table. Belshazzar eyed the garnet-colored wine in a pale glass flask, the cheese and date pastries next to it.

"Why all this attention on Nanna-Suen?" the shatammu asked. "And your father, suddenly such an expert."

"I'm sorry, but I don't know what you mean," Belshazzar said.

"I don't like the direction this is going." The shatammu walked around his desk. He fixed Belshazzar with steely eyes. "And I'm not alone. Some of the old families -- Marduk's most prominent and powerful supporters, suppliers of slave expertise, choice sacrifices, money... well you know their wealth -- are threatening to withhold their gifts unless they can be earmarked for Marduk alone. So, tell me, what is this? What's going on?"

"As you know, I don't condone every choice my father makes. He is an old man, sentimental, I suppose nostalgic about his childhood home..."

The shatammu did not look convinced.

Belshazzar took a breath. He narrowed his eyes. "Maybe he is not altogether..."

"Nabonidus is entirely within his mind," the shatammu said sharply, "and not unhappy about laying down royal edicts and the like."

"He is old," Belshazzar said firmly.

"I believe you know that he plans to divert important resources from Babylon to Ur, to rebuild Nanna-Suen's temple and actually install his daughter, the king's daughter as high priestess at the occasion of Nanna-Suen's New Year." The shatammu's voice rang off the stone walls. "That is not how do we things now, nor have we done for far longer than I can remember."

"I understand and would never make such a decision, myself," Belshazzar said, in as conciliatory a tone as he could muster.

"But it's not up to you, is it?" the shatammu asked.

This was not going in any way as Belshazzar had wished.

"What if he decides some time to celebrate Nanna-Suen's akitu... *in Babylon?*" The shatammu seemed accusing now.

Belshazzar leaned back, giving what he hoped was a look of suitable outrage, appalled. "That's unthinkable."

"Yet some have thought it." The shatammu returned to his desk but leaned across it toward the prince. "I am simply warning you that unless your father reins in this eagerness to promote the god of his childhood, there will be dire consequences for his future and for the future of Babylonia itself." The shatammu softened his voice, as if remembering that the man before him would himself be king one day. "I know that you recognize as I do Marduk's priority for the well-being of this great god's city and the empire at large. So, I'm telling you as a friend to the gods to correct this alarming trend."

"I understand," Belshazzar said, "And thank you." If only, the crown prince thought, I knew how. Wasn't he doing the best he could?

CHAPTER 24 (PARSA)

*C*yrus and Prexaspes talked of little else as they rode back to Parsa. In truth, it was Cyrus who did most of the talking. The young king was almost giddy with how successful their visit to Susa had been. And it cheered Prexaspes to see it, to relive the conversations, remember the wonders, and travel with Cyrus's imagination back in time – when Cyrus's grandfather had governed the region as a single polity.

"And," Cyrus said, turning in his saddle to appreciate the cart behind them, piled neatly and high with the best bows – pride of old Elam. He turned forward again. "Otanes will be thrilled. He'll have his hands full satisfying the desire of all those boys to grow up like him."

Cyrus sighed a happy breath. At the high call of a hawk, he reflexively looked to the sky in the direction of its call. It had been years since the falcon he'd raised as a youth had flown for the last time. But when his mind followed paths of the past, he caught himself looking for the companion who'd helped send the wicked groundsman away. Cyrus looked over at his friend, ever alert, the picture of strength. Prexaspes, haughty son of the Pasargadae chief. It was the cruelty of the groundsman that had thrown Cyrus and Prexaspes together. And to think that they were friends now... Cyrus shook his head. Life was so unpredictable.

Feeling Cyrus's eyes on him, Prexaspes turned to look at him. Prexaspes's expression, normally wary with caution, ever ready to defend, softened in fondness. Cyrus had heard the rumors but chose to ignore them. He simply didn't care.

"Are you looking forward to moving back to Pasargad?" Cyrus asked.

Prexaspes shrugged. "It's all the same to me."

Cyrus laughed. "I didn't even grow up there –"

"The zeal of a convert," Prexaspes observed with a grin.

"But you have to admit," Cyrus said, "It's the best place in the world."

"Even after seeing Susa?"

Cyrus shook his head. "Pasargad forever," he said, almost wistful in its tone. Cyrus looked again to the horizon. Just over that far set of hills lay the palace at Anshan... soon to be former palace, he thought.

"Cassandane and I can hardly wait," Cyrus said. He didn't see Prexaspes stiffen at the sound of Cassandane's name.

CHAPTER 25 (MEDIA)

"*Y*es, I assembled the troops," Astyages said to Amytis. "It's what good kings do from time to time."

From high on the down-stuffed throne Astyages had inherited, he spoke down to Amytis as if she were a child. Not that it was how he'd spoken to *her* when she was a child. That was all rebuke and rejection. But the patronizing tone was unmistakable. Amytis shifted on her feet, trying to figure out a tactful way to say, "That's why it's strange. In all the years of my childhood and since my returning from Babylon, you never once called up, polished, or reviewed Media's army," She didn't say that, of course. She didn't say, "You're not a good king." No, with age and a lot of experience in halls of power such as Amytis had never imagined seeing, she had learned to curb her impulsiveness... mostly. If she said anything to bruise her father's fragile ego now, his temper would have shut down any avenue for Amytis to learn what she needed to know.

And she needed to know.

As soon as Amytis had seen troops assembling in the great plaza just inside the outer gates, alarmed, she'd asked Harpagus to explain. He told her what he knew: not much. Because King

Astyages himself was there in the midst – barking orders, sending officers scrambling - Amytis didn't have a chance to confront her father until it was over: a review of the troops; chaotic, given the short notice, but grand nonetheless.

Now she stood here, ill-prepared, in Astyages's smoke-stuffed audience hall. Windowless, candle sconces flickered in yellow tallow bringing the wool tapestries – muted scenes of battle and conquest – into a garish kind of life.

"This doesn't have anything to do with... Parsa does it?" Amytis asked. She almost regretted naming Cyrus's tiny kingdom. Astyages had said nothing about it – not Cyrus, not visiting – since they'd returned from Susa. Amytis didn't want to remind him, but....

"Good relations," Astyages said, "Just as you wished. And I agree! Now, it's been a most exhausting afternoon – " He looked past her to the guard at the door, nodded for the man to open it.

Amytis turned. She didn't wait for the curt command, "Get out," that she knew would follow. But she heard it anyway.

CHAPTER 26 (BABYLONIA)

*I*n the weeks following the auspicious eclipse, Nabonidus exhausted every source to determine exactly was done in the past for such an occasion. What were the clothes that his daughter should have as high priestess of the moon god -- what jewelry, the proper form of the rituals, and so on down to the tiniest of details. It had been more than ten decades since the rites were observed. Anyone who might have remembered from first-hand experience was long dead.

King Nabonidus was determined to learn what he could and then follow it to the letter. What joy, when Nabonidus discovered the first high priestess's description of her own home adjacent to the temple! He ordered that Ur have an exact replica built.

It was easy to see that Nabonidus could have conducted such research for years. But finally, it was inevitable, clear: the days were getting shorter. Even in Babylon, the temperatures, at night anyway, had begun to hint of the seasons' turn. If he was going to have Susanni in place by the seventeenth day of Tashritu, he had to go.

So it was that Nabonidus departed, under the king's guard. The plan was first to collect his daughter from Ishtar's temple (and Nitocris's control) in Uruk. From there, he and Susanni would together continue on to Ur. He could hardly wait. Finally, they would celebrate Nanna-Suen's akitu... with a high priestess (he'd want to change her name) - the first time in what seemed like forever.

The only disappointment: to Nabonidus's dismay (but not surprise), Belshazzar wanted no part in it. Nabonidus told himself that it was just as well. Not without precedent, Nabonidus would leave matters in Babylon to the crown prince.

* * *

FLOATING out of Babylon with his small royal entourage was to Nabonidus relief. As he watched a cloud's reflection waver on the slow water's surface, he thought how different his sensibilities were from Belshazzar, his own son. Belshazzar soaked up the energy of the court with its hushed gossip, plots, and ostentatious luxuries as naturally and thirstily as bare ground soaks up the dew. Born and raised among the big city's wealthy, always jockeying for approval and favor in this city of Marduk, Belshazzar fit in, like Nabonidus never would. Belshazzar wore luxury with the air of entitlement. In his eyes was the glint of insatiable power-hunger. Nabonidus didn't fault him for it. But he did worry sometimes. Well, one day Belshazzar would indeed be king.

Nabonidus still marveled at times that it was on his own head that Babylonia's crown rested. Why he should have been surprised, he didn't know. After all, between Adad-guppi, a mother who had leveraged a peculiar savvy to become so indispensable to Nebuchadnezzar's court and every administration since, and this son who longed to inherit a throne, it had been almost inevitable that Nabonidus became king.

What's more, Nabonidus had married the daughter of Nebuchadnezzar. Bastard daughter and as ill-inclined to the court as Nabonidus himself, she was nevertheless the late great king's daughter. Nabonidus shook his head. What strange twists his life had taken. Now he was king. He sighed. But... he looked around at the barge, felt his heart lift to imagine the grand day... and noted that little as he desired it, the crown did have some advantages. Prioritizing Nanna-Suen was top among them.

Nabonidus relished the journey south along the Euphrates – the air's faint breeze redolent with ripe melons, pomegranates, and figs; herons working their stilt-legs along the shore, watching with focus as sharp as beaks for what only they could see; the sound of fiddling insects in the dark of night and heaven's dome wrapped all over the big sky. Eagerness for the upcoming akitu warred with his wish that this travel would never end.

Yes, it was a kind of bliss for this king of Babylonia – the travel, the destination. As they neared Uruk, Nabonidus requested that his singer-scribe recite the ancient story of Uruk's legendary king, Gilgamesh. Nabonidus found himself emotional – his throat ache, his eyes smarted – at all of it. The poignant tale, the circumstances in which he could hear it, the moments each so precious – and now to Uruk itself. The gods had blessed him indeed.

Close to the gulf with access from there to greater seas and peoples and goods, Uruk was a huge and marvelous city with a history older than writing itself. Nabonidus could easily spend a happy lifetime studying it.

The city had long been the home of the goddess Ishtar. Hundreds of years ago, she shared it with the sky-god An. But today, it was she, the lion goddess of love and war who dominated the place. The huge terrace on which An's White Temple had been built still remained, but the city's ancient architecture was in a constant state of disrepair. Still, it was beautiful.

Most of Uruk was gardens, and canals were the city's roadways. So Nabonidus's party passed the final miles of their journey, traveling through the city in smaller boats. The crew was quiet – even for those who cared less about history than King Nabonidus were awed by the ancient city. They passed first through the tanners' neighborhood on the outskirts, then the weavers', metalsmiths', butchers', and bakers'. They passed through the Royal Orchard district, where true to its name, fruit trees bent heavy with their yields. Finally, the boats parked on a quay bordering the walls that enclosed the sacred Eanna district. There they disembarked. From there, it was only a short walk to the temple. But Nabonidus wouldn't have been able to prepare himself even if he'd had longer time to do so.

CHAPTER 27 (MEDIA)

"*B*ut surely we have more than *that!*" Astyages said. Harpagus found his eyes wandering to a small door in a wall behind Astyages's throne – the passage through which he came and went in service to the king. And oh, how he wanted to go. Ever since Astyages had conducted the review of Median troops – an army that Harpagus had trained... and refreshed so recently at the king's command, Astyages had been obsessed with how many fewer soldiers were there than the grandiose numbers that he'd imagined.

"We do, for certain," Harpagus explained. "But as your lordship knows – and at his earlier command – they are stationed throughout the empire. Defense, protection of assets, securing the passage of merchants from whom we gain so much... has been of utmost concern."

Astyages scowled. "Well maybe it's time we bring some of them here."

"Here, sir?"

"Do it."

Such certainty in the king was rare, Harpagus knew.

"Now."
And it usually spelled trouble.

CHAPTER 28 (BABYLONIA)

$\mathcal{T}$he reception Nabonidus got in Uruk was a jarring counterpoint to the peace of the journey. Nitocris stormed out of the Eanna temple as Nabonidus's party approached, her gray hair still streaked with brown tumbling down from a linen band she had loosely tied in a vain effort to control it. A spotted panther padded quietly behind her.

"What business do you have removing my daughter from the goddess's service?" Nitocris demanded. She threw heavy leather gloves to the ground and impatiently brushed a wispy bunch of fur from a long apron of bronze plate fastened on linen. She put her hands on her hips, the metal pieces jangling.

"Good to see you, too, wife," Nabonidus said. "It's been a long time." He glanced warily at the panther trying not to catch its unblinking yellow eyes.

Nitocris shook her head. "Get your people settled and meet me back here -- the inner courtyard, if it please. I have wildcats to feed and a litter of cubs not yet weaned." She spun away, not waiting for a reply.

There were times, the king thought, when Nitocris was every bit Nebuchadnezzar's daughter. He knew it was hard-won and not the only thing he respected. "You heard the queen," Nabonidus to the stunned people who had come with him. As if woken from a dream, Nabonidus's staff clipped into action.

While the barges were unloaded and the entourage settled as instructed, Nabonidus looked around. Finally, he drew a young temple oblate aside. "Where is my daughter?" he asked.

The girl knitted her eyebrows.

"Nitocris's daughter," he said.

"Oh! In the sanctuary, my lord," the girl replied. "Praying to the goddess. At least that's what her mother, the lion-lady priestess, directed her to do."

"I see. In that case, will you take me to the courtyard where I am to meet Ni-, the lion-lady priestess?"

They passed through the temple's outer gate and into the public courtyard. A stand of trees so old their limbs had twisted back on themselves cast shade over the ancient stone patio. He didn't have to wait long before Nitocris returned, without the gloves and apron this time. But behind her the panther remained, a fluid part of her shadow.

"It's not too late to repent," Nitocris said. "I warned you. Ishtar, the star of our mornings and of our nights, great goddess of this empire and bloody warrior of battles old and new will not look kindly on your establishing the princess of Babylon as priestess to another god."

"I respectfully fear the great goddess. But it is Nanna-Suen's wish that our daughter go to Ur. The priests and sages of Babylon agree."

"Those old men?" Nitocris spat. "They have never understood the ways of the goddess. They think her some weakling of the heavens, I suspect. And will suffer for it, if they don't already. How many can get a woman other than at the *akitu*," she asked. She raised her arm and let her wrist drop suggestively.

"It's not about one god or another," Nabonidus said. "Not necessarily. It's what the eclipse and omens mean."

"It was a bad sign, like every eclipse," Nitocris said. "Apparently this time, even the copper kettledrums couldn't keep the danger away." She sighed. The panther rubbed its cheek against her thigh, a pointed incisor flashing in the sunlight. She stroked its head absently. The purr was a rumble. "Of course if I cannot change your mind," Nitocris said.

"You cannot."

"Well then." Nitocris looked Nabonidus full in the face, searching his eyes. He held her gaze. She exhaled in a long breath. "The girl is ready. In truth, she's excited. She's been asking me about her new duties... trying on some of the garments you sent ahead..." Nitocris shook her head. "I only wish I could agree that this is the right thing, that Nanna-Suen has somehow appeased our lady of the stars. If not, you'll be the one to pay first, of course. It isn't right for kings to so tamper with the business of the gods." Nitocris threaded her fingers through the graying hair at her temples.

"You know it used to be like this," Nabonidus said, "the king's daughter as priestess to Nanna-Suen. Before Marduk became Babylonia's high god."

Nitocris rewarded Nabonidus with a small smile. "The historian, as always," she said, almost pitying. Nitocris pulled off the linen band from around her forehead and her hair spilled over her shoulders. Most women her age had cut their hair short. They wore wigs restyled for different occasions or hung pendants, beads, or jewels from silver bands around cropped heads. "I don't know why I care." She turned her eyes on him and was suddenly the deliciously strong daughter of Nebuchadnezzar that Nabonidus had married decades ago.

"I would take dinner with you."

Nitocris stepped back. "Is that a confession, or a royal command?"

Nabonidus shrugged. "We'll leave tomorrow morning."

Nitocris nodded and walked away.

Nabonidus remained in the courtyard. Nitocris didn't turn again before she disappeared around the temple's corner. The panther's twitching tail was the last Nabonidus saw of her. His life, with its surprising delights and heavy griefs, Nabonidus thought, was finally such a small thing. He thought about the thousands of years of people who had passed through this place, of the city's revolutionary past -- the first monumental public buildings, the first attempts at writing -- how much had changed for human beings from this particular place. And how much remained exactly the same.

He heard the temple doors squeak open and turned to look. He caught his breath. There in the doorway was Nitocris – no, the mirror image of the girl Nitocris -- when Nabonidus had first laid eyes on her. The young woman walked toward him with the same lilting gait and looked up at him with the same dark eyes flecked with gold. Her lips turned up at the corners with the same hint of a grin. She bowed deeply. "My lord," she said. Not identical, then, Nabonidus thought.

CHAPTER 29 (BABYLONIA)

$\mathcal{T}$he temple complex was a sprawling area into which Nabonidus's small party was easily absorbed and accommodated. Less than a quarter of its dining room, large enough to host Ishtar's holiday feasts, needed to be set for dinner; but that quarter was elegantly laid with fine glazed stoneware, glass goblets for wine with bowls of fruit and flowers running down the center of each table. Nabonidus entered with his daughter. He took the central seat, or course, gestured to Susanni to sit at his left; and the rest of the company sat down. The grand seat to the king's right remained empty.

Servers bustled in with platters of fish, pulled from the gulf not an hour earlier, roasted with fresh herbs and dressed in tangy flower petals. Heaps of grilled bread with sesame oil lay within reach of each person, as did bowls of bitter cress lightly dressed with honeyed wine vinegar and sea salt.

Nabonidus lifted his silver fork and his eyes and froze. Without lowering his gaze from the far doorway, Nabonidus returned the utensil slowly to his plate. He watched Nitocris walk in. She wore a long gown of green silk into which, visible only if one looked closely, Ishtar's rosettes had been woven. Fur from a lion's mane draped a low neck and circled the cuffs of three quarter length sleeves, each hatched to the elbow. Her hair -- carefully brushed, loose strands oiled in place -- shone gray-black in a high, loose bun. Nabonidus stood quickly, catching his chair behind him as it tipped. Everyone else stood, too.

Nabonidus – and the others – only sat again after Nitocris had. She took the seat to Nabonidus's right. After people had resumed conversations and the eating and drinking of a dinner long in the works, after Nabonidus had followed his wife in savoring the delicacies of Uruk that filled their places, she spoke.

"Belshazzar is well," King Nabonidus said. "In charge of the other of Babylonia's royal affairs while I'm gone. Ably, I hope."

"Happily, anyway, I'm sure," Nitocris said.

Nabonidus waited while a boy refilled Nitocris's cup with wine. He waited until the boy had stepped well away again. Then, "Will you come," Nabonidus asked, "for Marduk's Akitu this year?"

But Nitocris wasn't listening. She scowled at a man seated not far from them and intent on hearing as much of their conversation as he could, then let her eyes pass nonchalant over the rest of company. When his neighbor interrupted with a request for something or another, Nitocris leaned over to the king. As she reached for the cress, under her breath, she said, "Don't look, but who is that man?"

Nabonidus swung his head around the tables, as if appraising the entire group. "A representative from the Esagil," he answered as quietly.

"Doesn't trust you, does he?"

"I'm making some changes. Not everyone is pleased."

Nitocris sat back. "Well, your daughter is not among them."

"I'm eager to go, Father," Susanni said, grinning.

Nabonidus smiled. He pushed his chair back and stood. When the rest of company moved to join him, Nabonidus waved for them to sit down again. When they had, he extended a hand to his daughter, which she took. Nabonidus raised Susanni to stand beside him.

When the crowd was quiet, and all eyes on the king and his daughter, Nabonidus spoke. "This girl who was known until now as Susanni shall henceforth and for the rest of her life be called Ennigaldi-Nanna," he announced as if in defiance of the man Nitocris had noted or any who doubted his piety, "to reflect the divine office she is prepared to take."

The assembly remained quiet some moments longer than was comfortable. But Nabonidus waited. It was his daughter herself who broke the silence to elicit, with a beaming smile of happy acceptance, the cheer that the king's announcement deserved.

When Nabonidus was seated again by her side, Nitocris huffed and took up her wine. She shook her head lightly. She drank and lowered the cup again. "Your Egibis were here a short time ago." At her signal, an oblate removed Nitocris's plate.

"They are not mine," Nabonidus said and handed the girl his plate, too.

"Well, they've been working for you, as I understand it, for a long time," Nitocris said.

"For your father first. It was Nebuchadnezzar who really gave them a start, then Amel-Marduk, then Igliss. But really, they work for no one but themselves."

"Whatever the case, they are reliable. We can always count on them for timely delivery. Iddina, I think, was the Egibi in charge last time."

Nabonidus nodded. "He's the eldest son of Khai, your father's one time scribe and judge, the man who began the business."

"Right. Khai -- much more circumspect. Iddina, on the other hand, is full of news and colorful stories. This time, they arrived via Susa. He told me that the new king of Parsa, Cyrus son of Cam, has been cultivating a relationship with Susa, with all of Elam, from what I gathered. Does it worry you?"

"Not really," Nabonidus said. "Your father tried to assert more control over Elam, years ago. There are still bricks stamped 'Neb-uchadnezzar' there. Anyway, your father recognized their deter-mination for independence... and history for fighting fiercely for it. He didn't push it further – not worth the trouble. If anything, I'm glad this Cyrus is reaching out to them. If they cause trouble, it'll occupy Media, keep them out of our hair."

"Harran, you mean," Nitocris said.

CHAPTER 30 (MEDIA)

"*W*hat's this I hear about withdrawing troops from the outlying areas?" Amytis demanded.

Despite himself, Astyages dropped his eyes from her gaze. He forced himself to raise them again. "My counselors tell me they're not needed there."

"... and we need them <u>here</u>?!"

Astyages pursed his lips. When did this woman become such a ... person? She'd been such a little thing, bastard girl – and her mother, running away like that. He hated when slaves got away with it, disappeared. And left this girl, unremarkable except for her durability. Back in the day, it seemed she was always getting hurt. But useful, the child – she protected Mandane, the true princess. No one could have guessed that it would be the scruffy bastard Amytis who married Nebuchadnezzar, but there it was. He almost laughed. But now here she was so... involved.

"It just doesn't make sense," Amytis said. "The Scythians are a chronic threat along the northern border; in the west, there's Croesus –"

"We have a treaty with Lydia, and –" Astyages sighed a great, audible exhale. "Listen. You were the one who wanted to establish good, strong relations with Parsa. "I'm sure you agree, then, that Cyrus – my grandson – will be even more eager to appreciate the benefits of vassalage – the great Median empire backing his admittedly insignificant country – when he sees the might that stands behind little Parsa. After all, it's what we do, protect our vassals... like a father for his family."

There were so many ironies, hypocrisies, and blind spots in what Astyages said, especially to her, that Amytis almost dismissed the whole message. And yet. There was truth in it. Some. Amytis narrowed her eyes. Finally, "I don't like it," Amytis said. "Diplomacy doesn't require a demonstration. Plus, armies are hard on the land they travel through."

Astyages muttered, "Always 'the land this' and the wild that'." Then he looked straight at Amytis. "You don't have to like it," Astyages said. "You're not coming."

"What?!"

"You're not coming."

In hindsight, Amytis would berate herself for not acting on her suspicions, especially when Astyages said, "You'll need to manage things here – be the crown – from Ecbatana, in my stead." Astyages never allowed anything that might even hint of his not being in every moment the Median empire's great king.

CHAPTER 31 (BABYLONIA)

*N*abonidus's company traveled the fifty miles south southeast between Uruk and Ur by barges compliments of Ishtar. When they neared Ur, the boatmen steered into narrower channels. Tall reeds made green alleyways. Herds of water buffalo, loosed from their morning milking grazed among the river grass. They swam channels, nostrils snorting, and lumbered along the muddy banks.

As they went, King Nabonidus led the boatmen in singing the ancient praise songs of Nanna-Suen whose white crescent moon marked the forehead of each beast, light or dark. "The Glory of Heaven has loosed all their halters, a teeming herd. He has poured out milk from the beautiful cows at the offering table; his bright hands ever pour the milk."

The king learned from his daughter that Nitocris had had little role in raising the girl. Susanni had instead served the temple in a variety of ways as her age allowed, beginning in the laundry, graduating to the kitchen, then the fields. She tended the temple's flocks for a time, assisted her mother with the wildcats, and after her first blood, took the oath of the priestesses. At that point, she began to learn Ishtar's sacred songs, stories, and secret rites. She performed the daily service and helped prepare and observe the festivals.

But Susanni never went to Marduk's Akitu in Babylon. After Susanni's uncle Ean, crown prince to Nebuchadnezzar's throne, became sick (and the young man's mother, queen at the time, killed on suspicion of witchcraft), Nitocris forbade the girl from leaving Uruk. When the prince died, Nitocris came under suspicion and was demoted from the high priestess to keeper of the great cats. No one took notice of the girl.

Rumors of witchcraft died down over the ensuing years. So when Nabonidus took the throne and installed Nitocris according to tradition as the high priestess of Ishtar's temple no one protested. By then, Susanni was a young woman and had served in every area of the temple. Nabonidus was confident that this next move was exactly right.

They traveled south past Larsa. When the Euphrates widened into fields and swamps, Nabonidus knew they were close to Ur and very near the great Gulf. So they pressed on past dusk. When they arrived at Ur, the crescent of the city's patron god shone clear in the sky. "City of the finest divine powers," Nabonidus said as they pulled ashore, "abode of Nanna, built in a pure place! City, beautiful as the sky! Your lofty palace is the E-kiš-nu-ĝal, where Nanna-Suen's sacred table lies and in which the fates are determined! Your pilasters, heavy with radiance, tower over all!, like a white cloud, a spectacle in the midst of heaven, like flashing lightning it shines."

* * *

SUSANNI'S INSTALLATION as the high priestess Ennigaldi-Nanna would be on the next day just after Shamash yielded the sky to moon and stars. It would be an auspicious night. Ishtar in her evening form, the feminine goddess of bounty and love, would share the sky with her father, the luminous prince of heaven, Nanna-Suen.

In the morning, temple slaves began erecting a dais across the broad courtyard of Nanna-Suen from the staircase of the ziggurat temple. People gathered early. At sunset, Nabonidus took the dais and addressed the crowd.

"When Nanna-Suen requested a high priestess, on the thirteenth day of Ulūlu, in the month when goddesses purify themselves in the river, the Bright-Light moon god showed his sign and made its meaning known to me. I heeded the word of Nanna-Suen, the great god, my creator. But terrible difficulties and obstacles had to be overcome." Nabonidus paused and looked around. "As you now know, for a very long time the office of high priestess here in Ur had been forgotten. One day, a day that the gods had appointed, I looked anew at an ancient stele, fashioned and carved by a king of the past. On it was depicted an image of the high priestess. What's more, written upon the stele were lists of her clothing, her jewelry, and all the accessories of her office. I carefully replicated every one.

"But that wasn't all. This place had been abandoned and the temple itself a heap of ruins. And no one knew the original plans. Many of you here helped to clear and excavate. Soon, the temple's foundation became visible. In the meantime I discovered an inscription by the first high priestess, Sargon's daughter Enheduanna. She also had renovated and restored the temple. She also built her own house What you see here," Nabonidus swung his arms wide, "is Nanna-Suen's temple home and the palace lodgings of his high priestess exactly as they were in the olden days. I had it all rebuilt just as it had been then, and next to it, the house wherein my beloved daughter shall dwell."

Murmurs of approval rippled through the crowd.

While the sky was still soft with ebbing day, Ishtar began to emerge, glimmering and glittering against the darkening sky. Nabonidus prayed toward the evening star. "Lady Ishtar, graciously release this girl from service that she might answer the request which cannot be denied. The prince of night and creator of all, Nanna-Suen, wishes her to be his high priestess."

Nabonidus turned and stood looking off the dais behind him toward the courtyard's main gate. Great stone guardians, winged bulls with silver orbs between their horns, and the serene faces of human sages, flanked the entrance. A horn sounded from the wall, and Susanni appeared. The crowd sighed as one. The young woman stood, a tiny spot of grace, between the massive *lamassu*.

* * *

SUSANNI LOOKED every bit the princess that she was, and every bit the daughter of a man enamored of the past. She walked forward slowly to stand just in front of the *lamassu's* gentle gaze. Her hair was styled in a simple but magnificent sweep. Only on such an exquisite coiffure could the headdress identical to that worn by Queen Puabi, almost 2,000 years earlier, hope to rest. Nabonidus knew the weight of what she wore, but the girl didn't wince or flinch.

Three tiers -- each a triple beaded strand of lapis, carnelian, and gold -- hung from brow to crown. Along the lowest tier rings of pure gold hung over her forehead and around her head. On the next tier were strung pendants of gold sheet fashioned like beech leaves, each twice as big as the girl's eyes. On the top, golden willow leaves in clusters of three through which golden flowers with white and blue inlay on their petals ran in whimsical randomness. Above and behind it all towered a bouquet of seven lapis-centered golden flowers, held aloft by thin golden stems and fixed by a hidden comb. On either side of the whole hung a strand of large, square stone beads. Each ended in a lapis amulet -- on the left, a seated bull; on the right, a calf. A broad gold ribbon, looping around and over, back and forth, held it all in place.

From the girl's earlobes double hoops of gold, shaped like the heavy crescent of Nanna-Suen, dropped and brushed the skin above her shoulders. Around her bare neck were three parallel strings of lapis, carnelian, and gold beads in the middle of which was a pointed star encircled by a twisted ring of silver.

Susanni stood still in the hush until the crescent of Nanna-Suen lifted from the horizon. When its horns showed bright and sharp against the darkening sky, Nabonidus stepped down. Susanni walked forward to meet him, like a leaf floating down the Euphrates. Nabonidus offered his arm and glanced up at him briefly. Dabs of white makeup in the inside corners of her eyes made them stand out in striking contrast to the heavy black kohl that ran around their rims. Green eye shadow, the color of the gulf at dawn softened them. Together they walked to the temple steps, turned, and faced the crowd.

"On this auspicious evening," Nabonidus said, "I hereby dedicate my daughter to my lord and lady Nanna-Suen and Ningal, heavenly parents of sun and star, of Shamash and Ishtar. Would the consecrated personnel of this great temple, Ekishnugal, and its accompanying shrines now step forward: the high priest, the purification, priest, the *zabardubbu*, the diviner, the cook, the miller, the master builder, the builder, the courtyard sweeper, the chief doorkeeper, the court attendant, the priest who performs rites of homage, the singers who gladden the gods' hearts?" As each man and woman approached, whispering in the crowd grew to a murmur.

"The collegium here enumerated, I now release from their obligations." Nabonidus had to raise his voice to be heard over the crowd. "I hereby free these persons from service and give them, without burden or delay, to my lord and lady Suen and Ningal. Come forward and deposit your signs of office." No one moved. Nabonidus did not repeat himself. Susanni lifted her chin, and the first one came forward. The others followed until one by one the former officials had laid their seals, bronze breastplates, amulets and more at Susanni's feet.

After the last of the former officials had disappeared back into the crowd, king and daughter climbed the stairs. Beaten gold covered the heavy wooden panels of the temple's broad doorway. Nabonidus said, "I hereby pledge generous offerings to this temple complex, abundant fields, orchards, slaves, cattle, and sheep. I will ensure that the high priestess's place is secure. I pledge to increase the regular offerings threefold and install in this temple all kinds of goods and treasures." With each declaration, the crowd cheered. Nabonidus raised his hands, palms out, and they grew silent again.

As Nabonidus lowered his hands, the great doors swung inward, groaning on their hinges and rumbling against the pivot stones. Out of the darkness stepped two girls dressed in robes to match Susanni's. They stood on either side of her.

Nabonidus declared, "Through the exorcists' art, I have purified my daughter and do this day consecrate her as high priestess exactly as in the days of old." Nabonidus nodded to one of the girls who reached out and lifted the elaborate headdress from Susanni's head. The crowd gasped. For with the stunning headdress came the magnificent coiffure. Susanni's own hair tumbled down in long dark waves strung through with golden rings and beads of precious gems.

The other girl lifted from off her arm a flat band of soft white leather sewn with thousands of tiny lapis lazuli beads. A row of golden animals -- stags, gazelles, bulls, and goats -- strode against the blue background. Between them hung pomegranate fruits in clusters of three. The branches of a tree with golden stems and carnelian fruits as well as golden rosettes were sewn at regular intervals, and all along the bottom of the strip hung palmettes of twisted gold wire. Susanni nodded to the girl, who fastened the band around the new high priestess's head. The girls stepped back into the shadows.

"From this time forward," Nabonidus said, "my daughter shall no longer be called Susanni but Ennigaldi-Nanna, High Priestess requested by Nanna-Suen." The crowd cheered. Nabonidus turned his palms from the crowd to the sky, facing the brilliant crescent moon.

"Nanna-Suen," he prayed, "holy god, lord of the crown, light of mankind, supreme god whose every command is true. May Ennigaldi-Nanna, my own beloved daughter, live happily in your presence and may her every command be reliable and true, may her actions please you, may she commit no wrong. And in the days to come, I promise that your temple in Harran shall also be rebuilt." He looked out into the crowd, "And that one day we may celebrate the Akitu of the great god Nanna-Suen in every one of his temples."

There was hushed murmuring in the crowd. "Did he say 'every'? Are there not only two?" neighbor asked neighbor, until someone called out, "one day, Babylon?" But Nabonidus was already walking toward the banqueting space.

* * *

IT WASN'T easy for Nabonidus to tear himself away from Ur. Still miles from Babylon, Nabonidus dreaded being back in the capital again. He didn't mind the logistics themselves, found satisfaction in fulfilling the man disparate tasks expected of the king. It was just... Babylon. It was the expectations that to his mind had nothing to do with ruling, nothing to do with proper management – repairs, improvements, economy... It was all the thousands of unstated micro-expectations of social life, displays of wealth and power... that wore him out. The very things that Belshazzar relished.

The closer they got, and the less he wanted to arrive, the more clearly Nabonidus imagined his next move.

This time away, the exhilarating installation of his daughter as priestess to Nanna-Suen, the whole religious experience reminded him of just how important such things were. Not only to the empire – even those with whom he disagreed on details believed this – but also to him, personally. He was a quest-er, ever hungry for the food that only the gods could give, spiritual sustenance. For that, like so many other seekers before and after him, he would go to the desert.

No one had been able to subdue the wild Arab tribes of the peninsula to the southwest. Yet there were among those people some who held in highest esteem a god much like his own Nanna-Suen. Being in Ur reminded him: it was hard to underestimate the ease of being among people of like mind… and heart. Besides, opening up trade routes through the area would be beneficial to the empire. No one could fault him for that. And he'd be out of the snake-pit of Babylon. If only his son Belshazzar seemed as wise as his daughter, Nabonidus lamented. Then again, he thought with a smile, Belshazzar might be more the son he needed than Nabonidus had ever recognized before. Yes, he'd leave Babylon to the crown prince again.

The only thing that rankled (and it was a familiar itch), was Harran. Namely, the dilapidated state of the Elhulhul. Medes controlled the area and had since Nebuchadnezzar was merely crown prince. And the Medes didn't care about Nanna-Suen, much less the moon god's temple there. Well, Nabonidus sighed, it was the gods' expectation that kings would keep up the care and maintenance of their temples. Nabonidus searched the sky for an arc of the moon, half-full it was, against the pale end-of-day sky. Finding it, he sent up a quick prayer that Nanna-Suen would make it possible for Nabonidus to fulfill that sacred duty – that the Babylonian crown have the kind of access they needed to renovate the sacred Elhulhul.

So, when Nabonidus bolted awake in the middle of the night, breathless with astonishment, he wondered if the dream had indeed been a promise from the gods. Or had it been merely the product of the last night's imagining? It took the king a long time to fall asleep again.

CHAPTER 32 (MEDIA)

*I*n the weeks before her father's journey south to Parsa, Amytis took every opportunity to remind King Astyages of what he'd agreed. Just as she didn't cease reminding Astyages of the benefits of seeing the mission through – laying the groundwork for peace, friendly relations with and even support for Parsa – Astyages didn't cease reassuring her that he would do that. She had his word. And she had said what she could to Harpagus, her old friend. So, when the king and his troops, an impressive army indeed, pulled out of Media, Amytis let them go.

Harpagus looked back once – Media's proxy sovereign standing at the silver gate, uncharacteristically attired in the jeweled crown of the empire's monarch. Amytis normally eschewed the burden of it, the display. But she'd been in palaces enough to know now the value of such a signal. A golden jackal robe lay over Amytis's narrow shoulders, embroidered boots fur-lined rose to the knee. He knew that tucked into Amytis's boots were the blousy trousers of Median riders. She'd be worried, he knew; and as soon as they were gone, as soon as she'd made sure that the palace's daily duties had been satisfied, she would ride.

Harpagus sighed. Before they left, Amytis had taken him aside.

"If it happens..." Amytis said, "though he's given me his word it's all in peace... But. I remember what my father did to you. If it comes to that... you have my blessing, my orders, if you need that."

Harpagus didn't ask for clarification, didn't ask exactly to what Amytis had alluded. But he could guess. And the thought, delicious as it might be, was impossible to imagine in reality. He sighed. If only he could simply have stayed. If Astyages had given him the choice, Harpagus wouldn't have hesitated to be steward to Amytis instead of Astyages, to remain in Ecbatana rather than see the young man his own son was not. (Not a day went by that Harpagus didn't imagine what his would be like... were the boy still alive.) But the king had commanded Harpagus's presence. So. Harpagus turned back to the front.

Ahead of him, the thousand booted warriors, the caravan of provisions, including gifts Amytis insisted they bring to Cyrus's family, and at the front of all of that, the carriage that held King Astyages. Far apart as they were, Harpagus couldn't know that within that carriage, barely half a mile out of Ecbatana, Astyages was busy dictating a message. "To be delivered directly to Cyrus," Astyages said. The brevity of the message didn't reflect the amount of time Astyages had spent figuring out precisely what to say. "Tell him that I've decided even a vassalage is too great an honor for such a petty place. He is to forfeit the crown. Parsa shall no longer have status as a kingdom. Any independence is a thing of the past." Astyages had calculated correctly: This was something that Cyrus could not accept. Astyages smirked. With enough time for Cyrus to gather all his troops, the punishment would be brutal. Genocide.

CHAPTER 33 (BABYLONIA)

"*A*nd we didn't even have to get involved," Nabonidus shook his head in wonder at the news.

It had seemed impossible. The Medes had occupied Harran exactly as they had from the time that his mother Adad-guppi, as priestess highly educated, had been removed with her boy Nabonidus to Babylon.

"Any sense of when the troops will be clear?" Nabonidus asked.

The young man who had brought the information – rumors of the Medes' withdrawal from Harran – was the same as observed now that that was all it would take allow the Babylonians to rebuild Nanna-Suen's northern temple.

"They're gone, sir."

With Media centralizing its troops for a southeastern campaign, Harran was open for renovation.

Nabonidus looked up at the sky, to where the moon would be, were it visible (it was not). "So, that dream," Nabonidus said quietly, "It came from you, after all."

To the youth, Nabonidus said, "Bring Belshazzar to me."

CHAPTER 34 (PARSA)

" *R*iders from the west, sir!" A young scout from Cyrus's outlying guards hurried into the king's audience room. "Nearly one hundred, and twice their number of armed men on foot."

"The Medes, already?" Cyrus asked. He had indeed rejected Astyages's so-called offer. Immediately. That accepting would have meant giving up Pasargad was reason enough alone to Cyrus. As for the rest of Parsa, its tribal leaders agreed: they would not give up their independence. Not without a fight.

"We can't tell, sir."

"Saddle my horse. I'll meet you at the gate."

Despite the determination of its leaders, knowledge of Astyages's intention to attack Anshan became a common source of consternation among the general population before the Median army was even close. In some corners, talk turned to escape. Crushing defeat seemed inevitable. How to get out of the region alive in the face of this impending monster was the topic of many hushed conversations.

When Cyrus learned this, he encouraged the people who

wished to leave to do so and assured them that there would be no shame in it.

"You are free," he said, "and must decide as your conscience and circumstances dictate."

Few left, and all such conversations ceased. In the meantime, Cyrus stepped up the Parsan troops' training. He could not make the men more, but he could try to make them better.

Now, Cyrus rode to meet a different army – not huge, but under the circumstances of Astyages's advance, they could ill-afford even a skirmish with anyone else.

So it was that Cyrus rode now with only the scout and their weapons stowed away.

Pounding hooves behind made Cyrus turn. Prexaspes reined in next to the trotting horses, a stave strapped to his saddle, short bow and arrows on his back. A long spear hung against his thigh. "Where are you going?"

Cyrus took in his friend's ostentatious weaponry, the neat arrangement of his clothes, his heavy jaw clean-shaven as usual, the concern in his narrow eyes. "To meet a band," Cyrus said. "We don't know whom yet. And still some distance?" Cyrus asked the scout.

"Yes, sir." The scout shifted in his saddle under Prexaspes's glare.

"What kind of a band?" Prexaspes fired his question at the scout.

"We'll find out soon," Cyrus said.

"I asked him," Prexaspes said, still glaring at the scout.

Cyrus shrugged.

"Armed?" Prexaspes asked.

"Yes, sir," the scout said and quickly added, "some riders, some on foot --" He glanced anxiously at Cyrus. "A few hundred from what we could see."

"'A few *hundred*?!" Prexaspes exclaimed. He turned his ire on Cyrus. "Why you - the king, then, and why alone?!" The horses' formerly steady trot broke at his shouting. Prexaspes grabbed the reins of Cyrus's horse and brought them to a halt.

"It wasn't his decision to make, Prexaspes. You know that. Now let go of my horse."

Prexaspes dropped the reins. "You should have sent someone – me, Pharn, anyone."

"I don't want trouble. To show myself as a friend, without threat..." he gave Prexaspes a hard look. "That's best." Cyrus nudged his mare back into a trot. The others fell in beside him. "Besides, I'm curious. I don't want to wait to find out."

"I'm coming, then."

Cyrus sighed. "At least drop the stave."

Prexaspes frowned but loosened the straps and tossed it into the plateau's tall grass, tamping a gap in the waving stalks.

CHAPTER 35 (BABYLONIA)

They stood as it seemed they'd done so often, in all these decades before: father and son in a tense face-off. Nabonidus noticed that Belshazzar had hardly even stepped a foot or two inside the door, so certain was he that he'd want to be leaving soon. And Nabonidus as usual, felt defeated before they'd even begun. He'd succeed, of course, in furthering his plans – Nabonidus was the king after all – but with his son...? That was a different matter.

"You know that we've begun renovations at the sun god's temple in Sippar."

Belshazzar squinted under heavy lids. "Yes," he said, lifting his voice as if to say, "go on."

"Archaeologists uncovered an even older foundation than Nebuchadnezzar had found. Plus an inscription, dating back hundreds of years, to Hammurabi himself. Frankly, I am in awe."

"You love those old things."

"History is the future, Shazzi. Don't forget it."

"As you say."

Nabonidus took an equalizing breath. "I've been thinking that it's time Babylonia explores trade possibilities through the south,"

Nabonidus said. "Babylon would benefit from direct routes from the gulf to the sea."

Belshazzar crossed his arms over his chest. "No one traverses the Arabs' desert, Father."

"Maybe not, but –"

Belshazzar shook his head. 'We've got Gutium... that pass through the Zagros available, already in Babylonian control..."

"I want to go myself," Nabonidus said.

Belshazzar dropped his arms to his sides.

"You can manage things in my absence, like you did when I went to Ur."

"Proxy king?" he asked, trying to keep the eagerness from his voice.

Nabonidus nodded absently. "I'll be gone, I don't know how long."

Belshazzar smiled. "You can count on me."

"I hope so."

Belshazzar opened his mouth.

"I trust so," Nabonidus said firmly.

Belshazzar shut his mouth.

"I want you to continue the work in Sippar while I'm gone."

"Of course. It's expected of kings."

Nabonidus raised his eyebrows.

"Not that I presume to the crown," Belshazzar said, tossing his head back and forth with each word.

"Right. Because I will rule from the desert just as I would from Babylon, however long it takes," Nabonidus said. He narrowed his eyes. "There are two other things." Nabonidus looked hard at Belshazzar, as if reevaluating a private decision.

"What?" Belshazzar asked, as if he were already judged.

"I will not perform Marduk's akitu."

"What?!" Belshazzar shouted. "It is the most fundamental act of Babylonian kingship."

"I know. But I cannot return only for that."

"'Only?, only?!'"

"I am formally appointing you to be my substitute in the ceremony."

Belshazzar's eyes opened wide, all indignation evaporated. "You wish me to act as king in the akitu?"

"It's not unheard of."

"As long as the qipu gives formal and public approval..." At the thought of it, Belshazzar actually smiled. It wasn't to last. "And the other thing?"

Nabonidus took a deep breath. "Last night I had a dream. Both Nanna-Suen and Marduk appeared. The gods promised that the Medes and their king, Astyages, would be removed from Harran."

Belshazzar smirked. "Did they say when?"

"Come on, Shazzi. You know it doesn't work that way. And yet I just learned that the troops are indeed pulling out."

Belshazzar looked incredulous.

"There was more," Nabonidus said. "Marduk and Nanna-Suen stood together and ordered me to rebuild the Elhulhul, Nanna-Suen's temple in Harran." Nabonidus watched Belshazzar's face closely. It was unreadable.

"I know the Elhulhul, father. Grandmother has been talking about it all my life. You, too."

"I'm sending a team of engineers and archaeologists to begin exploring what is necessary to rebuild. We're keeping it quiet, presently. I tell you now because if you are to be my regent while I'm gone, you must be prepared and willing to act, should the opportunity arise. You know what that means, right?"

"The king is to carry the bricks himself," Belshazzar answered, bitterly. "This has been your plan all along, hasn't it, father?"

"Marduk stood with Nanna-Suen to command this of me."

"Then you should be the one to do it."

"If you are managing affairs in my stead, Shazzi, you are acting for the king."

"In other words, you won't leave the throne to me unless I promise to rebuild your precious god's temple."

Nabonidus sighed and shook his head. "It is not only me – "

"Of course not. It's you and Grandmother."

"It's the gods, Shazzi. Now do I have your word?"

Belshazzar glowered at Nabonidus. He took in his father's elegant robe, the heavy ring of kingship, the golden crown. His eyes lingered on the silver medallion that hung from Nabonidus's neck -- a lion-headed griffin in hand-to-hand combat with a hero-warrior – embossed precious gems caught the light and threw their colors around the room. "Yes," Belshazzar said. "But only if the Medes are gone from the place."

"The gods promised it."

* * *

AS SOON AS Belshazzar had left, Nabonidus slumped into a chair. He took off the crown and laid it on a table. The old king bent over, his head in his gnarled hands. The medallion swung free beneath his neck. The image of a lion-headed griffin in hand-to-hand combat with a dagger wielding hero-warrior graced one side. On the other were the insignia of three gods – the winged disk of Shamash, the star of Ishtar, and above them both the round moon of Nanna-Suen.

After a few moments, he looked up. The moon, waxing nearly to full was bright against the night sky. Slowly, he got to his feet. With his face upturned, eyes closed, he prayed, "O Sîn, lord of the gods, king of the gods of heaven an underworld, god of the gods who dwell in the highest heaven, when you joyfully enter the temple may there be on your lips blessings for Esagil, Ezida, and Egushnugal, the temples of your great divinity. Reverence for your great divinity instill in my people that they might not sin against your great divinity. May their foundations be as firm as those of heaven. Deliver me, Nabonidus, king of Babylon, from sinning and grant me long life." He opened his eyes, put his hands to his cheeks and said, "In Belshazzar, my own offspring, my eldest son, instill reverence for your great divinity that he might have no sin and enjoy an abundant life."

CHAPTER 36 (PARSA)

"Just around this hill," the scout said, "in the next valley we should be able to see them."

Sure enough as soon as they'd rounded a stony outcropping, one of the Zagros Mountains' last sighs as the range leveled out to the south, Cyrus could see the approaching army. Elamites. He urged his mare into a canter and called Prexaspes and the scout to follow behind him. As they closed the distance, Cyrus assessed the group. Foot soldiers led, about two hundred strong. Men on sturdy ponies and heavy horses followed. At the back of the company were three open wagons, pulled by oxen.

Suddenly, Cyrus threw up his arms and called out, "Mardonius!" He took the reins again as a man on the cavalry's flank broke to meet him. They clapped each other's shoulders as the horses danced around.

"Cyrus!" Mardonius grinned. Then he sobered, looking at Prexaspes and the scout. "I would have thought you'd send a guard."

Prexaspes nodded. "See?"

"Prexaspes, you remember Mardonius, from Susa?"

"I do. I thought you were out of the army."

"We heard about Astyages, about the Medes bearing down on you. It's big news. I've been bored out of my skull so safe and slow in the palace. It was a great opportunity. I asked Tepti to release me, to release us." He nodded to Gobryas, riding in a small wagon behind. "He agreed and added this contingent, too. Astyages is not popular. The Elamites are on your side."

As they rode back to Anshan, Mardonius and Cyrus talked strategy. Cyrus was grateful to have someone with experience and knowledge of war. Prexaspes rode close to his king, glancing back every so often at the army that followed. When he saw the dip in the grass where he'd dropped his stave, he rode head, dismounted to scoop it up, reattached the weapon, and resumed his position next to Cyrus.

Mardonius agreed that Astyages's troops were far too formidable in number, arms, and training to meet head-on. "Do you have a plan?"

"I'm thinking of removing everyone to the hills north of Anshan."

"And leave the homes and farms undefended?"

"Yes."

"If we cannot hold Astyages off..." Prexaspes said, "If we lose, it will all be Median, anyway."

"We won't lose," Cyrus said.

The men, flanking Cyrus, turned their heads simultaneously and looked at him, incredulous. Prexaspes was the first to shift his gaze ahead.

Mardonius shrugged. "Have you told the people?"

"Not yet."

CHAPTER 37 (MEDIA)

*A*styages's army moved slowly not for lack of strength and resources but because of it. They started out with thousands of men, many fresh and sharp from service in challenging regions, summoned back for this punitive blow in Anshan. The king gained more troops along the way. For they passed through territories said to be vassal states to Media, where Astyages called up yet more men pledged to arms.

The Medes' reception by these vassals was lukewarm, Astyages noticed with a disappointment that he tried to hide. He fancied himself the popular leader of a huge empire; but it was easy to see that Media was less unified than he wanted to believe. In some cases, he had to force the men to join his troops. That the army consumed nearly everything from the territories they crossed didn't make them any more welcome. Not only did the men require common items -- weapons repaired, new clothing, armor, and tons of food every day -- but also the Median chargers, Nisean horses, famous for centuries (they were indispensable to Assyria's war machine) as the very best war horses, required supplemental grain and still denuded whatever grasslands the army passed through.

The army's wake was dust and waste, just as Amytis had predicted... and lamented. But their passing gave Astyages an opportunity to remind the peoples of greater Media of his presence and demands. He didn't tell anyone the message he'd sent to Cyrus... nor the message he'd received in reply. Cyrus was assembling every force he could. Astyages grinned. Let him finish, and they'd slaughter every viable man in that damned place. So the Mede took his time.

* * *

BACK IN ECBATANA, Amytis did indeed ride often and far. The mountain air, the primal strength of the horse beneath her, and the sheer magnitude of this place she called home were – if not balm – then clarifying. She'd sent a messenger with Astyages's troops, of course, a youth who promised to bring her news immediately, if Astyages departed from the plan she so clearly described. The young man hadn't yet returned. Thankfully, Amytis thought, because she'd heard from Median tribesman in the southwest that Babylonians were poking around the temple ruins in Harran.

"Let them," she said. She knew Nabonidus, was fond of Adad-guppi. "Tell me if they bring soldiers or take over other areas of the city. Otherwise, let them work. They'll improve the place." Far more troubling were hints and rumors of a restlessness to the west. Nathan's wife's cousins – scattered throughout territories – confirmed it.

CHAPTER 38 (LYDIA)

*C*roesus gathered his advisors together. Birdsong from the parks of Sardis trilled through the palace's open windows on breezes softened by the Mediterranean air. Croesus waggled his double chin in an effort to convince them that the journey must be undertaken. He was sure of the outcome – Lydian control of all those resources, all that wealth just sitting in the Median mountains, never mind the trade. Media should belong to Lydia, he declared, and now was the time. But they needed allies.

No one doubted that Croesus would forge ahead with his intentions, whatever anyone else may have thought. Nevertheless, Croesus would go through the motions of consulting, and they of saying what someone must: there's no need; the conscripts will be unhappy about leaving their comfortable settlements along the blue sea coast; it will stir up trouble where there isn't any... and so on. Besides – and they tried to put this delicately -- what more do you want? But Croesus was Croesus: if there was more to be had, he wanted it.

So draped in gold and jewels that he could hardly move but for the countless slaves and servants who moved for him, King

Croesus still wanted more. In this case, he saw an opportunity finally to gain full control of the entire east-west trade along the northern corridor, land and sea, from the farthest east, west even beyond Sardis to the ocean itself. And not only that – all those precious metals, gems, and more that lay under Media's ground... all that old-growth timber... Croesus swiped the back of his hand across his mouth.

"Media is fragmented," he said, "weak. Look, the Babylonians have already moved into the vacuum at Harran. If we don't act now, Babylonia could trump us this golden opportunity."

Finally, one of them dared to speak the obvious. "But wouldn't that break the Halys treaty?" he asked.

All of his life, Croesus had been stymied by that damn treaty. It was not of his making. But when he inherited his father's kingdom, so he'd inherited that agreement, and it rankled for him even as his wealth increased and his holdings grew.

Until recently, it hadn't mattered. Treaty or no, he couldn't have expanded east. The Median empire was too strong. But now... Now... yes! Croesus's scowl turned into a great big grin.

"That's just it! *I* wouldn't be breaking the treaty. If that young man prevails, the treaty would be null. If this Cyrus defeats Astyages, the young man on Media's throne would be a usurper." In a display of righteous indignation, Croesus flung his hand, golden fingers gaining their own momentum, and cried out, "He would have killed my brother!... in-law," he added under his breath, quickly going on, "the very one in whose name the treaty was forged. Should we move against this usurper, we would simply be avenging the death of my peace-loving family."

The three advisors looked at each other.

"Cyrus *is* Astyages grandson," one said.

"By blood," another added, wincing with the truth of it.

"And the marriage of your sister," the third said, "gods grace her memory, to Astyages -"

"Short as it was," the first advisor piped in. They all nodded.

"Was simply the sign of the agreement between your fathers—"

"That neither Lydia, we, nor the Medes should ever cross the Halys in aggression against the other again."

Croesus narrowed his eyes at the three. "Well, I think the others – Babylonia, Egypt, Greece – will take my side."

Again, the advisors looked at each other: which one would speak the next most obvious? When they looked at the man who'd dared before, he buttoned his lips, sat back, and shook his head. Croesus watched it unfold and finally demanded. "What. What now?"

"It's just that there's a possibility..." one advisor began.

"Yes," the another said, "what if..."

"There is no way," the bravest said impatiently. "This... Cyrus. He can't defeat the Medes. An empire versus... a village."

Croesus stewed in his chair.

"Well, not exactly a village," one of the men said.

Then Croesus stood. "You're right." He shrugged. "I don't know all the details. But I do know that Median forces have pulled back everywhere. There are opportunities on the horizon. We should be ready. I'll secure allies. Media *will* be mine."

Croesus was right that the Babylonians were already in Harran. But their king, Nabonidus, was not. Neither was he in Babylon. So when Croesus sent for an audience with the king, it was the crown prince who received the request.

CHAPTER 39 (PARSA)

"*I*'m not going."

The girl had entered the chief's tent without apology or ceremony. The only child of one of the most well-respected members of the tribe, Zarin had grown up with an air of entitlement that seemed only to make the young men want her more. She was easily the prettiest eligible young woman of the Pasargadae. She knew it and used it. Only she could, only she would, burst in on the tribal chief like this and with such a declaration.

"Everyone must go," the *zapanitu* said. "It's not only the king's command in a time of war. It's also the single best way to protect you, and the other women, children, too."

"Prexaspes wouldn't make me, if he were the *zapanitu*."

"Well he's not. Sorry to disappoint, but I am still very much alive. Besides, he is quicker than anyone to follow Cyrus."

"I know," the girl said, frowning. "Cyrus this, Cyrus that. Everywhere that Cyrus goes, Prexaspes follows."

Even pouting, she's pretty, the chief of the Pasargad thought. Why his son didn't move on her, he couldn't say. Though she does prove to be difficult. "Does your father know you're here?"

"No. He told me to pack lightly."

"Listen, Zarin. Until only recently, we have always been a people on the move."

"Well I haven't," Zarin said, tossing her head and stomping her foot.

"We still live in tents."

"But they're nice tents, and they have all the things we need."

The *zapanitu* gave her a critical look.

"To be comfortable!"

"You're wasting my time. Go. Pack as your father said."

* * *

THE FOOTHILLS NORTH of Parsa's plateaus were rugged and pocked. Shepherds knew them well, even many miles into the wild. Cyrus, too, knew them from his days escaping the dysfunction of the palace and the abuse he suffered at the hands of the groundsman who had brought Cyrus's father under his control with opiated relief for King Cam's grief.

It was in those hills years ago that Cyrus had stumbled on the simple dwelling of Mit and Spaco. Walking here now, he could feel the mix of affection and anger rise. He could never reconcile their tenderness and love toward him (he had never doubted that he was their son) with the knowledge that it had all been a lie. They had betrayed the palace -- his poor mother, his *real* mother, and the king himself. Not that Cyrus held any affection for Astyages. But the shepherd slaves, as dear to him as true parents had betrayed Cyrus. That thought more than any other kept him from embracing them fully, despite the surprising reunion in Parsa.

Now, Cyrus walked with his beloved family into the hills of home, hoping that here they and all the other Parsan innocents would be safe.

"Are you alright?" Sanda asked, when his pace slowed. "This is the right thing to do."

"I know it is. It's just that this place --" his eyes jumped to a goat path on their right.

"Ah. Mit. Spaco." She nodded. "You need to let it go." Her tone was gentle.

"How can I?"

"Don't take it so personally. They wanted a baby." She leaned her hand against a tree, catching her breath. "Besides, now you know a thing or two about how to get around in the mountains."

He smiled. "Are you tired?"

"I'm pretty much a flat-lands girl."

"I wish you had learned to ride. A horse would make this so much easier for you."

Sanda thought about the colt born the night of their wedding, jet black and wobbly. "He has become a beautiful horse."

"Far easier to manage than his mother!"

The mare was a cast-off that the boy Cyrus had insisted on taking from Media. No one had wanted her -- small, dish-faced and mean -- except the boy prince, raised as a slave. Years later, Cyrus had ridden that horse into Pasargad. That was when Sanda had first seen him. Cyrus was different in ways that she wanted to know the rest of her life. The rendezvous she secretly arranged that night between his mare and a stallion treasured by her tribe brought Cyrus back to her. The colt was their offspring.

Pasargad had few horses. These two were exceptional -- nimble, intelligent, and far stronger than their modest size suggested. Over the years, together with the native horses, Cyrus had increased the animals and distributed them among young men willing to spend time training for defense.

"Between the two of them you've bred a fine herd."

"*We* have," Cyrus said with a wink.

Cassandane rewarded him with a smile. Then she stepped back onto the trail. "Walking is good."

"But you're tired."

"I am." She turned to look at him. "I hope you'll be happy to know why."

Cyrus's eyes changed in an instant from query to delight. "Pregnant?"

"It seems. Yes."

Cyrus swept her up and kissed her deeply. He set her back down gently. "But now?" Cyrus's forehead creased in concern.

"As good a time as any." Sanda smiled.

After the women and the children were settled into tents, caves, and hidden copses tucked in the Parsan foothills, the soldiers bid them farewell. Mardonius stepped away from his Elamite warriors to find his son, to hug Gobryas before the battle began. But the pitiable boy couldn't be found. He'd slipped limping through the throng to a dark corner of the cave.

"Take courage, child," Mardonius whispered as he rode away. "Til I return."

The men made their way to the edge of the valley. The river was dry now, quiet and still. Word was that the Median troops were so great in number that they would fill it like a flood.

CHAPTER 40 (BABYLONIA)

*B*elshazzar had just heard Khai's report – the costs that renovations in Harran would incur – and resenting every bit of it, when he received the message.

From the west, King Croesus of Lydia declared, "terribly disturbing news – Media had come under assault from a foreign usurper."

Belshazzar read that opening part twice. This was not exactly as Belshazzar had understood events. It was Astyages's troops on the move, after all. In truth, Belshazzar didn't really care.

"I'll see him any time," Belshazzar said.

The messenger shuffled his feet. "King Croesus was quite insistent," he said, "that it be the king himself."

A crimson flush rose from Belshazzar's neck up into his eyes.

"King Nabonidus, sir."

Belshazzar threw his drinking cup to the ground, twisting its silver lion's snarl into a half-bent grin. "Fine. Tell your Croesus this: You'll find *King* Nabonidus in Teima. In the dead middle of barbaric nowhere... Don't write that last part," he said. "I'll assure safe docking in Ashkelon, if you wish to sail as far as you can. My father, *the king*... Yes, again... will see to your passage through the

desert from there." Belshazzar muttered, "Good luck with that."
Then seeing the messenger earnestly scribbling said, "Not that.
Just end with the desert. Then the usual blessings." Seeing the
scribe hesitate, Belshazzar said, "*Marduk*'s blessings. On our
continued friendship, the gods guide you, blah blah blah, and
so on."

CHAPTER 41 (PARSA)

The Elamite contingent was a welcome addition to Cyrus's Parsan troops; but their combined numbers were still a fraction of the army that Astyages marched toward them.

"They're too big, too many," Prexaspes said.

At only a day's march north, their estimate of Median force was irrefutable: Astyages's army was huge. And they would be in Parsa tomorrow.

Cyrus had assembled his commanding officers -- Otanes, Prexaspes, and Mardonius. Cyrus looked at them, such a small and virtually untried group.

Word had come from Astyages himself. No offer of concessions, invitation to reinforce vassal status, only this: "We will crush you."

For a moment, the men swam in Cyrus's eyes. Despite the threat, not a one had left, not a one had raised objection to defending Parsa, not a one. Now here they stood, ready to go over the battle plan.

Prexaspes, a dear friend forged from ugly enmity. Practical and realistic; but whatever his misgivings, he would not hesitate to back Cyrus. Cyrus looked with fondness at Otanes, his lanky frame a chiseled echo of his sister Sanda's lissome beauty. Cyrus's brother-in-law leaned lightly on his bow, a real work of art. Only Mardonius had seen real armed conflict before but never against so formidable and army. And Cyrus barely knew him, having met the man just the once in Susa. Well, he had proven circumspect and sage in his advice during the past days; and there was no time to test him now.

"Yes," Cyrus said. "They are too many. Too big to enter the plain without making themselves fatally vulnerable. That's why we're here." Cyrus swung his arm around the rugged hillsides. "To get to Anshan, they'll have to follow either the narrow valley to our east or the only slightly wider valley below us. They cannot maneuver chariots abreast, much less wide lines of troops. No matter what, they'll have to expose long flanks to our arrows and spears."

"But there are still too many."

"Tomorrow, when they move, we'll know which route they'll take. We have a size that can quickly adjust.

"Otanes, your archers will lead in the initial assault. Only after Astyages's men have advanced into the plain and the first 100 or so have passed at least to the middle of shooting range, should you give the signal to shoot. Remember, some of them will be on horses and those might be in the lead, advancing fast. After you've done your work, I'll give the signal for the cavalry to follow me into the field. If for some reason, the front line of the Medians advances out of your range, tell me immediately so that we can initiate the cavalry."

Cyrus smiled at Prexaspes, barrel-chested and slim-hipped, whose clothes as always were perfectly arranged. There were aunts among the Pasargad happy to fashion clothes for the chief's son, especially a youth as impressive as Prexaspes, even one as particular. Not even impending battle could persuade Prexaspes to cut corners with his wardrobe. Every hair in place, he had tied a yellow band around his head, a twisted fillet like he'd heard the Assyrian noblemen wore hundreds of years before.

"Prexaspes, you and I will each lead a contingent of horsemen to the front, intercepting Astyages's chargers. Their mounts may be heavier but ours are faster, and speed will be crucial here. We must get ahead of them." Prexaspes solemnly nodded his head, the cords in his neck giving and stretching with the effort.

"Mardonius, you will lead the infantry out after us to pummel the flanks and (hopefully) the rear." Cyrus laid his hand on the elder's shoulder, "Your courage and experience are invaluable. The men will be afraid. Let them see you before you advance. Actually, when we're done here, go and mingle with them. Let them see your assurance."

Cyrus turned back to his brother-in-law. "After Mardonius has advanced, Otanes, I want you to bring your archers with their swords and spears in behind Mardonius' men. Hopefully," he said, looking at each in turn, "we can put an end to this by nightfall. Meanwhile, sit. Eat, drink." The meal was simple – the same ordinary fare that the troops were accustomed to having at home – beans and barley, bitter greens with sweet onions, fruit and cheese.

At dinner, Cyrus called for their attention. "The Medes have come a long way," he said. "We all know their numbers are great; but remember, those men have to be fed. They will be tired and hungry, while we are rested and nourished by our own food. And who can defeat a pistaka-eater?" he added, eliciting a ripple of laughter. Cyrus went on, "They are far from home. Some are mercenaries with no investment in winning except some pay. Many of the rest don't even really consider themselves Medes. We, on the other hand, are fighting for the land and the people that we love. This place is our home."

A few men shouted assent.

"We have lived on this land," Cyrus continued, "We survived bad times, and we have made them good. Here, we have tended animals, planted trees and vines. We have made our land fruitful. We have made it strong." The men clapped. "We have made it beautiful. And the people here are our people – our wives and children, our parents, our brothers and sisters. This land," he said, "is ours." Over the cheering Cyrus concluded, "I for one will never give it up." The men shouted and beat their fists on the planks that served as tables. "I see you feel the same." They were still cheering as Cyrus returned to his tent. He hoped they were ready.

He left before any one of them could see: already he grieved. How many of these men – these good people, his people – would die in the fight tomorrow? Yet what was there to do but fight, defend this place they all called home? Oh, Pasargad, Cyrus thought. He would fight for the place itself. He would fight to make good on his promise to Cassandane - Pasargad. He would fight to the death.

CHAPTER 42 (ASHKELON AND TEIMA)

*F*rom the port at Ashkelon, on a padded divan, rich mosaic underfoot, under the shade a gossamer awning that rippled in a light sea breeze, Croesus reread the message. The dispatch that Croesus had received from Nabonidus was brief. Yes, Nabonidus would see Croesus, hear him out. In the desert. If Croesus chose indeed to come. "Bring no more than three persons – personal servants, if you must have them," Nabonidus had written.

The men that Croesus had taken this far with him were a select group, representatives from the Greek settlements that the Lydian had brought under his rule and the most physically impressive. In this quest to secure allies, he had wanted to be sure to communicate the strength of the Lydian forces without arriving in numbers that were in any way threatening. He'd planned it very carefully. But three, only *three... "personal attendants"?!* Croesus read the note yet again and lifted his eyes. Yes, that was the sum of it.

* * *

NABONIDUS HAD HAD time to consider Croesus's proposal. He considered it seriously. Allied with Lydia, Nabonidus could secure control of Harran the better to enable proper religious duties in service of Nanna-Suen. But. Even as it was now – Harran ostensibly in Median control – Babylonia had already been able to begin such work. If Astyages had a brain in his head, he could see that Nabonidus was actually engaged in improving a Median holding. And asking nothing but the liberty to do so. But *did* Astyages have a brain in his head? Nabonidus weighed the options.

"I led my people from remote mountains and took the road to my country Teima in peace," that is what he told any official who dared challenge his mission. Peace. Nabonidus thirsted for it. And he had found that it was the desert that quenched it for him. Now this alarm and request, which smacked of demand, from the king of Lydia. Nabonidus sighed. Let the man come, but only in peace. The desert brooked no excess. Maybe the desert would work its purifying fire on Croesus, too.

CHAPTER 43 (MEDIA)

"No," Amytis said, "no." And all the rage that ever should have welled up in her against this man the world knew as her father rose like the lava of a volcano that had been quiet too long. She didn't shout it, didn't scream the word. No, the sound from her mouth after that was beyond words, and it shook windows up and down the palace walls. But when Amytis's anger was spent – and the room in ruins – there was still nothing she could do.

CHAPTER 44 (PARSA)

*T*he armies clashed some miles north of Anshan, in the river valley. The terrain had slowed Astyages's troops, so the day was already closer to night when the fighting began.

Astyages's archers began shooting as soon as they saw men in the hills. Using the advantage of the low sun's glare, Otanes adjusted quickly. But the Medes were inexorable. They poured through the wide pass toward the plain. Behind the archers came a seemingly endless line of armored infantry, far more than Otanes's men could possibly take down. This was not at all what they'd planned. Cyrus shouted to Mardonius to lead the infantry ahead.

Astyages kept his own cavalry behind, holding them still out of sight. He rode at the very end, keeping his trusted general Harpagus close beside. Cyrus had to adapt. Rather than risk his own precious horses running into the flailing spears and swords of Astyages's army, Cyrus ordered half his cavalry contingent to dismount. He handed the reins of his steed to Prexaspes and said, "Get your men each to hold another horse, and stay here." Before Prexaspes could protest, Cyrus directed his men to leave their horses with Prexaspes's contingent and follow him. Then he ran off on foot, disappearing in front of the men who followed.

The battle was hard. Mardonius had succeeded in intercepting Astyages's front line, and his men fought beside him with unwavering determination. "Hold the line!" he shouted as he yanked his sword from a Mede's face and swung it into the neck of the man who battled the neighbor to his right. "Courage! Push!" Shield down, he drove forward into the Mede who had stepped on the bloody face of a screaming companion to slash at Mardonius with a dagger. As Mardonius deflected the thrust with his shield, he raised his sword overhead and brought it down with a crunch through the top of the man's skull. At the same time, he saw the youth to his left miss a strike and then the Mede he fought, sliced through the wrist that held the young man's shield. The boy screamed and Mardonius groaned as he watched the Mede cut him open chest to bowels. The young man looked surprised as he caught his heart with his one remaining hand before dropping dead. Mardonius fought on with renewed fury.

Cyrus thought he had fought hard before, when Harpagus had mercilessly pitted the ten-year-old shepherd against seasoned warriors, over and over. But this was a different kind of awful. ... Harpagus. Cyrus didn't have time to dwell on it now. When he could tear his eyes away from the bloody man he had dropped, Cyrus looked for Astyages but saw only a tide of identical iron masks, ugly and mean.

That, and on the Parsan side an extraordinary warrior whom Cyrus could not recognize. To watch the man fight, it was less like war than some fatal dance. He kept showing up in the edge of Cyrus's line of sight – a beautiful butcher. The man lifted and turned as if his body were made of water. A fountain of death, Cyrus thought, the man would parry and with a single stroke fell man after man.

Cyrus had to tear his eyes away, and each time just in time to block another crushing blow or thrusting spear. His arms ached and his legs became as stiff and heavy as stone columns. Cyrus signaled to Prexaspes, and the two cavalry battalions switched places. Cyrus's group extricated themselves one by one from the fighting. They returned to the horses, and Prexaspes's men entered the fray. Otanes's men spelled off Mardonius's troops as well as they could. Mardonius himself fought on, seeming never to tire but as if each man he confronted had dealt his wife's death, twisted his son's foot in the womb, as if he had everything to live for.

High hills brought the dark more quickly to the valley. Not fast enough, as far as Cyrus was concerned. Finally, Cyrus caught sight of Astyages, at the far edge of the army. The Median king had not fought at all. Cyrus signaled to Astyages for a halt to the fighting and a chance to speak. The Median king ignored him, and the battle raged on. Furious, Cyrus trotted back to the horses, dropped his weapons, even the *akinakes* dagger that seldom left his waist, grabbed the reins of his horse, and rode straight toward the Medes. Median archers took aim at him, but "Hold!" Astyages commanded. He couldn't lose the man yet.

"Had enough, boy?" Astyages called to Cyrus. Even from a distance, Cyrus could hear the taunt in the old king's voice.

Cyrus glanced around. "The day is late. Your men are at least as exhausted as ours," Cyrus called back. "Let us both tend our injured, remove the dead," Cyrus said. "But we will keep fighting as long as you do." Cyrus rode back to his troops without waiting for an answer. That his men had visibly relaxed by the time Cyrus met the line told him that Astyages had drawn away indeed.

Parsa and its Elamite ally had barely survived. But they hadn't lost. Yet.

* * *

As the soldiers made their weary way back to the tents, to what succor they might get with simple food and rest, "Who is that?" Cyrus asked, pointing to the soldier who had so captivated him with his skill and finesse.

"An Elamite like me," Mardonius said. He lifted his helmet off his head. "The name's Hystaspes -- Vishtaspa, if you prefer." He ran a hand through soaking hair. Unlike me, he's important. That is, his family's from Susa, well respected, rich. Word has it that they come from the line of kings that ruled the region before the Assyrians did them in, that he's one of the would-be princes of Elam." Mardonius tilted his head, considering Vishtaspa anew. "Most of their kind hire other people to do their military service," he said. "This guy could have. He has enough money. But he insisted on joining the fight himself."

"What's he like?" Cyrus asked.

"A hell of a warrior, that's for sure. As for his temperament, I don't know. He keeps to himself."

Prexaspes had joined them, falling into step beside Cyrus. He added, "You're talking about that guy, Vishtaspa?"

"Yes," Cyrus said. "Do you know him?"

"No," Prexaspes said. "But I did see him before we left the village. He brought his wife along all the way from Susa. I hear he doted on her the whole way here. It's unseemly, if you ask me. Women don't belong near fighting men. Just my opinion."

"Yes, it is," Cyrus said, "your opinion." He thought how often the knowledge of Sanda's proximity had kept him going that day.

"Can I ask you something?" Mardonius fixed worried eyes on Cyrus. He glanced anxiously at Prexaspes, hovering as usual nearby.

Cyrus nodded to Prexaspes, who stepped away.

When they were alone, "What is it?" Cyrus asked.

"My son," Mardonius said.

Cyrus thought of the club-footed little boy with the bitter demeanor and acid tongue.

"If something were to happen to me. If I were to die..." Mardonius said.

Cyrus shook his head. It was reflex. He couldn't allow that any of his men, these good men merely defending their families, their homes might die. Of course they could. They just did.

Mardonius said it aloud. "This is war, after all."

Cyrus's exhalation was his only concession.

"Would you look after Gobryas?"

Cyrus stopped. He considered the veteran before him. They hardly knew one another, having met only recently and only the once when Cyrus and Prexaspes had visited Susa. And yet, he saw now that they knew each other very well. Cyrus thought of the sacrifices Mardonius had made, the Elamite troops he had added to Cyrus's ranks... He saw the deep lines in Mardonius's forehead and thought about little Cambyses, how Cyrus would do anything to keep his son safe, even the unborn child that Sanda carried.

Cyrus gripped Mardonius's shoulder. "Like my own," he said, and felt Mardonius relax.

CHAPTER 45 (PARSA)

*A*fter the men had eaten, they returned to their tents to repair weapons, clothing, and bodies in the waning light. Cyrus had worked out the next day's strategy with Otanes, Prexaspes, and Mardonius and was sitting apart, looking out over the field when he saw a rider heading from camp into the hills where the women and children were. He could just make out the man they called Vishtaspa or Hystaspes.

"I suppose he hopes to 'wash his feet.'"

Cyrus jumped. "Prexaspes. You surprised me."

"That's why you should have a guard, dear king."

"Always nagging," Cyrus said.

Prexaspes sat next to Cyrus, shoulder to shoulder.

"Like I said," Prexaspes huffed in disgust. "Women… a soldier during war…" They watched Vishtaspa's form grow smaller in the distance. "It's not the time."

Cyrus had to allow that he was right. They needed to keep focused.

"You should, you know," Prexaspes said, "have a guard."

Cyrus turned to look at his friend's face.

Prexaspes shrugged. "Survive this, and people will still want to kill you. It happens with kings." Suddenly serious, Prexaspes took Cyrus's hands in his own. "I'll never let you fight without me again."

"You sound like a scolding old aunt," Cyrus said. Grinning, he extricated his hands. Then, sobering, even stern, "You were right to obey me. If you hadn't, I'd have had to make an example of you. And I'd hate to lose my closest friend."

Prexaspes couldn't tell if Cyrus were serious or not. He'd seen the fury of Cyrus -- rare but consuming -- and understood the necessity of military discipline. Still.

"Really," Cyrus said, as if reading his thoughts. Breaking the ensuing silence, Cyrus turned back to look toward the hills. "So that Vishtaspa. Some guy, after all, huh?" The exaggeration was clear.

"I know. If there's anything that should be women's business, it's birthing, for crying out loud."

Cyrus snapped his head back to Prexaspes. "Birthing, you say?"

"His wife. Vishtaspa's. The girl looked about ready to split when they rode into the village. A runner came and told him after the battle that her pains had started."

"You didn't tell me she was pregnant."

"Why should I?" Then, seeing Cyrus's face, Prexaspes said, "I didn't think it was important."

* * *

WHEN VISHTASPA RODE BACK to the camp a short while later, Cyrus met him. The man dismounted while Cyrus held his horse's head. "Nice work on the field today," Cyrus said, handing the reins back to Vishtaspa.

"Thank you, sir."

"You must be tired, and your weapons in need of some repair."

"I've already fixed and cleaned my weapons, sir. And I'm not so tired as half the other men, and thank the gods not wounded," he added.

Cyrus began to walk toward the camp, Vishtaspa beside him leading the weary horse.

"How is your wife?"

Vishtaspa started, causing the horse, nearly asleep on its feet as it walked, to toss its muzzle up. "She's fine, sir. Thank you for asking."

"I understand that she's expecting a baby."

"She is, indeed. Our first. I was told that her pains started this afternoon. But nothing's come of it after all." He patted the horse's neck.

"Still waiting, then?"

"Yes, sir." Vishtaspa didn't need to explain the worry that furrowed his brow.

Cyrus broke away, but he watched Vishtaspa lead his horse back to the camp. Suddenly feeling the ache of fatigue in his legs, Cyrus wondered if ten years ago he would have bounced back from such a hard day as Vishtaspa appeared to have done.

They had lost men today, men whose families would have to do without them for the rest of their lives. He hated the thought of putting his people in front of Astyages's troops again tomorrow. He hated the thought of Astyages at all, his own grandfather, so confident and smug with his countless troops.

War. It was all so stupid, that's how Cassandane had put it. He huffed a wry laugh. How ironic that here he was, in the thick of it... defending the chance to build a place of peace. And he, fighting as if the other's dying breath was all the air he'd ever wanted, when all he'd ever wanted was in those hills – Cassandane – and this place – home.

CHAPTER 46 (TEIMA)

*C*roesus felt as though he never stopped sweating, from the moment they left the breezy port until his arrival, safe, in Teima. Anxiety and heat – a dreadful combination. His Arab escorts revealed little of their faces and less of their thoughts but assumed absolute compliance as they silently ushered the corpulent king and his three "personal attendants" across the sands. Each morning, he awoke surprised to feel the skin across his neck uncut and his water skin newly full.

When he'd first stepped into the encampment that Nabonidus himself introduced as "the palace" (!), Croesus tried to hide his shock. The Babylonian king had constructed a satellite base in the middle of the desert, built of the same mud and plaster construction, tents all around, and furnished with the same woven wools, plush pillows for furniture as the native desert-dwellers. Arabs came and went throughout the so-called palace with a liberty Croesus later learned was born of common respect and shared beliefs. These people, he learned, worshiped a god that Nabonidus identified with his own Nanna-Suen.

The whole thing was deeply unsettling, even after he'd been installed in a (surprisingly comfortable) low cushioned chair, a platter of fruit and nutmeats (no wine here) next to him. Still, Croesus was clear about his mission. After he'd laid it all out, detailing in every way that he'd rehearsed the advantages to Babylonia in his proposal... Well, Croesus hoped he had convinced the old king. Though he had to admit that a more definite commitment from the Babylonians would have been nice.

CHAPTER 47 (MEDIA)

*A*mytis reined in her mount, its sides heaving. She leaned against its neck, its mane course under her hands. She could catch her breath more quickly now than when she'd first returned from Babylon. Her blood had thickened. Though why that came to mind, she didn't know. It had been years since her return.

The horse dipped its head into the alfalfa, tall now, in this high mountain field. Amytis looked around. Despite everything, her heart softened. She loved how the thin mountain air gave every color and every being a crystalline quality so different from the muted haze along the wide Euphrates. Media's landscape never failed to lift her spirits. Yet now it was exactly that – the beauty of the place that made her head thick with anxiety.

War ruined everything. It was ever and always devastating, not only to populations but to the land itself. And all those animals. She'd seen it. Everyone had. Armies tore through territories with no concern for a forest's sophisticated diversity, no regard for what made a stream run clear or the wildlife plentiful. They chopped and burned and trampled their way along – forward march with human strength trumped the value of anything else. War itself was a tyrant, creating crises that laughed at the long-view, scorned wisdom. Dominance now was all that mattered. It was always bad.

Amytis didn't need to see to know that Astyages's huge forces had already wreaked havoc on the fragile lands between Media and Parsa and dreaded learning the devastation to Cyrus's Parsa, too. Cyrus. Please gods, she prayed, let Astyages spare at least his life.

CHAPTER 48 (PARSA)

*T*he next day, they were back at it, numbers be damned. The Medes' famous war horses were fierce and powerful, biting and kicking in close combat with the Parsan cavalry. But Cyrus's eclectic herd was quicker. Parsan riders urged their mounts to dart and dash, catching opponents where possible in narrow wadis or boulder strewn hillsides. Still, the Parsans' were herding horses, at best used for hunting, and barely trained in war. By contrast, the steeds of Media seemed made of iron and animated with fury. Those horses, molded by particular human training and interests, knew – and loved – war.

Astyages's troops pressed forward, taking Parsan casualties to match their own. Cyrus saw Mardonius fall but had no time to grieve his friend. He fought on, replacing Mardonius' command of the Elamite infantry with Vishtaspa. The Anshanite archers kept Astyages's troops in enough disarray to fight through to the afternoon; but without replacements such as the Medes could make, they were exhausted. By mid-afternoon Astyages's Medes had advanced decisively. By any account, they had won.

Cyrus's army was demoralized. They had lost precious troops -- neighbors and friends -- and the Medes showed no sign of stopping. Yet when they heard Astyages call out that the Medes would take the palace at Anshan next, then Pasargad, and every inhabitant they could flush out, Cyrus's men fought with renewed fury.

Indeed, the threat of assault on a region that Cyrus held especially dear was too much. While Sanda and the other wives, sisters, and mothers watched from the nearby heights, prayed to their gods, looked after the children and the infirm, and encouraged each other, he fought furiously, leading his troops, wounded and weary, in a long and bloody battle.

But the men were overwhelmed and terrified by the inexorable and brutal advance of the Medes. As the sun tracked behind the highest peak, Cyrus's army fell to pieces. Finally, it happened. Whoever could run, did, back toward the hills that hid their women and children. Astyages cheered as his troops surged forward.

Suddenly, there was a great outcry from those hills. The women, the hems of their skirts in their hands, emerged in full view and began pouring down the hillsides straight into the path of their men, brothers, and sons. Cyrus groaned to see Sanda among them. Next to her, a woman who looked to have swallowed the moon. Vishtaspa's wife, Cyrus guessed.

When the men from both armies stared in disbelief, the women whooped and cried in ululating shouts to the defeated warriors. When they were certain to be seen, the women held up their skirts. "Are you such babies," they yelled, "that you would crawl back into the womb? Turn around and fight!"

Even from a distance, the gesture was unmistakable, the effect immediate. Shame. Shame on men ever or in any way going to war. Shame for failing in what they called honor, duty, defense. It would always be the women who suffered the most – all the women, but the defeated worst of all subjected to tortures of body and mind for unimaginable minutes, hours, weeks, months, and years, for the rest of their lives. They would face battles that never ended, unarmed in body and hostage to lives they loved. Shame. Cyrus's face flushed a deeper red than any physical exertion. Shame. He looked away. It was Vishtaspa who broke first, turned back toward the Medes and shouted a cry that set fire to the blood. Cyrus spun to join him and their whole ragged troops behind them. As the sun dipped below the ridge, Parsans and their Elamite allies flung their weary bodies back into battle – to a man, determined this time to leave the field only either victor or dead.

CHAPTER 49 (PARSA)

*M*any did die that day, and by night Astyages's army had pushed them right up against the mountains. But Cyrus's men did not surrender.

Inside the tent, redolent with the fresh roasted meat that Astyages required and the sour smell of spilled wine, Astyages raised his arms. His weapons-bearer, a youth from one or another of Ecbatana's important families, leapt forward to unclasp the silver chest plate – shiny and clean as the day it was forged – from his soft body.

"Those pistaka-eaters sure are brave," Astyages said.

From the corner, Harpagus heard himself reply, "Yes, sir." He clenched his teeth. Always, yes.

* * *

IN THE PARSAN camp that evening, the tired men tended the wounded. Cyrus walked among them, encouraging, praising, joking. But his mind was cluttered. He kept running through the options, what to do next... each time arriving at the same, impossible point. They couldn't leave; they'd all die if they stayed. They couldn't win, they couldn't lose... Finally, Cyrus gave Prexaspes a meaningful task and when Cyrus saw an opportunity to get away without notice, he did. He withdrew his mare from the temporary corral and rode into deeper into the hills. It had been a long time since he'd traveled these paths, narrowing to meandering threads where only goats' feet had trod. But he remembered the way. He missed the company of his falcon and wondered if the horse did, too, remembering when it was just the three of them escaping the claustrophobic stress of Anshan's palace years before. The night air was clear, and this time Cyrus rode with purpose. Once he thought he heard the snort of a horse – someone following – Prexaspes, Cyrus figured... if it were anyone at all. But his friend never appeared and the foothills spoke only the sounds of nonhuman kin.

After a while, Cyrus pulled up at the cottage. Its vegetable garden shone tidy in the moonlight. The simple pen next to it was empty, its sheep and goats safe inside a shed. Cyrus dismounted. An old man emerged in the doorway. Behind him stood a woman, her gray hair twisted and tied loose over one shoulder.

"Pop, Ma," Cyrus said as he embraced each one.

Spaco hugged him tight, then held him out, the length of her arms, tender eyes apprising him. He knew he was a mess. Cyrus's face was haggard and streaked with dirt. Dried sweat, and dust caught in his knotted beard. Above his eyebrow a black line marked a cut where the blood had stopped but the skin had yet to heal.

Spaco's eyes welled. "It's been hard, then," she said.

Cyrus nodded. "We're losing."

The old man led them in to the house.

"Mit wanted to go to you, when it was clear that Astyages would attack. I wouldn't let him. 'The gods will bring you to us, when the time is right,' I told him." Spaco patted the arm she held. "But even I doubted it."

Mit cleared his throat. "She was right. I might have made it worse." Cyrus looked into Mit's face, as etched as a dry riverbed.

"I don't understand," Cyrus said.

Spaco glanced at her husband. Mit nodded to her.

"I, we, need to tell you something. Please, sit."

They sat, the three of them around a rough table. Spaco shook her head with a wry smile. "All these years we didn't want to tell you precisely because we were afraid that *you* would attack *Astyages*. But now he's here... declared himself your enemy."

"But..." Cyrus didn't even know what to ask.

"Astyages is afraid of you. Before you were even born, he feared you. He was sure that the son of Mandane would conquer Media and take the kingdom from him -- a dream told him. So he brought your mother back to Media from Anshan to give birth there." She paused. "Where he would kill you."

Cyrus inhaled sharply.

"But he didn't want to do it himself. So, he told everyone that you had been born dead and secretly commanded his steward to kill you."

"Harpagus?" Cyrus asked in disbelief.

Spaco nodded. "Harpagus didn't want such blood on his hands. So he told my Mit," she put her hand over her husband's, "a shepherd slave, to do it. As it happened, I had just birthed a baby, dead... another." She shook her head. "A boy. We had tried so hard to have children. When you came along..."

"He wanted me dead," Cyrus's eyes were empty.

"Yes," Mit said. "But ten years later..." the old man's voice was bitter.

Cyrus's eyes cleared with recognition. "You didn't leave me in the palace, did you? Astyages took me from you."

Mit hung his head. "I was devastated. The king said he was happy you were alive. The magi told him that that game you played –"

"When the children made me king," Cyrus nodded, remembering.

"It fulfilled the dream. But just to be sure you'd be no trouble to him, he sent you here, to your father's place in Anshan."

"Like he did to my mother," Cyrus said. "Far away and too weak to be anything much." Cyrus looked into each of their eyes in turn, Spaco's and Mit's, the old couple he'd thought were his parents and then believed had betrayed him, abandoned as a child. "I have been angry with you for something you never did."

"It's true that we did not tell you who you were," Spaco said, matter-of-fact again. "We argued about that." She smiled at Mit. "But it seemed safer for you this way."

"Is that why you changed my name," Cyrus asked Mit, "when we went to the palace?"

Mit nodded. "Bartatua, 'with far-reaching strength'..." He shook his head. "Too threating. Better that you, the son of a shepherd slave be something like 'Kurash' or 'Cyrus,' one who bestows care.'"

"Did you know that my grandfather – on my father's side – had such a name?" Cyrus tugged a thin cord from around his neck and withdrew a small clay cylinder that had laid against his chest.

The old couple leaned in and marveled at the image, a victorious horseman in battle and the words, "Kurash the Anshanite, son of Shishpish. " They shook their heads.

"It's a good name," Mit said, "'to bestow care'."

"As is Bartatua," Cyrus said. "'With far-reaching strength.' I need it. Thank you for that," Cyrus said. "Thank you for everything."

"Now, you've been here too long," Mit said. He stood, his voice gruff. "You need to get back to your men. But I'm glad you know."

"First, a prayer," Spaco said.

Cyrus nodded.

She pressed into his hands a small measure of flour.

Gesturing Cyrus into the courtyard, she stepped back. Cyrus started a small fire using only the crudest implements just as Mit had taught him as a child. Over a low stack of cypress and laurel trunks, he offered the sacrifice of barley flour – simple and small. Suddenly a jagged thread of lightning cut the evening sky. Cyrus jumped. Thunder set the horse whinnying and tugging her tether in fright while the sheep and goats bleated in deafening fear. When they were finally quiet again, Cyrus heard Mit beside him catch his breath. He looked up to see the sky darken and roil with the wings of falcons, hawks, and eagles. Birds, more than he could count, alighted on the house.

CYRUS'S TROOPS had seen the lightning and heard the thunder. When they saw the cloud of birds following Cyrus, they knew that the gods were on their side. Their numbers were too few to win. But for tonight, this was enough. More than enough. Even Prexaspes was too overcome to berate Cyrus for going off alone. So the men made a great meal, using up all of the rest of what they had. They couldn't win. But when they went to bed, they slept soundly.

CHAPTER 50 (PARSA)

*S*hortly after Cyrus had left the first parents he'd ever known, two men – their boots the high boots of Media's cavalry – laid waste to the cottage in the hills. There, in the silence of the evening, they killed the old couple. They kicked the embers of Cyrus's sacrificial fire in the courtyard and took the sheep and goats back with them. Astyages would be pleased. It was hard to keep such a large army fed.

At their report, Astyages was pleased indeed, ever so pleased finally to be tying up loose ends. He dismissed the men and exhaled a long breath. That was done. Next. He inhaled and summoned Harpagus.

When the steward appeared, he noticed Astyages's weapons-bearer readying two sets of armor.

As the youth cleaned the one (not the king's) of blood and oiled the leather straps, Astyages said, almost absently, "Shame that Spitamas won't see the victory."

Harpagus nodded. He closed his eyes in a moment of sympathy. Spitamas had died on the field the day that day, and though Amytis hadn't loved him with any passion, Harpagus knew that she would grieve his death. He started to find the weapons-bearer at his back, measuring Harpagus for the chest-plate.

Harpagus looked at Astyages in surprise. He saw only satisfaction.

Astyages smiled. He did not say aloud what was so clear in his mind. In the morning, he would finish the problem that had plagued him for so many years – the curse of those damned dreams. Tomorrow he would put an end to Cyrus, an end to all of Parsa and anyone loyal to him. Astyages looked at the steward before him. It was time the man finish what his king had commanded on the day of that boy's birth.

"You're to take his place, Harpagus."

"Excuse me?"

"With Spitamas dead, I want you to head the troops, you to kill Cyrus."

And Harpagus heard himself say, "Yes, sir." Like always.

CHAPTER 51 (BABYLONIA)

*A*dad-guppi rushed into Belshazzar's rooms with the energy of a child. "Isn't it wonderful?!" she exclaimed.

Belshazzar scowled. He didn't need to ask.

"To be going back to the Elhulhul, I began to wonder if I'd ever see the day!" Indeed, at over eighty years old, his grandmother might well have died much earlier. But here she was spry as a girl and as excited as anyone could be.

As if it weren't bad enough to have to divert funds to Nabonidus's pet project, Belshazzar had gotten word, the king's command and a very clear one at that: he, the crown prince and acting in his father's stead, was to go himself. It was time for him to satisfy the ceremonial inauguration of sacred repairs. Belshazzar looked down at his pink hands – such grand rings, such soft skin, such perfectly trimmed nails... He would have to carry the bricks himself. Sure, a token stack. But, still. And not for Marduk, not for Nabu. The Babylonian pantheon was a powerful one, populated by several significant deities, among them Nanna-Suen. But people had begun to talk, they'd begun to see the favor Nabonidus gave to the god of his youth. They'd heard the insinuations, witnessed the removal of his daughter from Ishtar's temple and installed instead in Ur. Some were concerned.

Belshazzar found himself caught in hard place, impossible you might say. He had spent his life working himself into the elite circles of Old Babylon. Every minute of every day he had studiously conformed to the manners, the speech, the dress, the expectations of Babylonia's most powerful, generations-long families. He had exercised every charm and not a little money to ingratiate himself to Babylonia's highest levels of religious leadership in its most powerful temples – the Esagil in Babylon of course but also Nabu's temple in Borsippa. He'd become friends (!) with the shatammu in Sippar. It helped that Igliss had occupied that post before... Belshazzar had spent his life fitting perfectly to the Babylonian palace. There was nothing he wanted more than to be king. But he was not. That crown lay on his father Nabonidus's head. To fit in with the people who ran the empire... and to become its king. Yet now, for Belshazzar to act the king from *Nabonidus's* throne, he risked doing precisely what could alienate the people whose favor he had curried all the decades of his life.

Beaming, "When do we leave?" Adad-guppi asked. She fairly bounced on the balls of her feet, so eager was she.

Belshazzar groaned.

CHAPTER 52 (PARSA)

*T*hat morning, having risen with the soldiers before the sun – and before Astyages – Harpagus spoke to the troops. He hadn't had a dream, he had had no vision, no instruction from the gods. Rather, he'd tossed and turned with memories unbidden, all the reasons he'd wanted Cyrus dead. The images, the memories had exhausted him with anger and grief. So much grief. Yes, he'd wanted Cyrus dead. Dead like his own son, Harpagus's one and only child killed because of Cyrus's life. And he thought of Astyages, all these years in his service. Yes, always yes. Well, Harpagus had experience in battle, experience at the head of trained troops. Harpagus would lead them, this great Media force. The Median king had commanded it.

Harpagus spoke first to the officers. At the end of his brief speech, "I know how to finish this," Harpagus had said. "Follow me."

* * *

WHEN THE SUN crested the eastern foothills, Cyrus's scrappy army descended to fight their last fight. Their harbinger of death,

Astyages's troops, were already climbing toward them. It was a sight to see: a few tattered men on collision course with a brutal military machine.

From the back of the field, so preoccupied was King Astyages with his fantasy of victory – executing Cyrus, branding soldiers as slaves, the delicious spoils of Parsan women – that he failed to notice he was standing alone.

Harpagus had found his revenge.

When Harpagus had addressed the officers that morning, he did so not merely as their commanding general but as a Mede who knew the empire better than anyone except Amytis. He said first that he knew that few of them, indeed any of Astyages's subjects, respected the king. That had silenced them completely. They exchanged sheepish glances. Some looked at the floor. One man said, "Isn't that treason?"

"Astyages is an old man," Harpagus had said. "He has no sons. Now even Spitamas is dead. Astyages's death would leave Media in the disruptive chaos of would-be kings battling over its throne. It is already a fragile state." Harpagus spoke with authority. "I know better than anyone how fraught Media's future would be, if Astyages should die without an obvious heir."

Harpagus had let them contemplate this for a moment. Then he had said, "Yet there is an heir. And he is right in front of us. Cyrus. We are simply on the wrong side. You know that Cyrus is Astyages's grandson. Now, don't you agree that the youth's survival and prosperity demonstrate divine favor from infancy on? Besides, his subjects love him -- just look at them. Allies even volunteered to join his cause. I am speaking not of treason but the righting of a wrong. All I ask is that when we go, when we lead the troops forward, you indeed follow me."

Harpagus let his eyes find each officer in turn. "The battle has already been too long, too hard. I know how to finish this. Follow me."

CHAPTER 53 (PARSA)

*T*hat day, when Cyrus's meager troops tore down from the mountain with fatal determination and Astyages's army surged up the rocky slope, they never met. The Medes looked to their officers, who looked to Harpagus, who sought out Cyrus.

And when the old steward saw the young man over whom he had suffered such angst and ambivalence, he knew afresh that Cyrus was not guilty of the horrors Harpagus had endured. Cyrus was not responsible for Harpagus's son's death. While it's true that seeing Cyrus brought imagines of his own son, what his boy might be like now, if he'd been allowed to live, what Harpagus saw looking at the man now, was his king.

So, with a voice strong and clear, unmistakable full to the hills, Harpagus called, "We are with you, Bartatua!"

He saw Cyrus's eyes grow wide with surprise.

Then Harpagus signaled his men to join Cyrus's troops in surrender.

The battle was over before it had begun. Someone thrust a standard into Cyrus's hand. He lifted it, a crude golden falcon sewn onto a battered sheet.

No one noticed when King Astyages stripped off his chest-plate. No one saw him draw his dagger and fall upon it, driving the blade straight through his own heart. Someone shouted then, and Cyrus ran to the dying king.

"I know the truth, old man," was all Cyrus said.

Then, Cyrus turned to Harpagus, planted the standard, and enfolded the man in a fierce embrace.

* * *

THE WOMEN and children joined their men, and the foothills rang with relief and joy.

Cassandane found Cyrus like spring finds green. When he caught her up in his arms, poignantly aware of the bump in her belly and the boy at her side, he vowed yet again never to let this woman go. Into her ear, he whispered "Pasargad" in the very same moment as he heard in his, the same, magical word. Reluc-tantly, Cyrus returned his wife to earth. They lingered a moment longer in each other's arms. Then, with a heart as full for Cambyses waiting shy and quiet beside Cassandane, Cyrus bent and gently ruffled his son's hair. Straightening again, This child, Cyrus thought – his eldest son, crown prince of Parsa and now so much more... Cyrus's face clouded, wondering at the difficulty Cambyses's shaking fits posed. How could any commander control his troops much less lead an army with such an affliction?

Cassandane watched Cyrus's expression change. "That," she said as she tucked her arm into his, "is for another day. This day is for celebrating." Then, seeing her brother, she seized him in a bone-breaking hug.

Otanes laughed at her relief, then winced – he'd taken an arrow to the hip. Not a bad wound, but a new one. From behind him stepped Zarin as stunning as ever despite the deprivations of the caves. As Otanes drew her forward, Zarin rested her eyes soft and admiring on the handsome archer.

Cassandane and Cyrus exchanged puzzled looks.

"Zarin and I are getting married," Otanes said, making space under his arm for the young woman's snuggling frame.

"You? Her?" Cyrus stammered.

"That's wonderful news," Cassandane said. "We just had no idea."

"I know," Zarin said. Unlike her face, her frame, her form, her voice grated like a hoof on stone, struggling for purchase. Otanes grinning beside her didn't seem to notice a bit. "Everyone expected me to marry Prexaspes. Even me," she added, turning her lips down in a pout. Then she looked up at Otanes's smooth face and brightened. "But when I saw how adorable Otanes is – and every girl wants him -- I couldn't say 'no'!"

"You asked her?" Cyrus said.

"I've always wanted to," Otanes said.

Cassandane adjusted her expression from surprise to pleasure. "So we'll be sisters, then," she said to Zarin, smiling.

As Zarin tore her adoring eyes from Otanes, her own smile disappeared. She ran her eyes over Cassandane's long frame, Cassandane's dark hair and face of angles and edges..., and Zarin tilted her head to the side. "I guess."

Neither Cassandane nor Cyrus had time to be offended. The piercing scream of a child seized their attention. A little boy broke from small ring of adults and ran. But he was a wounded thing, lurching on one leg while the other its foot a misshapen mass, bumped and dragged behind. Cyrus retrieved him in an instant. The child would not be held, but when Cyrus lowered him to the ground, he kept a hand on each shoulder. Gobryas. His face red, with outrage was streaked with tears.

"Oh, child," Cassandane said. She knelt before the boy. "I am so sorry," she said gently.

"*You* didn't do it," Gobryas said. He looked at Cyrus.

Cyrus braced for the orphan's blame.

"You," Gobryas said, "didn't either." The child's voice was as bitter – if possible, even more – than when Cyrus had met him and Mardonius in Susa. "*He* did," Gobryas said, "my father. And who would blame him?" Gobryas asked defiant. He kicked the club foot out for all to see. "I'd rather die, too."

Cyrus hadn't been able to tell Cassandane the promise he'd made to Mardonius. And frankly, in the crush of battle, the thousand demands of leadership, and the utter shock of victory, he'd forgotten. But it was a promise just the same. So, Cyrus took a deep breath. He crouched down.

"Your father was a brave man," Cyrus said.

Gobryas pushed out his lower lip. As tears fell down his scowling face, Cyrus reached out to take the boy's hands in his own.

Gobryas wrenched them away.

Cyrus pursed his lips. "The day before your father was died – valiant and brave, he told me how much he cared about you." Cyrus glanced up quickly to see Cassandane listening carefully.

Cyrus sought Gobryas's eyes with his own and finding them, said, "I will take care of you now."

"I can take care of myself."

Cyrus looked at Cassandane.

She widened her eyes and shot Cyrus a wincing smile. Then she bent to Gobryas. "We will honor your father now," Cassandane said, "the sacrifice he made, and –" she glanced at Cyrus, then back to the boy, "his wishes. You are a part of our family now."

And for the millionth time, Cyrus felt himself beyond lucky to have married this wonderful woman.

"Now," Cassandane said rising to her feet, "for your father and for all those brave men dead and wounded, for their families – so many, grieving like you the loss of someone irreplaceable, we will celebrate the end this war."

Gobryas swiped a hand across his cheeks. Then, he let Cassandane lead him to where Cambyses all eyes and ears waited. Though Cambyses was the elder, the boys were about the same height. Cassandane said something to Cambyses, and with the boys side-by-side ahead, together they all walked back toward the tumult of camp.

"Just in time," Prexaspes said. He pulled Cyrus toward the band of officers who had gathered on the outskirts. There, Vishtaspa's wife, Hutaosa, presented the baby she had born in the night -- a boy.

"I've decided," Hutaosa said, her voice resonant with such self-assurance and strength that no one flinched at her use of the singular, "to give our son a name to reflect this moment." Watching her, listening to her, Cyrus thought that even had she not been ready to deliver, it was easy to see why Vishtaspa would want such a woman with him. Cyrus looped his arm around Cassandane's waist. He understood.

Hutaosa smiled at a beaming Vishtaspa. Then, shifting the baby in the crook of her arm, slowly she rotated him to take in the camp, brimming not only with Parsans and Elamites but also members of all the tribes of the wide Median empire.

"All that we had thought we'd lost," Hutaosa said, "has been gained. And more. His name," Hutaosa declared, "shall be Darius."

"It's perfect," Cassandane said quietly to Cyrus. Then, she exclaimed a tiny cry, laid a hand on her belly. Cyrus looked at his wife in alarm. But she smiled. "So early," she said, "but it felt like a kick."

PART II

(550 – CA. 549 BCE)

CHAPTER 54 (MEDIA)

*I*t would be impossible to overstate the relief that flooded Amytis's body when she got the news. No, not when she *heard* but rather when the news had finally sunken in. Before that, the report had been so astonishing, so unpredictable an outcome of Astyages's war – and the result so good, despite her father's ignominious end – that it took moments of disbelief, silent and long enough to stir Nathan to alarm. He called for tea – a bracing brew from the east – and guided her to the open window for the air that he'd seen invigorate her times before. Finally, she grinned.

* * *

THE PURITY of her relief was short-lived. Messengers reported from the east: rumors of religious upheaval, charismatic prophets and the like; in the north, always the ferocity of tribes stirred things up; to the south, Babylonia's crown prince himself had gone to Harran (the presence of Belshazzar, whom Amytis knew too well, not the temple renovation itself troubled her); and in the west, Croesus was on the move, courting allies she'd been told.

Under the circumstances – stressful – Amytis rode. She knew better than she wished how important it would be to restabilize the empire. Yet for that, her hands were tied. She was no longer its sovereign, proxy or otherwise. Amytis was now merely the daughter of its king, its defeated king. She'd been eager before to see Mandane's son, now a man. Now, it was urgent. There was so much to do. Amytis felt the horse's gathering of power, the spring of strength under her as they leapt a fallen log. Down they came, and with the horse's neck against her cheek, she spurred him to a drum-rolling gallop across the meadow. Amytis willed Cyrus to reach Ecbatana soon. If she could have yanked him there herself, she would have done it. Truth was, there was little she could do.

CHAPTER 55 (ASHKELON AND SAIS)

*W*hen Croesus returned to his ships at Ashkelon and got the news of Cyrus's unlikely (to say the least) victory, he felt vindicated. Wasn't it just as he'd suspected? That the upstart had unseated Media's rightful king (admittedly, the logic was a stretch) ... surely compromised if not negated the Halys Treaty prohibiting either from crossing the river with aggressive intent. Whatever the case, Cyrus would soon be heading to Ecbatana – dangerously close to Babylonia's northern territories, he hoped Nabonidus could see. Yes, Croesus felt especially vindicated, then, in having suggested to Nabonidus that Cyrus might have it in his mind to expand. But a more definite commitment from the Babylonians would have been nice.

Well. Croesus looked out at the sparkling sea. The Lydian king figured that he could count on a livelier reception in Egypt. At least it would be fun. Pharaoh Amasis had an international reputation for knowing how to party. And the journey easy. From Ashkelon to the Egyptian palace at Sais on the Nile delta, wasn't far, and they could make the journey comfortably by boat.

* * *

ALL THE WAY, waves lapping the reed hulls a gentle breeze
tugging them along – so nice to be sitting in real chairs again! –
Croesus imagined the feasts, the girls, the gifts. So, when they
arrived in Sais only to learn that the pharaoh had gone some
hundreds of miles southwest -- into the desert -- Croesus seriously considered turning around and heading home. Discord
among his sea-loving troops would have been enough. Only the
prospect of (the former) Media's natural resources and all the
wealth it enjoyed simply because of its high-trade location drove
him on.

Amasis had indeed traveled to the interior. Egypt's pharaoh
had gone to build a shrine to the god Ammon, whom local
tribesmen revered. The support of those tribes had proved deci-
sive in Amasis's coup, and the pharaoh wished to thank them.
Not only might this keep them on his side but he could justify it
to the Egyptians as a shrine to their Amun. So, the pharaoh was
in the desert. There was no choice for Croesus but to meet him
there.

"We know this god," one of the Greeks in Croesus's party
offered as Croesus stood despondently watching the troops
transfer from boats (so breezy, so restful) to camels (ugh).

"Oh?"

"Not personally," the man said. "But they say that Ammon is
really Zeus with great ram's horns curling around his ears." The
man circled his hands around his own ears to demonstrate. As he
trotted off to his place in the caravan, he tossed back over his
shoulder, "Greek merchants called him Zeus *ammon*, 'Sandy
Zeus.'"

Amun, sand... Croesus groaned. How he dreaded the thought
of another desert journey ("Sandy Zeus," indeed). But. If Croesus
had to face the young Parsan, if it came to a fight, it would do to
have as many friends as possible. And Amasis was a particularly
powerful, if flighty one, to have. So, Croesus had directed his

men to shift from ship to camels. He could hear the men grumbling as they set out across the sand.

CHAPTER 56 (PARSA)

ith the battle over and their lands secure, the Elamites prepared to go. They left Parsa with Cyrus's insistence ringing in their ears that he would send of Media's riches to Susa. Their people would be friends and allies, a return to the old Susa-and-Anshan. Soon, he'd host delegations in Pasargad, Cyrus promised. Indeed, strong personal friendships between them had been forged. Refined in the crucible of battle, they'd hold forever. In the case of Vishtaspa's family a particularly deep bond had been established. Besides the men, Hutaosa and Cassandane had also become fast friends. So it was that Vishtaspa's family stayed behind. They would continue as a part of the crown's inner circle.

* * *

CYRUS ALSO SENT the Median forces back, specifying that Harpagus be at their head. To Harpagus, Cyrus gave instructions that any of the troops who wished to return to homes in territories along the way were welcome to go. Immediately after the battle was done and he could speak with Astyages's troops, Cyrus had learned the pressure Astyages had put them under to conscript them, how reluctant they'd been to fight for such a man, for such an "empire" at all. Cyrus was surprised, then, when Harpagus reported disagreement in the ranks.

"The soldiers are confused, sir. Some argue that we should remain together, return to Ecbatana and report as a single force. Others, eager to return to their particular tribal regions, say that they're done."

"I said that they could do that – return home," Cyrus said. "Is that confusing?"

Harpagus opened his mouth then shut it again. "No sir. I'll confirm with the men."

Cyrus turned to go.

"And you?" Harpagus asked.

Cyrus turned back.

"When will you come to Ecbatana?"

"Why?" The question left Cyrus's lips before he'd given it much thought.

Until that moment, Cyrus's goal had been simply to repulse the Median king, to protect Parsa's nominal independence, a modest nation... and to build Pasargad, a simple and beautiful home, an open-air palace for his queen Cassandane and their growing family. But, while Harpagus stood patiently waiting an answer, Cyrus saw the reality for what it was. Like it or not, with Astyages's defeat, Cyrus had become king of that sprawling empire, and its capital was far to the north in mountains he'd known so well as a child – son of shepherds, slave to the very palace that was now his. Cyrus sighed.

"I'll talk to Cassandane," he said.

As it happened, Cassandane saw the necessity of going to Ecbatana to formalize Cyrus's victory and reestablish Parsa as part of the greater empire. "We'll do what needs doing – " she said.

"It might take a while," Cyrus said.

"But we'll be doing it together."

Relief spilled over Cyrus's face. He actually smiled.

"And when it's settled," Cassandane said, "we'll return... Pasargad," she finished with a grin.

"Pasargad," Cyrus said and kissed her. "Forever."

* * *

OTANES AND ZARIN married at the end of the month -- a far more ostentatious wedding than Cyrus's had been to Sanda. When Otanes expressed misgivings about how grand (and expenseive) were Zarin's plans for the event, she said, "Times are different now, sweetheart. Parsa was so poor and depressed back then."

In the midst of the revelry, Vishtaspa leaned over to Cyrus and said with a wink, "I guess you'll need to prepare for another wedding yourself."

Cyrus sat back. "What?"

"Sorry. I assumed you knew. Didn't Astyages leave a daughter behind?"

"Yes. Amytis. But she's my mother's sister."

Vishtaspa nodded. "They say she's been managing Media since Astyages left."

The celebration going on around the men was in full swing. Though they sat next to each other, it was difficult to hear. Cyrus stood and gestured for Vishtaspa to follow him to a quieter spot.

"I know that she returned to Ecbatana after her son was assassinated in Babylon..." Cyrus's expression was a mix of bewilderment and disbelief. "She's probably married again. And even if she's not –"

"May I speak freely?"

"For certain."

"You need to make her your wife."

Cyrus would have laughed if Vishtaspa's intelligent face weren't so serious.

"I *am* going there, to Ecbatana. With my family – Cassandane and Cambyses. Gobryas too. Is that not enough?"

Vishtaspa shook his head. "This marriage – you, to the daughter of the defeated king – is crucial to show that you have joined the Median empire to the Parsan kingdom that you rule."

"Vishtaspa, I *have* a wife. And no interest in an empire."

"Listen," Vishtaspa said gently, "I love Hutaosa as you love Sanda. That doesn't change. But –"

Cyrus's face was hard, angry.

Nevertheless, "Without such clarity," Vishtaspa said, "Media and Parsa unified as one strong empire…"

Cyrus snarled at him and walked away, back toward laughing crowd.

"… you could lose it all," Vishtaspa said into the empty air.

CHAPTER 57 (SIWA)

$\mathcal{T}$he trip was cruel – dry, hot, and punctuated by sandstorms that blinded even the camels with their long lashes. One advantage that Croesus saw, though it was crude comfort: the men could not defect. To break from the group now would be suicide. Following the direction of their desert guides – so silent they evoked a suspicion that didn't help matters – Croesus drove his men on. For their morale, Croesus plied them with promises of rich reward when they got back to cool and breezy Lydia. After days of hard travel, a guide reported that they should arrive the next day. That evening, the usually taciturn guides told the men of wonders that awaited them at the oasis in Siwa. By then, Croesus's troops had been subjected to so many teasing mirages that the group fell silent when the oasis finally came into sight. It seemed too good to be true.

But it was true. In this most unlikely place with sand all around in every direction as far as the eye could see, there were actual lakes. And surrounding those lakes was silt so rich that olive groves ran wide, and tall palms dangled clusters of plump dates. Sweet water bubbled up endlessly from nearly 300 wells. The men were speechless. They found Amasis at the shrine site, observing a most un-Egyptian-looking building operation, directed by a man who turned out to be the oasis's ruler. Amasis greeted Croesus enthusiastically and directed an attendant to show the Lydian king to his lodgings. The pharaoh saw Croesus's disgruntled men and with a great grin and expansive gesture, invited the travelers to enjoy the lakes. Croesus's men stripped then and there and jumped splashing straight into the "Spring of the Sun."

Amasis shared a joke with the oasis's ruler and then returned with Croesus to the pharaoh's temporary house on the oasis. After Croesus had had a chance to clean – divine – in a great private bath, after he had donned the long robe, light and fresh that an attendant handed to him, and strolled to the pharaoh's tent, Croesus found Amasis already reclining in the shade. He could get used to this, Croesus thought, indeed.

"I'd like to introduce you to my new wife," Amasis said, and indicated that she should be brought. "You'll like her," he said. "She's Greek."

Ladice was nothing like Amasis. After a time, she entered, her back straight, arms loose at her sides. Croesus couldn't decide if she was pretty or not, couldn't tell if her pride was off-putting or arousing to him. Despite Amasis's teasing, Ladice didn't smile. She greeted the men, said she hoped Croesus would be comfortable here, and then she left.

Amasis sighed. "Lovely, isn't she?" he said, leaning back on his couch. "Her mother, you know, is the ruler of Cyrene." He winked at Croesus. "With a daughter like that, I'm happy to make alliances. Now, where were we?"

In the moment, Croesus regretted that he had no available offspring but as the conversation proceeded – it was so much easier to talk to this man than to Nabonidus! – he made sure to drop references to his considerable material wealth. Its effect was clear, far more predictable, more *normal*, than it had been with that ascetic Babylonian king. Croesus made sure the conversation ranged also to include world affairs, specifically that surprising (alarming?) new player, Cyrus.

When it came time to leave, Croesus found himself reluctant to go. It had been so *pleasant* here. But the greater goal lay ahead. The day before leaving, Croesus returned with Amasis to the shrine. He visited the god's oracle and offered sacrifices of food items carried from Lydia and spices from caravanners in Teima. He hoped he'd checked all the boxes of wooing Amasis. It was time to for his big ask.

"I doubt there's much threat in the Persian," Croesus began, as they walked back to the camp. "I simply... knowing of your interest in areas to the north – Judah, Syria... wanted to assure you of our friendship."

Amasis's eyes danced. "Of course, dear king. And you of ours!" he added, slapping Croesus's shoulder. "I'm sure that with your considerable resources, skilled navy and numerous armed troops, you've nothing to worry about. And then there's that treaty you mentioned that your father made with the former Median king. If as you say this Anshanite has Median roots and is posing as the natural Median successor, then you won't even need to call out the forces. He wouldn't dare attack. Nothing to worry about, my friend."

It wasn't exactly the endorsement of Croesus's offensive that the Lydian king had hoped for; but the "friendship" part was good to hear. Good enough, for now. When Croesus and his men finally saw the light browns of their hot and land-bound journey give way to the Mediterranean's deep blue, it felt to them almost as if they were already home. Croesus had other plans, though. One more stop. At risk of mutiny, he nevertheless commanded the lead ship to make for the Greek mainland. First, he would renew connections with Sparta.

CHAPTER 58 (PARSA)

*I*t took some weeks to settle things in Parsa before they could begin to move Cyrus's household up the mountain range from the foothills around Anshan and Pasargad to the high peaks of Media. Finally, they were ready.

"You should leave more horses," Gobryas said. "Weapons, too."

"That's a stupid idea," Cambyses said.

The argument escalated louder and louder until exasperated Cassandane raised her hands. "Hush!"

Gobryas had been absorbed into the royal household just as Cyrus had promised to his father, the dead Mardonius. A kind of step-brother to Cambyses, Cyrus had hoped that the boys might be friends. They were about the same age. Cambyses, small and quiet, had had no real comrades, none that lasted. That he was the crown prince set him apart (though palace life in Anshan was not much different than that of the local chieftains), but it was his epilepsy that fully alienated him. Cyrus had hoped that Gobryas's own birth defect might make the boys more inclined to bond in friendship. The opposite proved to be true. They were rivals immediately.

Nevertheless, like Cambyses, Gobryas was included in all the conversations about governance and logistics of rule along with the crown prince. Unlike Cambyses, Gobryas was fascinated by the logistics of governance and the workings of things in general. But as strong as his interest and aptitude were, stronger still were his opinions and his temper. Cassandane told Cyrus to be patient - the boy had just lost his father, understandable that he'd be prickly and angry. But even she was relieved when Gobryas would wander off by himself to ponder some logistical challenge or another -- how to build this or that, how many people or animals it would take and how long...

CHAPTER 59(MEDIA)

*W*ith Media, Cyrus was suddenly transformed from the petty king of Parsa, governing from a rude palace in Anshan, into the monarch and commander of a formidable empire. For by gaining control and the allegiance of the Medes, Cyrus had also acquired territory, material wealth, and military power far exceeding what he had governed from Anshan. Although it would take more than a generation for people to refer to the former Media by its new identity as a part of Cyrus's empire, the small kingdom of Parsa that he had ruled became with Astyages's defeat, almost overnight, the Persian empire.

To Amytis, names meant nothing. The land she loved – this wild place – the land that she had devoted her life to protect was beyond any name. This land – mountains, ravines, lakes, and meadows – had existed before there were names and she hoped would endure long after. What mattered was that this place with its wildly diverse nonhuman inhabitants not be ravaged by human greed, abused for the short-term gain she'd watched her kind sacrifice everything else to get. The rule of nations mattered. Cyrus had better hurry.

CHAPTER 60 (PARSA TO MEDIA)

*W*hen Cyrus left Anshan, he left his father-in-law, the capable Pharnaspes, in charge of the region as a kind of governor. Cyrus had leaned on Pharnaspes's practical wisdom in the past and was confident that establishing him at Anshan while Cyrus ruled from Ecbatana would keep the peace among Parsa's local tribes and ensure the stability so hard won in recent years. They had talked through all such things in the past as Cyrus struggled to transform the Parsa he inherited back into a strong and prosperous one.

He did not, however, talk to Pharnaspes now about the matter of marrying Amytis, about whether or not Vishtaspa was right. Neither did Cyrus talk with Cassandane about it, even when their household journeyed toward its new home. She could tell that he was troubled, and more so for not talking. But he didn't know what to say or how to explain beyond what Vishtaspa had said. And she had never not known how to ask. Thankfully, the business of moving, all the logistics and decisions of suddenly managing a huge and wealthy territory were distracting enough. That, and Cassandane's pregnancy – this one made her more sick, more tired, more swollen than the first – gave them both reason enough not to talk.

CHAPTER 61 (BABYLONIA)

*B*elshazzar worried that despite a lifetime's effort to demonstrate his Babylonian-ness his own loyalty to Marduk may now be in question. Yes, he was the crown prince and his father King Nabonidus's regent. But his father had been in the desert for months now and for all Belshazzar could tell, it might be years.

"And now, here I am in far-north-nowhere Harran," Belshazzar complained, " just as he had planned. It is I who has to 'carry the bricks'." The scribe waited patiently as the middle-aged prince let his eyes wander restlessly around the dilapidated mansion – the best available – that he had taken over for his home. Temple renovations would take a long time. As crown prince, Belshazzar's hands were tied. Nabonidus was still king.

"Have you heard, tell me – are they talking about me in Babylon?"

"How so, my lord?"

Belshazzar pursed his lips tightly then huffed. "Are they saying… do people question…"

The scribe raised his eyebrows.

"I'm concerned that rumors, utterly unfounded, might be circulating... About my... about the throne. You know."

The scribe nodded, understanding, then said, "I can't say, sir, for sure since I'm here with you. But I really don't think so."

Belshazzar brushed away the man's reply. "Well. Of course, it's no worry. I am the crown prince and have Babylonia's best interest in always in mind. That should be clear."

"I never doubt it," the scribe said. He paused. "Was there something that you needed from me?"

"Yes. Right." Belshazzar bustled his hefty frame around the table in front of them. "Another of my father's missives. Requires a bit of editing. As before." He handed the document to the scribe.

The scribe's eyes widened. "This is King Nabonidus' dedicatory inscription for the Elhulhul, the temple itself. And you wish me.... to make some changes?"

"It's not satisfactory, as is. You can see that," Belshazzar said. "Not right, elevating Nanna-Suen like that. A few small tweaks is all I ask – bring the language down a bit. As we know, the moon god is a mere member of Marduk's pantheon, not head of it." Belshazzar snorted as if the idea were preposterous.

But it was exhausting, a constant battle, proving his allegiance to Marduk above all, while Nabonidus seemed constantly to be undermining it. The stakes were high. So Belshazzar altered his father's controversial intentions where he could in a constant effort to demonstrate his own fitness to Babylon's great throne.

CHAPTER 62 (MEDIA)

The news was clear: King Croesus of Lydia was courting allies. Amytis bent over the withers of her horse and ran her hands through the rich grass. She hadn't seen it for herself, but Amytis had heard that his kind, the Greeks anyway, salted the fields they conquered, rendering the land sterile for as good as forever. Yet another example of the stupidities war engendered. Amytis straightened again. They had to keep Media together. Thank goodness Cyrus was on his way. Amytis put her heels to the horse's flanks and turned back toward the palace. She had a wedding to plan.

*A*s they approached, the palace at Ecbatana seemed even grander than Cyrus remembered. Surrounded by a series of walls, each painted a different color, it was nothing like the barely fortified Anshan, despite the work Cyrus had done to renovate and rebuild there. Ecbatana's palace was huge, covering a full square kilometer. Cassandane was eager to see it, built of wood and stone from the mountain forests around and furnished with the most exquisite items from the farthest reaches. Ecbatana stood at a prime location for east-west trade, and Astyages had capitalized on this. The former king loved fine things, grand and unique. He collected exotic spices, linens, and jewels from places far to the east and nearly as far again to the west. Now all of that was theirs.

Harpagus met Cyrus's caravan. "There's something you should know," Harpagus said as they passed through the final gate. "Amytis didn't know that her father was going to attack Parsa."

Cyrus looked at him in surprise.

"She wanted to establish friendly relations, draw Parsa back into Median control with diplomacy and the promise of shared security, even wealth."

Cyrus pulled his horse to a stop. Harpagus reined in, too.

Cyrus studied the man. "And you didn't tell her because…"

Harpagus opened his mouth to speak.

But Cyrus stopped him with a hand. "You weren't sure whose side you'd take."

Harpagus met Cyrus's eyes and held them. "I'm not proud of it," he said. " But yes."

They stood like that, silently apprising one another.

Finally, "I understand," Cyrus said.

Cyrus didn't need to ask if he could be sure that Harpagus would give Cyrus and the new Persian empire his full loyalty. And Harpagus didn't need to vow that he would. Each of them knew it to be so.

* * *

WALKING into the palace at Ecbatana again, no longer a slave boy but its king, Cyrus was struck by its cosmopolitan grandeur.

In the great hall, Cassandane turned around and around, her eyes bright with wonder. "It's not what I imagined, not what I heard. It's more." She ran a hand down one of the columns and gazed around at the others. "This place is amazing. The palace, the city, the mountains."

Cyrus, sober, watched her.

Cassandane walked to him and wrapped her arms around his neck. "And you must love all the horses! You're probably already plotting which to bring back with us to Anshan… to Pasargad."

Cassandane's delight at the wonders of the Median palace – showy and big – evaporated when Cyrus told her what Harpagus had said.

"And you believe him?"

"Why shouldn't I?"

"I don't know where to start to answer that," Cassandane said. "Maybe with the fact that Harpagus didn't do anything to stop the fighting from its start. You would have lost Parsa entirely if it hadn't been for the women shaming the men to keep on. All those lives, lost! And then there's Amytis herself. I've heard that she's been at least as instrumental in the leadership of Media as her father the king. And why wouldn't she be? She was only married to the most powerful man in the world and mother to his successor – years in the Babylonian courts of power. She probably master-minded the whole thing. So. No. I don't believe she was ignorant of Astyages's intent to attack." Cassandane laughed ruefully. "But she can hardly admit that now, not with her father dead, not with you – with us – here as the victors, unlikely as it is."

CHAPTER 64 (BABYLONIA)

*K*hai struggled to balance the books, drawing from both the crown's private holdings and the state's greater budget. From Harran, Belshazzar had sent word: "A diplomatic event..." the crown prince had said, "so, yes... from the national treasury..." He was planning a lion hunt.For what could be more traditionally monarchal than that, Belshazzar thought to himself, and to be invited was the greatest privilege and one that reminded everyone what prestige there was in gaining the crown's favor.

The event itself, the danger of it, unnerved Belshazzar. But its benefit to his image, his reputation, his profile far outweighed the trepidation (which he hid quite well). Belshazzar was confident that when the oldest families' sons, the noblemen, outlying tribal chiefs, army and administrative officials were invited to participate in a royal hunt of many days that would take them into the green hills of Gutium, any who might be questioning his position, his fitness to the role... they'd come around. He was right. None could resist the honor, and Belshazzar made certain that anyone who was anyone in the up-and-coming generation of elite Babylonians got an invitation.

* * *

AT LEAST, Khai thought, he wasn't also running the family business. Two years earlier, Khai had turned the reins of the Egibi corporation over to Iddina. He had seen too many enterprises fail when the senior executive died and the business inherited by someone who hadn't ever led it. Iddina didn't often ask his father for help or advice but managed well… in his own style.

And that style included a lot of travel that, Khai wryly observed, couldn't do much to help Nupta's barrenness. Iddina's wife still hadn't conceived, and the frustration made her temperament, already spoiled, ever more difficult. So, even when Iddina was in Babylon, he turned more and more to his sex-trained slaves for satisfaction.

At the same time, Khai's own daughter Davcina, whose delicacy and sweet temper had delighted him all of her life, became terribly ill. Just when Khai agreed to Qudashu's urging that they find a suitable husband for Davcina, her hands and feet twisted in on themselves. She moaned that her brain felt like it was bursting against her aching skull and that pain radiated from every joint. The girl became incapable of leaving the house or indeed of doing anything at all. Khai was spending a fortune on Babylonian magicians and doctors, hoping that one might finally cure his little girl. The stress of Belshazzar's demands took Khai's mind off of his daughter during the day; so whenever he returned home he was newly devastated to find that Davcina's condition hadn't improved. If anything, it was growing worse. Between Nupta's infertility and Davcina's peculiarly cruel disease, their houses seemed an extension of the doctors' temple quarters. The smell of fish from the physician-sages' uniforms was ever present.

The only upside to all the trouble and worry, as Khai saw it, was that he had little time to think about Amytis, to wonder how she was and where. He'd heard about Astyages's defeat of course and only hoped that she'd gain a better partner with Cyrus on the throne than her father had been.

CHAPTER 65 (MEDIA)

*A*mytis met them in a grand entrance hall, where fires, roaring in its three hearths, cast long shadows against the walls. Amytis wore the white linen shift of mourning, honoring the deaths of her husband and father. But over one shoulder a cape of golden jackal pelts dropped to the floor. Variations in its fur blended with the gray that streaked through her light brown hair. Widow of Nebuchadnezzar, queen mother of a former Babylonian king, who stood so straight and proud, was actually much shorter up close than she seemed.

"Welcome, nephew," Amytis said. She stood still, her arms at her sides, but her eyes were both searching and judging, quickly evaluating the young king even as they sought familiarity. As they lingered on the swoop in Cyrus's lower lip, in her eyes tiny pools caught the firelight. Amytis sniffed once, bit back the tears. Amytis followed his glance to the tall woman, clearly pregnant, who smiled back at Cyrus with dark eyes.

"You must be Sanda," Amytis said.

The smile evaporated. "Cassandane to you," Sanda said.

The frosty glare that Amytis got couldn't be missed.

"As you wish," Amytis said. Then, without any change to her

demeanor, "I can't imagine you would ever believe I had no knowledge much less desire of my father's attack on your country." Amytis tactfully ignored the look of surprise Cassandane shot Cyrus. "Well. You'll have to judge me by my actions and intentions from here on." She didn't wait for a response, didn't see the ice in Cassandane's expression crack with uncertainty. Amytis had turned toward the door.

Amytis signaled a man forward. He was of such average height and build, in clothes of plain woolen weave, that he had seemed to Cyrus simply a fixture next to the far fireplace. "This is Nathan, our best scribe. He will show you the records and archives."

The man dipped his head, "Sir," he said. "I also wish to welcome you -- back, as I understand it, though I wasn't here when you were a boy. I assume that you didn't see much of the records then, and they've changed for certain over the years since."

"I suppose they have," Cyrus said, finding his voice in the face of this scribe whose bright demeanor and intelligent eyes put the lie to his unremarkable appearance.

"I will gladly introduce you to the empire's records, such as they are."

"Thank you, Nathan. Nathan -- what kind of a name is that?"

"Hebrew, sir. Elnathan 'gift of God.'"

"Of what god?"

"Sir?"

"'Gift of' what god, which god?"

"El, sir. Simply 'God.'"

"I see," Cyrus said, though it was clear that he didn't.

Nathan looked at Cyrus's weary company and said, "Perhaps the others can get settled. You and I can go over the records, archives, perhaps my notes." His spoke as if planning a great adventure.

"I'm not much for records." Then seeing the scribe's face fall,

Cyrus said, "But you can show me, explain some things. That would be helpful."

Amytis said, "I will meet you there. We have a lot to discuss." She looked long at Cyrus with that statement. When Cyrus, under her gaze, shifted on his feet, Amytis said, "Harpagus, will you help Cassandane and the others find their places? I'll find someone to summon midwives." She saw Sanda start with surprise. "To have them here, so that you can get acquainted. I have a few in mind, the best of course."

Sanda nodded. "That would be good. Thank you."

* * *

NATHAN WAS reluctant to discuss any state business until Amytis had joined them. While they waited, Cyrus learned instead about the communities of Jews in Ecbatana and Media, many dating back to the time of Assyrian dominance, nearly two hundred years earlier. Cyrus wondered at the tenacity of traditions, reshaped for a life without temple or nation, and at how much emphasis Nathan and others in his community placed on what could be written.

For his part, Cyrus mistrusted literature. It seemed to fix artificially what was by nature dynamic. He and Nathan argued about this, Nathan taking the position that the literature was itself dynamic because it had meaning only as it was interpreted by people whose experiences and lives were dynamic by definition.

"One day," Nathan said, "Yahweh will return us to our land -- Israel, Judah. We will be again not only prosperous but be a blessing to other peoples, too."

"But that land is not yours. It's in Babylonia's Beyond-the-Rivers territory."

"That land belongs to the people of God," Nathan said.

"... and who is that determines who those people are?" Amytis walked in. This was clearly a topic the two had debated many times before. Their tone friendly banter, a topic whose debating had no end.

Amytis took the heavy seat that her father used to use, and pulled it up to the table. Nathan didn't meet Cyrus's glance as they took others.

"Nathan's records lay out the details," Amytis said, "But you'll see that Media's – the former Media's – holdings are widespread. I have worked hard to keep peace between disparate tribes and, despite my father's inclinations otherwise, to allow each to enjoy some of the riches of our empire."

Cyrus pulled his chair in closer.

"There's always trouble, of course. But you should know that there are rumors that after my father's… defeat, the empire has become weak. Weak-er. He was no great leader, as you experienced yourself, though you might have been too young to recognize it at the time. Anyway," she said, "some of the more independent and self-sufficient territories may wish to break away. That cannot happen for the well-being of everyone." Amytis glanced at Nathan and tipped her head toward a scroll on the table. "It will be important to reestablish a strong relationship with the tribes of the Parthian steppes to our east."

Nathan unrolled a map, and Amytis ran her finger over a broad territory some miles east of Ecbatana.

"They've always been edgy. They need a strong but respectful hand." She sat back. "There's a Babylonian contingent in Harran – it includes the crown prince – but they seem entirely focused on the Elhulhul –" Seeing Cyrus's confusion, "a temple complex dedicated to the god of King Nabonidus's youth – Nanna-Suen, part of the Babylonian pantheon, but not as prominent a deity as Nabu or of course Marduk. Anyway, unless they try to control the city or otherwise bring military there, it doesn't seem worth rebuffing them."

"And you know them personally – the king, the crown prince."

Clear-eyed, Amytis said, "I do." She said it without arrogance or smug superiority. A simple face. "Which is why I'm not concerned.

"Much more troubling," Amytis leaned forward, "I've learned that the Lydians are looking to supplement their already considerable army with allies... excluding us." She waited.

Cyrus raised his eyebrows.

"There is a treaty in place forbidding them from attacking us," Amytis explained. "And us from them. Neither should cross the Halys River with aggressive intent."

Cyrus nodded.

"But I don't trust them."

Cyrus cleared his throat. "I appreciate this." He pushed his chair back. "I do. But Media is part of Parsa, now, a Persian not Median empire. And I am its king." He stood.

Amytis leaned back. She took a deep breath. "These people, all of the people of the *former* Media, now greater Persia, know me. They looked to me when my father's policies were negligent or offensive. And I sought to make things right. For this land. You *did* defeat Astyages." Amytis stood to face Cyrus. "But it was Harpagus... on my secret orders," she heard Nathan inhale quickly, "that made that happen."

Cyrus sat back down.

"The people must see that we are together." Amytis closed her eyes in a long blink, then looked Cyrus in the eye. "I have made the arrangements for us to marry."

"No," Cyrus said.

Amytis pursed her lips.

"I said No." Cyrus stood up again.

But before he'd reached the door, he found Amytis standing in his way. He stopped, as much out of shock – she was quiet and swift as an owl – as the physical obstacle she presented.

"We don't know each other," Amytis said. "I accept that. Until we become better acquainted in the ways that time makes possible, know this. I have faced far more formidable challenges than your squeamishness, in defense of this wild and beautiful land. The welfare of its inhabitants – nonhuman, at least as much as human – is why I live. We *will* marry. How that affects your – other relationships – is up to you."

Cyrus clenched his jaw. His eyes sparked with defiance.

Seeing that, "Dangerous as it is," Amytis said, "I'll give you this: time. Not a lot of it. Threats to the empire are constant, as I think even this briefing has made clear. But I understand. You didn't plan to become king of ... and empire. And even if you had, you have no experience managing such a huge and diverse state. Plus –" Amytis's body softened. She loosened her stance. "You've only just arrived." She stepped aside. "Make yourself at home."

CHAPTER 66 (SPARTA)

*C*roesus knew better than to inundate the Spartans with luxurious gifts from his travels or the plush garments and delicacies that merchants brought through Lydia. When he arrived at the Spartan port of Gytheio, he offered practical basins (of handsomely beaten copper) and simply complimented the leaders on the organization and discipline of the men. During the succeeding days, he gave honor to their gods – their Apollo statue was a bit... dull, Croesus couldn't help but notice – with sacrifice and prayers. He also talked about the Parsans. "Rather like the Spartans in their rough circumstances, 'called pistaka-eaters,' after all... But without any of the same discipline or resilience," he was quick to add.

Croesus didn't let on that he was actually worried about Cyrus – by what astonishing strength had he defeated the Median might? Instead, Croesus used Cyrus's unlikely victory as vindication that the youth might get it into his head to concoct yet bigger designs. At the least, the young king had demonstrated that he was unpredictable.

The Spartan general let him talk. When Croesus was done,

"Why don't you simply preempt any possible attack by finishing him off yourself?" the Spartan asked.

Croesus glanced down at his lap, shuffled in his seat, and rearranged his robe. "You may know that the late Median king's wife was my sister. You see, some decades ago," he cleared his throat, "there was war between our people. Astyages's father got it in his head to attack us. My father met him with a force of comparable strength. Where the Halys River cuts across the land, they fought a bitter battle, both sides losing a great number of men and horses, but neither willing to surrender. The gods must have grown tired. That day, they say, the sky went dark -- an eclipse of the sun. Both men agreed that it was a sign to truce, that they should quite fighting. They agreed that neither one would cross the Halys River with offensive intent. To secure the treaty, the two kings wed their children -- Aryenis, for the Lydian side to Astyages from the Median side."

"Just to be clear, that was your sister."

"Aryenis, yes."

"Wedded not to Cyrus but to Astyages?"

"It was a while ago." Croesus quickly added, "That's correct."

"And Astyages is no longer king. This Cyrus now controls his former holdings."

"Yes, and by such a remarkable..." Croesus began, immediately regretting it. He finished with a bland, "turn of events."

The Spartan sat back.

Croesus was still. Then, brightening, he said, "So actually," bringing his hand down on the chair's arm, "it was a treaty that neither I nor Cyrus had any part in making."

"That may be true." The Spartan shook his square head, hair cut so close that Croesus could see the red scars on his skull. "But such agreements are promises between whole peoples, not individuals. It would be a breach for either to attack."

"But is the other even Media anymore?" Croesus mused aloud.

The Spartan stood up without a sound. "Now, if Cyrus should

be so arrogant and unethical as to cross the Halys River with aggressive intent, the treaty is void. In that case, you would have not only the right to defend yourself but the duty to correct him. As for the other, if this Cyrus has indeed usurped the throne..." He began to walk toward the door, then turned. "We would join you in *that* fight."

Left alone, Croesus sat silently, his brow pulled tight by the implications of the question unanswered. After a time, he nodded to himself and stood. He returned to his men. "The Spartans are in," he said. "Get ready. We sail tomorrow."

The men were ecstatic. Few of them cared about the arrangement with Sparta. What they cared about was home. They'd been gone too long.

Croesus hardly noticed their glee. He was preoccupied with the question he'd so absently posed. If Astyages were king of the Median empire... and Astyages were defeated... and the victor was not himself Median but insisted on an independent identity – Parsa, was it?... then that treaty – the agreement between Media and Lydia... Was Media even Media anymore? Not only that, but if it were a usurper – this grandson, who defeated – nay, killed! – Astyages... The more he thought on it, the happier Croesus became. He had found a way. Meanwhile, he'd send someone to gild that statue of Apollo – god of the sun, after all. If just *happened*... he grinned, sure that even the Spartans wouldn't mind a bit of gold.

CHAPTER 67 (MEDIA)

$\mathcal{I}$n the coming weeks, Cyrus hosted delegations of peoples from the greater empire. He knew that they were testing his commitment to maintaining Media's sprawling control. Among the first he met were the Parthians just to the east of Media, a territory through which one of the most important trading routes ran -- east across high plains farther than Cyrus could imagine. The Parthian delegation also brought double-humped camels as gifts on behalf of the Bactrians, whose land lay even farther east. One day, posted guards raced toward the palace to alert Cyrus that several stone-faced warriors from the freezing steppes of Scythia wished to see him. They were heavily armed but made a show of releasing their weapons into Cyrus's control, an act that revealed the marvelous tattoos Cyrus remembered seeing on a merchant guard from his childhood. They reported that they also came in friendship. Still, Cyrus felt their reservation.

His personal attendant, the eunuch Bagapates (recommended by Harpagus) helped Cyrus understand. There was talk, or rumor of it anyway, that Cyrus would return to Parsa, let Amytis keep Ecbatana, and release the other tribes from obligation... and protection. With each of the empire's diverse and far-flung contingents, Cyrus did his best to reassure them that he intended nothing of the kind – this was to be a new *Persian* empire. And they could count on fewer demands and greater support than they'd ever had before. But nothing he could say – or do – would be enough. It was clear that they were accustomed to dealing with Amytis, and she had made herself scarce.

It hadn't been an easy decision. But Amytis could see no other way. Amytis's very presence made Cassandane uncomfortable, which made Cyrus uncomfortable. Amytis knew that right now, Cyrus needed to present the strongest possible face of leadership. And he couldn't do that with her beside him. It was a gamble. Not really a choice at all. She just had to keep her head. So, the morning watch saw her depart – the rattle of hooves over the bridge, the call to open the next gate, and the next, and the next. And the night watch – and Harpagus with Nathan, too, always waiting on the wall – saw her return, tired enough they hoped for sleep.

Cyrus pressed on. He tried to express his respect for Amytis's counsel, if ever that were necessary, even as he sought to reassure the tribes, pressing them to pledge loyalty to his greater empire. But without her beside him... Some said it outright: they'd make promises only if she were there.

* * *

SANDA WINCED, then grabbed Cyrus's hand to lay on her belly. "Can you feel him kicking?"

"Not long now, I suppose," Cyrus said. He smiled with his mouth, but his voice was flat.

"I thought you'd be happier."

Cyrus looked at the face he found so dear, the edges of high cheekbones, softened by dark eyes and a full mouth. Cyrus drew Sanda to him, an embrace made awkward by the third, pounding its feet against the great arc of its mother's belly. "I am happy," he said. "I just worry for you."

They'd talked about it – that Amytis was herself a skilled midwife, like her sister had been before her was common knowledge. But Cassandane wouldn't hear of asking the woman she believed lay behind the Medes' attack to attend the birth of her baby. And Amytis didn't offer. And Cyrus never brought up the matter of marrying Amytis.

CHAPTER 68 (MEDIA)

*I*t was indeed a difficult birth. Despite the number of highly experienced midwives, the assurance of the magi that Sanda's labor began at an auspicious time, and the fact that this was not her first baby (Cambyses had arrived without complication), Sanda grew more anxious with each contraction. At her insistence, the midwives let Cyrus into the room. He dashed to the bedside, while the midwives were in hushed and constant motion around him.

"I can't stop thinking about your own mother," Sanda confessed during a lull. "She, too, had come from Parsa to Media to deliver a baby." Sanda grimaced with a wave of pain. "She killed herself, Cy." Cassandane's eyes were frantic with worry.

"But she thought that the baby, that I, was dead," Cyrus said. "She was sad and desperate. Besides, my father wasn't with her. I am here with you."

"Yes." But when another series of contractions came and went without any sign of the baby's entry, Cassandane wept. "I'm so afraid." Sanda's face contorted with another spasm of pain. She paled,

"Losing blood," one of midwives said, pumping Cassandane's wrists.

"I cannot leave Cambyses now – he's just a boy – and this baby..." Her voice trailed off.

Cyrus clutched Cassandane's sweating palm in his. When she slipped into unconsciousness, "Nooooo," he cried out.

"She cannot deliver if she's out."

Cyrus looked up to find Amytis in the doorway. One of midwives, desperate, had fetched her. The girl dropped her eyes, feeling the rebuke. It didn't come.

"Can you –"

But Amytis was already at Cassandane's head. "Lower it, keep up the pressure here, here..." She mobilized the midwives to stimulate Cassandane's circulation, move blood into her head. When Cassandane came to, Amytis was behind her. She said nothing, and Cyrus ignored her even as Cassandane pushed through another contraction.

Amytis stayed with Sanda throughout the birth. In and out of consciousness, Cassandane never knew the hands that held her head just so, the hands that smoothed sweat-smeared hair back from her eyes, the hands that wiped her forehead, her cheeks and neck with a soft, cool cloth belonged the woman she hated.

If asked, Amytis would have said that she did it for Mandane. She did it for the sister she couldn't save, the girl Amytis had protected for years, the sister she loved... and lost. She did it for Cyrus's mother, who herself had been so determined to help women in just this situation that she would have put the whole empire at risk. Amytis would have said she did it all for her. So when the baby finally slipped from Cassandane's body in a bloody rush – a squalling girl with two tiny hands, two tiny feet each with ten digits and wee toenails – when a midwife thrust the baby to Amytis (Cassandane had lost consciousness again), and the girl seized her finger with surprising strength and fiercely fixed her still unseeing eyes on Amytis's face, Amytis whispered in her ear, "I'd do it all again. For you."

But no one asked. And by the time Cassandane, red-cheeked and laughing held the baby to her breast, Amytis was gone.

* * *

THAT EVENING in Ecbatana's great dining hall, Cyrus told again how he came to know Vishtaspa – the extraordinary warrior who fought as though the battle were a dance – and his wife, Hutaosa. He told the story yet again of how, nearly ready to deliver a baby herself, Hutaosa had nevertheless traveled with Vishtaspa from Susa to join the Parsans against a seemingly impossible foe. At a critical moment in the battle, she was at the front of the women who rushed forward to urge the men on to what would become victory.

"Cassandane and I have decided to name our baby daughter in honor of this most admirable woman and friend. She shall be called Atossa after the brave and gracious Hutaosa, mother of Darius and wife of Vishtaspa.

"What's more," Cyrus said, "Vishtaspa has agreed to serve as governor of Parthia. With Hutaosa beside him and their robust son Darius, too – already walking – I am confident that we will maintain the good relationship that Amytis and I have worked to establish."

There, he'd said it. Actually, the installation was Amytis's idea, informed by Cyrus's assessment of the Susian's strengths.

But.

* * *

"IT'S NOT ENOUGH," Amytis told Cyrus later. "People are defecting. The Urartians..." At Cyrus's blank look she knew they hadn't come to Ecbatana, hadn't introduced themselves to him. "They're on our western-most edge... named for the mountain Ararat... "

Cyrus nodded, recognizing that.

"There's rumbling about secession. They claim Media is fracturing and that they should be as independent as in the days of Assyrians, of Elam, and the Manneans. People are calling it an uprising."

"I'll take care of it."

"You won't without marrying me."

Cyrus pursed his lips and stormed away.

CHAPTER 69 (DELPHI)

*A*fter clearing the cape, Croesus's ships swung east then north, up into the familiar waters of the Aegean Sea. When he commanded that they bear west again to dock at Marathon on the Greek mainland, the men nearly mutinied.

"It is for the gods," Croesus explained. "You've heard of the famous oracle of Delphi, but how many have had a chance to see it for yourself?"

None answered, though a mood of curiosity replaced the sullen knowledge that it would still be longer before they'd be home.

"This is your chance. The shrine is only a few miles inland, an easy trek for such resilient men as you. We can make it in a day." The men looked from the port at the mountainous terrain beyond. Croesus said, "a day each way. We'll stay only long enough to see the famous shrine and to hear the god's words as from Apollo himself. Then, you have my word, it'll be straight for home, a short sail east." Ignoring the resignation on their faces, Croesus said, "I knew that you'd appreciate this as much as me. So, let's get on with it. The sooner there, the sooner home, and what an opportunity!"

They packed light bags for the next days' hikes and turned in early.

When the morning sun shot across the water, Croesus roused the men calling, "Apollo rides! Ready yourselves to meet the god."

Easing the men's discontent, they arrived to the welcome of a wealthy benefactor. Croesus's Lydia had taken care to gift regularly to Delphi and to the other mainland Greek temples and oracles. But as they neared the site of the oracle, all the elegant vessels and golden statues that he'd sent to win the god's favor couldn't dissipate the stench. The god's mouthpiece, an old prophetess, sat on a tripod over a fissure in the ground. A noxious gas constantly leaked from it. More than one of the troops, eyes watering, thought anyone would feel overcome by some numinous force sitting there day after day.

"The dragon's breath is strong today," Croesus said, gagging, "a good omen." He recalled the massive silver basins and solid gold statue of the goddess Kybele, as large as a woman, that he'd sent to Delphi some months earlier and thought, "It better be good."

Croesus tried neither to breathe nor to look too closely at the woman, whose eyes rolled aimlessly in her head in a manner he found most disconcerting. Worse still, the oracle's eyes suddenly dropped straight ahead, fixing on some invisible spot to the left of the Lydian king. When she spoke, her voice was surprisingly clear, strong, and low. "Cross the Halys, and Croesus will destroy a great empire."

Despite himself, Croesus let out a whoop. He gathered his men, even more eager than they to return. He was elated – he'd heard it here, from the god's own mouth. He was right – that treaty was null. The former Media – all that gold, the gems, the trade! – would be his. It was as good as done.

CHAPTER 70 (MEDIA)

*C*yrus found Amytis at the stables walking out a horse that she'd ridden hard. After Amytis had insisted over and over on cooling a horse herself, the grooms and stable-hands accepted, grew accustomed, and left her to it. When she wasn't beset by worry, Amytis liked walking alongside a horse's ambling form -- muzzle low and soft, both of them deliciously tired – at least as much as she liked the riding itself.

But she was worried.

Cyrus fell into step beside them. The horse's hooves thumped softly. Fwump, fwump. Its breath was heavy but even.

"You really think that we have to marry?"

Amytis put her hand against the horse's neck. "I don't want to any more than you do." She ran her fingers up into the horse's dark mane and tugged at a small burr lodged in its hair. "But it's the way these things are done." The horse huffed once, lightly.

"And I'm asking you," Cyrus said. "Do you think it's necessary?"

Amytis stopped. The horse chunked a light divot from the path, halting, and hung its head. She stepped in front of the dappled stallion, stroked its broad face and ruffled its forelock.

"I'm hardly a model for doing things simply because that's the way they've always been," Amytis said. Finally, she looked at her nephew -- tall, with the deep dark eyes and curly hair that she recognized from the Parsan people. His nose was strong, arched a little like the heavy Nisean charger she walked. And his mouth, it arrested her every time, was identical to his mother's, her sister Mandane's. Amytis would never stop missing her.

"In this case?" From her earliest memories, Amytis lived her life protecting Mandane so that Mandane would protect Media until it became clear that Amytis would have to do it herself. To protect the place she loved more than anything, Amytis had had to leave it. She didn't wish such sacrifice on anyone. But. This land, she'd do anything.

"I just hope it's not too late," Amytis said.

CHAPTER 71 (MEDIA)

$\mathcal{I}$t took Cyrus a full week to approach Sanda with the news. The pounding in his heart made Cyrus's voice uneven. Sanda heard him out with a face he hardly recognized. Her expression was hard, her eyes empty.

Cyrus edged into the window seat next to Sanda. "It's a diplomatic necessity, Sanda," Cyrus said. "Please understand."

"And what of Pasargad." Cassandane asked. It was less question than accusation. "I suppose there's no necessity there."

"We will still go. It's all I've wanted – Pasargad with you."

"And her."

Cyrus shook his head emphatically, desperately. "One day, you and I and are family..." He took her hands, so cold, and sought Cassandane's eyes.

But she wouldn't look at him.

"You are my only, the only one I love. Sanda, please look at me."

Cassandane didn't turn her head.

Cyrus looked down at their hands, her fingers long and smooth, her palms narrow in his. He shook them lightly. "Sanda, I have to do this. This must be done to hold together an empire that I did not choose to have but whose stability now depends on me."

She said nothing.

"You know that," he said.

Sanda pulled her hands away. As soon as she met his eyes, Cyrus wished that she had not. They took away breath and thought as completely as the sea over a drowning man.

"I do *not* know that. I don't know you." And with that, Cassandane turned her face to the window again. "Leave me."

Cyrus took a ragged breath and stood. Still the woman whose laugh was fresh water to him, whose eyes were more precious than any gem, whose whole self fit to his like a part of his side... Cassandane didn't turn from the window. Cyrus walked back to his suite as heavily as a porter lugging stones from the mountains.

Outside the door of his suite, he was still so preoccupied that Vishtaspa had to grab his arm to get his attention.

"What is it?" Cyrus asked, seeing Vishtaspa's troubled expression.

"It's Prexaspes."

Cyrus grabbed his friend's shoulders. "No! What happened?"

"He got married."

"What?!" Cyrus's face relaxed into confusion and then a bewildered smile. "Married?"

"No one knew. He just met her -- a Mede, the daughter of some official or another."

"When?"

"Last night."

"But --"

Bagapates stepped into the hallway. "Sir, if you're to be ready..."

THE END

CAST OF CHARACTERS

*A*few things to note: Even for historical characters, there may be some question or disagreement regarding specific details. I do not provide here dates of death or other details that don't transpire during the course of this particular narrative. With the exception of Iddina, nicknames are my own. An asterisk (*) denotes non-historical characters, i.e. people that I've totally made up.

Adad-guppi: Aramean (from the defeated Harran); attendant in the Babylonian courts of Nebuchadnezzar and Amel-Marduk; mother of Nabonidus, grandmother of Belshazzar.

Amasis: Egyptian king (pharaoh) from 570-526 B.C.E.

Amel-Marduk (Bushu), born Nabu-shuma-ukin: son of Amytis and Nebuchadnezzar II; succeedes Nebuchadnezzar as king of Babylon 562 B.C.E. until his assassination in 560 B.C.E. In the Bible, his name appears as Evil-Merodach.

Amytis: daughter of Astyages, king of Media; twin sister of Mandane; wife of Nebuchadnezzar, king of Babylon; mother of Amel-Marduk; aunt of Cyrus II.

Astyages: son of Cyaxares; king of Media; father of Amytis and Mandane; grandfather of Cyrus II.

Atossa (named for Hutaosa): daughter of Cyrus and Cassandane; sister of Cambyses II.

Belshazzar: son of Nabonidus and Nitocris and so the (illegitimate, I imagine) grandson of Nebuchadnezzar.

Cambyses I (King Cam): King of Anshan (Parsa); husband of Mandane; father of Cyrus II.

Cassandane (Sanda): of the Pasargadae, Achaemenid clan; daughter of Pharnaspes; sister of Otanes; wife of Cyrus II, mother of Cambyses II and Atossa.

Cassiya/Kassiya: daughter of Nebuchadnezzar; wife of Neriglissar; mother of Labashi-Marduk; (half-, I imagine) sister of Nitocris and Eanna-sharra-utsur (sharing the father Nebuchadnezzar).

Croesus: king of Lydia from 585–547/546 B.C.E.

Cyrus II: son of Cambyses I and Mandane; niece of Amytis; grandson of Astyages; raised by Median slaves Spaco and *Mit(hradates) who called him Bartatua until he was ten years old, then returned to Parsa; husband of Cassandane; father of Cambyses II and Atossa; succeeds his father as king of Anshan (Parsa); becomes king also of Media when he defeats Astyages (550 B.C.E.).

*Davcina: Babylonian daughter of Qudashu and Khai; sister of Iddina.

Egibi: family name of Babylonian entrepreneurial family that becomes a powerful corporation beginning with **Nabu-ahhe-iddin (Khai)** and endures for several generations.

Gobryas: from Susa; club-footed son of Mardonius; as a boy, becomes Cyrus's and Cassandane's ward after Mardonius is killed.

Harpagus: palace steward to King Astyages.

Hutaosa: from Susa; wife of Vishtaspa/Hystaspes; mother of Darius (I).

Itti-Marduk-balatu (Iddina -- this nickname is historical): eldest son of Nabu-ahhe-iddin (Khai) and Qudashu; heir to the

Egibi estate.

Labashi-Marduk: son of Cassiya and Neriglissar; becomes king of Babylonia after Neriglissar; assassinated within months of taking the throne (556 B.C.E.).

Mandane: (legitimate) daughter of Astyages, hence princess of Media; half-sister of Amytis; wife of Cambyses I; mother of Cyrus II; I imagine that she commits suicide upon being told of her newborn's (Cyrus's) death.

Mardonius: army veteran who served in the Elamite palace in Susa; father of club-footed Gobryas.

Mithradates (Mit): Shepherd slave to Astyages's palace who with his wife Spaco raised Cyrus II (whom they called Bartatua) from infancy until Cyrus was ten years old.

Nabonidus: Aramean from defeated Harran; son of Adad-guppi; courtier in the Babylonian court; husband of Nitocris; father of Belshazzar; becomes king of Babylonia after Labashi-Marduk is assassinated.

Nabu-ahhe-iddin (Khai): son of Babylonian farmer Shula Egibi; scribe, entrepreneur; husband of Qudashu; father of Itti-Marduk-balatu (Iddina); founder of the Egibi family corporation.

*Nahhunte: head of the palace in Anshan.

*Nathan: from Nippur, Jewish scribe for Nebuchadnezzar; son of *Rabbi Yakov ben-Isaiah and *Michal; moves with Amytis to Media.

Nebuchadnezzar II: son of Nabopolassar; king of Babylon/Babylonia from 605 B.C.E. until his death in 5462 B.C.E.; father of Nitocris (illegit, I imagine), Eanna-sharra-utsur (Ean), and Cassiya by an Ishtar temple slave from Uruk (I made up this unnamed earlier woman/wife); husband of Amytis; father of Amel-Marduk by Amytis.

Neriglissar (Igliss): probably served with Nebuchadnezzar on campaign against Jerusalem in 587 B.C.; husband of Cassiya (so, Nebuchadnezzar's son-in-law); father of Labashi-Marduk;

king of Babylonia after Amel-Marduk; reigned from 560 B.C.E. until his death in 556 B.C.E.

Nitocris: daughter of Nebuchadnezzar; wife of Nabonidus; mother of Belshazzar; high priestess of the goddess Ishtar at the Eanna temple in Uruk.

Nupta: of the Babylonian Nur-Sin family; wife of Iddina.

Otanes: Achaemenid; son of Pharnaspes; younger brother of Cassandane; brother-in-law of Cyrus.

Pharnaspes: Achaemenid; father of Otanes and Cassandane; father-in-law of Cyrus

Prexaspes: son of the chief (zapanitu) of the Pasargadae.

*Sadeghi: the evil groundsman of Cambyses I's Anshan.

Šilhak-Inšušinak: king in Susa of Elam.

Spaco (probably itself a nickname; means simply "Dog"): Shepherd slave to Astyages's palace who with her husband *Mit(hradates) raised Cyrus II (whom they called Bartatua) from infancy until Cyrus was ten years old.

Spitamas: Median army veteran; husband of Amytis (after Nebuchadnezzar had died and she'd returned to Ecbatana).

Ennigaldi-Nanna (born *Susanni): daughter of Nabonidus and Nitocris; becomes high priestess of the Babylonian god Nann-Suen's temple in Ur.

Tepti-Huban Inšušinak: crown prince in Susa of Elam.

Vishtaspa/Hystaspes: from Susa; joins Cyrus's army; husband of Hutaosa; father of Darius (I).

Zarin: of the Pasargadae; marries Otanes.

CITATIONS FOR QUOTES

P. 12 "There's a big plot of land, an estate actually, four brothers..." C. Wunsch, "The Egibi Family's Real Estate in Babylon (6th Century BC)," 1999, *Urbanization and Land Ownership in the Ancient Near East,* 404.

p. 12 "already planted with date palms. Bright green..." G. Van Driel, "The Rise of the House of Egibi," 1985, *Jaarbericht van het Vooraziatisch-Egyptisch Genootschap Ex Oriente Lux* 29: 63.

p. 16 "Although it was a rightful succession..." Nabonidus's Inscription 1, cited by Paul-Alain Beaulieu, *The Reign of Nabonidus, King of Babylon, 556-539 BC,* 1989, Yale, 106.

p. 16 "Within only a few months, the boy-king's..." Berossus cited by Paul-Alain Beaulieu, *The Reign of Nabonidus, King of Babylon, 556-539 BC,* 1989, Yale.

"The heavens declare the glory of God." The Bible, Psalm 19:1.

p. 33 "The chiefs of each Parsan tribe were there..." Herodotus's *Histories* I, 25; cited by Pierre Briant, *From Cyrus to Alexander: A History of the Persian Empire,* translated by Peter T. Daniels; 2002, Eisenbrauns, 18.

p. 39-40 "'I had no thought of kingship for myself,...'"

Nabonidus's Inscription 13, in the context of a prayer: Col. VII, lines 38-56, cited by Paul-Alain Beaulieu, *The Reign of Nabonidus, King of Babylon, 556-539 BC*, 1989, Yale, 89.

p. 44 "3 GAR 1/3 *qa* palace of Amel-Marduk..." Daniel T. Potts, *The Archaeology of Elam: Formation and Transformation of an Ancient Iranian State*, 1999, Cambridge, 293.

p. 49 "Maybe some combination of people from highlands and lowlands..." Based in part on the Bible, Daniel chap. 8. Biblical prophets spoke out of their times and places. They were less fortune-tellers than wise and pious people of an invisible god. "Prophecies" in the book of Daniel likely came from times long after the events they purported to predict. Perhaps it happened something like this. I.e., an educated Yahweh-worshiper observed events, interpreted them as the doing of God. When they came to pass as so "predicted," they were remembered and maybe to those yet others were later added. Also informed by Henkelman's definition of Persians (Wouter Henkelman, *The Other Gods Who Are: Studies in Elamite-Iranian Acculturation Based on the Persepolis Fortification Texts*, 2008 Nederlands Instituut voor het Nabije Oosten). Lowland urban Elamites met with highland agro-pastoralist Iranians; note the dimorphic zone in eastern Khuzestan.

p. 58 "Just because I did not attend your schools..." In anti-Nabonidus rhetoric, he's described as making much of his literacy though unlearned. He uses the symbolic language of days and months to add weight to particular events. "Nabonidus also quotes the learned name of the month Ulilu in his inscription commemorating the elevation of his daughter to the high-priesteshood of Nanna-Sin," (Paul-Alain Beaulieu, "An Episode in the Fall of Babylon to the Persians," *Journal of Near Eastern Studies* 255, citing Erica Reiner, *Your Thwarts in Pieces Your Mooring Rope Cut: Poetry from Babylonia and Assyria*, Michigan Studies in the Humanities 5 (Ann Arbor, 1985, p. 8). Beaulieu. writes, "Similar quotations of hemerologies by

Nabonidus were, as already pointed out, more purposeful, although the king probably also relished the aura of learned sophistication and obscurity they created" (Beaulieu, *JNES*, 256).

p. 72 "'City of the finest divine powers,' Nabonidus said...'" "A Praise Poem of Ur-Namma C" for text see https://etcsl.orinst. ox.ac.uk/cgi-bin/etcsl.cgi?simplesearchword=Suen&simple search=translation&searchword=&charenc=gcirc&lists= accessed (again) Jan. 24, 2024.

p. 74 "tiny lapis lazuli beads. A row..." Based on descriptions of a headdress discovered at Ur by Sir Leonard Wooley, *Excavations at Ur*, (1929; latest edition 2013) Routledge, 67.

p. 80 "I am in awe." Nabonidus said exactly that: "I am in awe" in response to these discoveries, cited by Ronald H. Sack, *Images of Nebuchadnezzar: The Emergence of a Legend*, 2004, Susquehanna, 90

p. 81 "'Last night I had a dream. Both Nanna-Suen...'" Inscription 15 (Paul-Alain Beaulieu, *The Reign of Nabonidus, King of Babylon, 556-539 BC*, 1989, Yale, 240).

p. 81-82 "'O Sîn, lord of the gods,...'" See Ronald H. Sack, *Images of Nebuchadnezzar: The Emergence of a Legend*, 2004, Susquehanna, 91.

p. 92 "I led my people from remote mountains... peace." Nabonidus's Inscription 13, Col. III, 15-17; mention of Akkad and Syria in Col. II, 6-10.

p. 101 "The women whooped and cried in ululating shouts..." Justin I.6.13-15; cited by Amélie Kuhrt, "Women and War," 2001, *Journal of Gender Studies in Antiquity* 2: 9.

p. 103 "Those pistaka-eaters sure are brave" Nicolaus of Damascus probably following Ctesias *FGH* 90 F66.34. Astyages calls them "terebinth-eaters," but the word translated "terebinth" likely refers to a nut very like but not identical to pistachios (Heleen Sancisi-Weerdenburg, "Persian Food and Political Identity," in *Food in Antiquity* - J. Wilkins et al. eds. - Exeter, 1995).

According to the Greeks, it was associated with masculinity and wild nature.

p. 104 "Kurash the Anshanite, son of Shishpish." This seal (PFS 0093) was discovered at Persepolis, an heirloom that has lasted until today. Whether or not the Elamite Kurash on this cylinder is the same as the Kurash called "king" In the Assyrian annals continues to be debated. I believe with many scholars that the image depicts Cyrus II's grandfather, the first Cyrus. It reads "Kurash the Anshanite, son of Shishpish (Teispes)." See Daniel Potts, "Cyrus the Great and the Kingdom of Anshan" in *Birth of the Persian Empire*, 2005, British Museum, 18. It might come from a time before he was king (Matt Waters, *"Parsumaš, Anšan, and Cyrus,"* in *Elam and Persia*, 2003, Eisenbrauns, 292).

p. 105 "Suddenly a jagged thread of lightning...on the house." Nicolaus of Damascus tells this *FGrH* 90 F66 (41) cited by Pierre Briant, *From Cyrus to Alexander: A History of the Persian Empire*, translated by Peter T. Daniels; 2002, Eisenbrauns, 240. Nicholaus of Damascus' account does not specify the types of birds much less Cyrus's falcon. It does tell, however that predatory birds alighted on the house -- a good sign. And he includes notice that they made a great meal on the mountain and the next day, "made confident by these birds," they fought -- *FGrH* 90 F66 (41).

p. 106 "I want you to head the troops..." "So reckless was he," Herodotus writes, that Astyages put the wise and seasoned old general, Harpagus, at the head of the troops, "forgetting what he had done to him" Herodotus I, 127; cited by Amélie Kuhrt, *The Persian Empire: A Corpus of Sources from the Achaemenid Period*, vol. 2, 2007, Routledge, vol 1, p. 57.

p. 122 "King Nabonidus's dedicatory inscription..." From Paul-Alain Beaulieu, *Legal and Administrative Texts from the Reign of Nabonidus*, 2000, Yale, 240-241: "A newly discovered fragment (3) concerning rebuilding the Elhulhul in Harran elevates Marduk in a way consistent with inscriptions from the time of

Belshazzar's regency. ("Among the monumental inscriptions of Nabonidus, only those written during Belshazzar's regency fully acknowledge Marduk as supreme god with a befitting array of titles and epithets, while relegating Sin to a subordinate position" p. 240). "The position of Marduk in fragment 3 is compatible only with the 'orthodox inscriptions' written under Belshazzar's auspices during his father's stay in Teima." It's possible either that "rebuilding the temple was entirely Belshazzar's responsibility and was completed while the king was still in Teima, or it was initiated by Belshazzar but completed by Nabonidus after his return to Babylon. The second alternative has the advantage of harmonizing the contradictory data of the Elhulhul inscriptions in that it explains how Nabonidus could claim in inscription 13 to have restored Elhulhul after he left Teima, while at the same time the funerary stela of Ada-guppi could insist that she witnessed the rebuilding before her death in the middle of Belshazzar's regency."

p. 132 "They'd make promises only if she were there..." It was intriguing to me to find ancient historians prioritize Amytis in comments about Cyrus's conquest of Media – that the peoples of central Asia (Parthians, Saka and Bactrians, in particular) "spontaneously submitted to Amytis and Cyrus" when they learned "that Astyages had become the father of Cyrus and Amytis... his wife" (Nicholaus of Damascus FGrH 90 F66.46 and Ctesias, Persica, parag. 2; cited by Pierre Briant, From Cyrus to Alexander: A History of the Persian Empire, translated by Peter T. Daniels; 2002, Eisenbrauns, 33). Ctesias writes that after conquering Astyages, Cyrus kept him and Amytis in his palace where Astyages was like a father and Amytis was more like a mother than a wife to Cyrus (FGrH 68 F 9[2]; cited by Maria Brosius, Women in Ancient Persia, 559-331 BC, 1996, Oxford, 21).

p. 135 "'Cross the Halys, and Croesus...'" Herodotus tells this in his The Histories (I.53).

p. 142 "As for Elam... relationships." See Wouter Henkelman,

The Other Gods Who Are: Studies in Elamite-Iranian Acculturation Based on the Persepolis Fortification Texts, 2008 Nederlands Instituut voor het Nabije Oosten, 10-17.

p. 144 "in excellent Sumerian -- revealing her..." Joan Oates, *Babylon,* revised ed., 1986, Thames & Hudson, 38-39.

For details about the Akitu ceremony, I've drawn heavily from J. Bidmead, *The Akitu Festival: Religious Continuity and Royal Legitimation in Mesopotamia,* 2004, Gorgias.

A few of the resources I leaned on for details about the looks and layout of ancient Babylon include Andrew R. George, "A Tour of Nebuchadnezzar's Babylon," in *Babylon: Myth and Reality,* 2008, British Museum, 54-59; Joachim Marzhan, "Koldeway's Babylon," in *Babylon,* 2009, Oxford, 46-53; and Marc Mierhoop, "Reading Babylon," in *The American Journal of Archaeology,* 2003, 107:257-275. The following description of the Akitu festival is heavily dependent on J. Bidmead, *The Akitu Festival: Religious Continuity and Royal Legitimation in Mesopotamia,* 2004, Gorgias.

SOME OF MY SOURCES FOR INFORMATION

J am tremendously grateful to those scholars of ancient Near Eastern history and literature who have made troves of information available and keep adding to what we know and how we think about the people, the places, and times that these narratives so lightly brush. I'm deeply sorry not to provide exhaustive documentation for all the research that informs these books. In lieu of even a bibliography, here is a list (itself incomplete) of some of the hundreds of scholars, past and present, whose work informed the story I tell.

ABRAHAM, Kathleen
  Abusch, Tzvi
  Ackerman, Susan
  Ackroyd, Peter
  Adams, Robert McCormick
  Ahn, J. J.
  Aiken Littauer, M.
  Albenda, Pauline
  Albertz, Rainer

Albright, William F.
Alexander, Robert L.
Algaze, Guillermo
Allen, Lindsay
Al-Rawi, F. N. H.
Álvarez-Mon, Javier
Amiet, P.
Aminzadeh, B.
Anthony, David W.
Ataç, M. A.
Austin, M. M.
Avigad, N.
Axworthy, Michael
Bahrami, B.
Bahrani, Zainab
Baker, H. D.
Balcer, Jack Martin
Bandstra, Andrew J.
Barkworth, P. R.
Barnett, R. D.
Barr, James
Basham, A. L.
Basirov, Oric
Beach, Eleanor F.
Beaulieu, Paul-Alain
Beckwith, Christopher I.
Bedford, Peter Ross
Berman, Joshua
Betlyon, John W.
Bidmead, J.
Bivar, A. D. H.
Black, Jeremy A.
Boardman, John
Boda, Mark J.

Elgood, C.
Errington, Elizabeth
Eshel, Esther
Eskenazi, Tamara Cohn
Farazmand, Ali
Farrokh, Kaveh
Finkel, Irving L.
Flattery, David Stophlet
Fleming, D. E.
Foltz, Richard
Forsyth, Neil
Foster, Benjamin R.
Foster, Karen Polinger
Fried, Lisbeth S.
Frye, Richard N.
Fuchs, Esther
Gabrielli, Marcel
Galil, Gershon
Garrison, Mark B.
George, A. R.
Gese, Hartmut
Gopnik, Hilary
Goulder, M.
Grabbe, Lester L.
Gray, Louis H.
Grayson, Albert Kirk
Green, Anthony
Green, Jack
Griffiths, A.
Guliaev, Valeri I.
Gurney, O. R.
Hallo, William W.
Handley, Morrison
Harmatta, J.

Kratz, Reinhard
Kriwaczek, Paul
Kuhrt, Amélie
Lacocque, André
Lambert, W. G.
Landes, David S.
Lang, Mabel L.
Langdon, S.
Lavī, Ḥabīb
Leach, E. R.
Leiden, W. H. C.
Leloux, Kevin
Lemaire, André
Lerner, G.
Lincoln, Bruce
Linssen, M. J. H.
Lipiński, Edward
Littman, Robert J.
Liverani, Mario
Lloyd, Alan B.
Lloyd, Seton
Lucas, C. J.
Luckenbill, Daniel David
Lukonin, Vladimir G.
MacGinnis, John
Machinist, Peter
Malandra, William W.
Malbran-Labat, F.
Marzhan, Joachim
Master, Daniel M.
Matsushima, E.
Mattila, R.
McGovern, Patrick E.
Meier, S. A.

Pham, Xuan Huong Thi
Pinches, T. G.
Poebel, A.
Polosmak, Natalya
Pongratz-Leisten, B.
Potts, Daniel T.
Powell, Marvin A.
Pritchard, James B.
Oeming, Manfred
Rainey, A. F.
Reiner, Erica
Rolle, Renate
Röllig, W.
Rollinger, Robert
Root, Margaret Cool
Roth, Martha T.
Sack, Ronald H.
Salonen, A.
Sancisi-Weerdenburg, Heleen
Sanders-Goebel, P.
Sandison, AT
Sarraf, M. R.
Sarshar, Houman
Sasson, J. M.
Schaudig, Hanspeter
Schauensee, D.E.
Schmid, H.
Schmidt, H. P.
Schwartz, Martin
Schwemer, Daniel
Scurlock, Joann
Seymour, M. J.
Shahgolzari, SM
Shea, William H.

Shiff, L. B.
Simpson, St John
Skjærvø, P. O.
Soudavar, A.
Stadter, P. A.
Stausberg, Michael
Stein, Gil J.
Stevens, Marty E.
Stol, Martin
Stolper, Matthew W.
Stott, Katherine
Stronach, David B.
Sumner, William M.
Suter, David W.
Tavernier, J.
Thomas, D. R. A.
Thureau-Dangin, F.
Trotter, James M.
Tuplin, Christopher
Ulansey, David
Ungnad, A.
Vallat, F.
Van de Mieroop, Marc
Van Driel, G.
Vargyas, P.
Vaughn, Andrew G.
Veen, J. E. van der
Vogelsang, W. J.
Waerzeggers, C.
Waters, Matthew W.
Watts, James W.
Weiershauser, Frauke
Weinfeld, M.
Weisberg, David B.

Weiss, L.
Weitzman, Steven
Widengren, G.
Wiesehöfer, J.
Wiggermann, F. A. M.
Williamson, H. G. M.
Winter, Irene J.
Wiseman, D. J.
Wunsch, C.
Yamauchi, E.
Yavari, A.
Younger, K. Lawson
Zaccagnini, Carlo
Zadok, Ran
Zawadzki, S.
Zevit, Z.
Zimansky, Paul E.
Zimmern, H.

AUTHOR'S NOTE

*S*poiler alert
    Without Cyrus, we may never have had a Bible. And without Amytis, we may never have had such a Cyrus. But few people have heard of Cyrus much less of Amytis. And the role of Babylon in biblical development remains largely the purview of scholars and academics. I excuse our collective ignorance in part because the relevant facts are few, hard to come by, and riddled with uncertainties. That doesn't mean, however, that they can't make for a good story.

This book – and the others in what has become a multi-volume (and could be many more) saga – happened because I started making things up. I had intended to write a nonfiction tome about a momentous period in human history (the transition from Babylonian to Persian rule) and the figure who stands at its center (Cyrus II, a.k.a. Cyrus the Great). But the more I learned, the more intriguing the women became. And the more I learned, the more I was forced to accept what all the experts say: we know very little... concretely, that is. But oh, so much was possible.

I threw myself into the research. At some point, what I was learning reached a critical mass and slipped its academic bonds.

Turns out, the research had been seducing my imagination all along. Finally, I had to face it: they'd eloped. I found myself filling in the long blanks between certainties with imagining what might have been. Ancient characters had become real people. Events and places began to take the shape of a novel. Also, I have a terrible memory. In all that research, I was finding associations and connections that no one seemed to have made before, and I didn't want to forget them. My best vehicle for keeping track was story.

I agonized. My agent at the time pointed out the cold truth. We simply could not sell a book of nonfiction with, er, fictional elements no matter how extensive the disclaimers. So, I ordered the facts back into their house, and tried to send my imagination packing. Alas, the two would not be parted. Finally, a friend of mine who had herself recently made a shift from nonfiction to historical fiction confronted me. "Why are clinging to nonfiction?!" she said. "Accept it. It's a novel."

Once I did, the project became pure delight... and a full-blown series with Amytis, my tree-hugging bastard princess, their through-line (though the second book focuses on Cyrus's story – birth and coming into the kingship of Anshan). That said, this particular book – which weaves together coincidental stories focused on Amytis (in Media), Nabonidus and company (in Babylonia), and Cyrus and Cassandane (from Anshan/Parsa as the empire expands) – stands (or falls) on its own.

How much of the book is true? I understand the question, I do. And my best short answer is: all of it and none of it. This is a work of fiction. I made it up. That said, it is entirely based on huge amounts of hard-core research undertaken over the many years that this particular project has demanded and over decades before that as a student of the history and literature of the ancient Near East (what today we call the Middle East), earning a Ph.D. on the topic and a tenured appointment as a professor of it.

The question deserves a longer answer. First, a warning: the information here is best read *after* the novel itself for a couple of reasons. Most obviously, it will spoil the suspense. Equally serious, your brain might break. There are so many odd names and potentially unfamiliar references below that without having a story to hang them on... well, consider yourself warned.

Second, a quick note about sources. This story takes place 2500 years ago. Many relevant records, such as there ever were, are long gone. But many remain. Sources for modern researchers are wildly diverse, some primary and many derivative. They range from ancient histories (such as Nabonidus's *Chronicles*, Herodotus's *The Histories*, and to a lesser extent Xenophon's *Cyropaedia*) to modern archaeological excavation reports, from business records of the Egibi family and incantations and prayers of Babylonia to the Bible's Psalm 137, from an ancient world map drawn on clay (now housed in the British Museum) to a palace gate in stunningly beautiful tile (now housed in Berlin).

No one knows it all. Much about the period and its people is still in question. Hints and rumors abound. Ancient histories followed different rules than what we might wish. For such as Herodotus, one of our most important sources, reporting absolute fact was not always as important as telling a good story. And not all of the sources, ancient and otherwise, agree with each other.

For example, of Cyrus's birth and even lineage, we cannot be sure. We don't know the date of his birth, whether he came from royal or peasant parentage, or even what the name Cyrus means. As to the latter, I follow the logic represented in the novel – that it is Elamite and connotes protection. As for Elam, there is considerable disagreement about the state of Elam before Cyrus (and after Assyria). For a long time, the prevailing view was that it had been destroyed by Assyria or in severe decline; some (Matt Waters, Esther Fuchs, Daniel Potts) believe that it was fragmented into independent polities; and some (Wouter Henkelman and Mario Liverani) that it may have continued to be central to a strong network of relationships.

Concerning Cyrus's parentage, I follow Herodotus and others in naming Mandane as his mother and Cambyses I as his father. Both Cambyses I and Cyrus II called themselves kings by the Elamite title "king of Anshan" not "of Persia." I understand Anshan to have been a city (the modern archaeological site of Tel el-Malyan) within what was a relatively small and loosely confederated country of Parsa, itself arguably within the greater control of Media (and so of Astyages). In this fiction series, I follow Herodotus's dramatic and gruesome tale of Cyrus's birth and rise.

Then there's Amytis. That she is historical we can agree. But exactly who she was, not so much. Even her lineage is in question. Was she the daughter of Cyaxares or of Astyages? The (very few) records differ, and her mother is consistently nameless. That she is remembered as marrying Nebuchadnezzar II to satisfy the treaty established by Cyaxares and (Nebuchadnezzar's father) Nabopolassar allows me (almost) to have it both ways: I represent her as the daughter of Astyages, married to Nebuchadnezzar only because Cyaxares did not have any daughters. (I don't know if the historical Cyaxares did or didn't have daughters.) There is no record of Amytis being a bastard.

As daughter of Astyages, Amytis would have been sister to Mandane, Cyrus's mother. Herodotus tells the story hinted at here about Astyages's paranoia leading him first to get Mandane married off to Cambyses of Parsa and then of attempting to kill Mandane's infant son (the newborn Cyrus). I made up Mandane's subsequent suicide.

Herodotus tells that Nebuchadnezzar built the Hanging Gardens of Babylon for Amytis, homesick for the forested mountains of her beloved home, Media. There is reason to believe that such Hanging Gardens never existed, or if they did that they refer to gardens far north of Babylon built by an earlier monarch.

But the legend was enough for me, and enough to imagine a young woman committed to protecting (by virtue of Nebuchadnezzar's honoring the historical treaty) her native land from Babylonian development.

Ancient Media (in modern Iran) was indeed a wild, biodiverse, naturally rich and beautiful place, even more so than I could describe in the novel. And ancient Babylonia (in modern Iraq), especially under Nebuchadnezzar had a reputation even greater than I show for destroying places in the course of conquest and building like mad. It is hardly a stretch to imagine the clash between what we now call environmental preservation and "development.

I don't think it's a stretch to imagine a tension (timeless and human) in the Babylonia of these stories between those I think of as blue-blood traditionalists and the diverse peoples that Nebuchadnezzar imported and who continued to immigrate for decades after him. Or rather, the tension Babylonian citizens for generation back felt in the face of foreign elements. We know that Nebuchadnezzar's policy in war was to take from conquered nations the best and brightest, to bring them back to Babylonia and put their smarts and skills to work. Babylonian exiles such as those from the defeated nation of Judah were given positions throughout the empire, including the palace, as important tradespeople and intellectuals. What's more, these "foreigners" bore descendants many of whom identified more and more as Babylonian (rather than, say, Judahite). Nebuchadnezzar's court was cosmopolitan, and not all Babylonians were happy about that. Some native Babylonians, especially of the higher classes and with a stake in the nation's face and future would have had issues with such integration. That a foreign woman might bear the crown prince, as in this story, may have been intolerable for some people.

We don't know for certain that Amytis was the mother of the historical Amel-Marduk (my Bushu). But among other things (timing, e.g.), it appears that after the historical Amel-Marduk succeeded his father, Nebuchadnezzar, to the throne of Babylon, there was a wave of Median immigrants. Many Babylonians didn't like it. There is evidence that Amel-Marduk was sympathetic to these Medians, which supports the possibility that he was (half) Median himself.

I follow the scholar Irving Finkel in believing that a document recovered from this time, "The Lament of Nabu-shuma-ukin," is Amel-Marduk's. (Some of that historical text is in this novel.) Its composer, a finely trained poet, calls himself the son of Nebuchadnezzar and says he was wrongfully imprisoned. He promises to devote himself to the god Marduk, if the god would only secure his release. Hence, the name-change to Amel-Marduk, "servant of Marduk." In ancient Hebrew (transliterated), Amel-Marduk is Evil-Merodach and shows up in the Bible as the Babylonian king who released the Jewish king from prison and accorded him an honorable place "at the king's table." (Because of how easily English-speaking readers might confuse the English "evil" with the Hebrew "Evil," the transliteration [not to be confused with translation] of a name meaning "servant of," I chose to spell it differently [erroneously] as Evel.) This Evil-Merodach, nee Nabu-shuma-ukin, may well have met the Jewish king in prison.

Jewish legend also lands Amel-Marduk in prison (and furious with Nebuchadnezzar ever after). We do not know why the prince was imprisoned, but the most likely reason would be an attempt to usurp the throne. Sleeping with the king's women would have demonstrated such an effort. I made up the love story that supports it.

I also made up the love story between Amytis and Khai. But I didn't make up Khai and admit that I fell a little in love with the historical man myself. As I note in the character list, Khai is based on a Babylonian by the name of Nabu-ahhe-iddin, from the family Egibi. Nebuchadnezzar's near manic building – walls,

temples, palace, quays – surely created a lot of work and opportunity. (This likely dropped off under subsequent monarchs,
further exacerbating conflict between long-time citizens and
people of foreign descent.) Babylonian society was stratified,
with "citizens" (from among which politically powerful elders
came) at the top. But – during Nebuchadnezzar's reign in particular – for industrious, intelligent, and entrepreneurial people,
advancement was possible.

The historical Nabu-ahhe-iddin (my Khai) was such a person.
We have a remarkably large repository of records from his busi-
nesses spanning generations and including some family information. From humble beginnings with a small family farm, this man
developed a full-blown corporation with holdings in transporta-
tion, real estate (including rentals), banking, and of course farm-
ing. We know that he served for a time as a palace scribe and may
well have had close dealings with Amytis during the course of a
long and dynamic career.

The historical [Khai] also worked for the historical Neriglissar, whom I call Igliss. As per this story, Neriglissar appears to
have participated in the Babylonian campaign against Judah (see
below). Neriglissar was a member of the prominent Babylonian
Nur-Sin family and did marry Kassiya (or Cassiya), daughter of
Nebuchadnezzar, to become the king's son-in-law. His son with
Kassiya was indeed Labashi-Marduk for whom [Igliss] had lofty
ambitions.

The family of Adad-guppi, Nabonidus, and Belshazzar is
historical. I found the historical Adad-guppi to be so intriguing
and her name not too difficult that I decided not to call her
anything else. No one but a handful of scholars knows about
Adad-guppi, so I wanted to give her a chance out in the wider
world. Adad-guppi is sometimes called a priestess. Indeed the
historical record of her devotion to the moon god of her native
place, Harran, is striking. Also, we know that she secured and
maintained an important position in the Babylonian court lasting

through several kings. Adad-guppi had been taken by the Babylonians along with her son, Nabonidus, from Harran, when the Babylonians and Medes together brought the Assyrian empire to its knees. Without, I hope, giving away what's to come in the next books, Adad-guppi lived, according to an inscription that we still have, in good health until the ripe old age of 104 years old.

Incidentally, those familiar with the biblical narratives might recognize the place name of Harran and maybe even link it with Ur. A whole lot of the greater biblical story begins in those sites. Abraham (then Abram) departs from Ur with his family, including father Terah, wife Sarah, and nephew Lot and settles in Harran, where Abraham is said to have heard God's call to "Go... to the land that I will show you." Ur and Harran were the two cities of the moon god. I'm not sure what to make of these connections, but there's yet another story in there somewhere. Oh, and Abraham's leaving Ur and then Harran appears in the Bible right after the Tower of Babel story. (Babel/Babylon – not a coincidence. See below.)

When I first began this project, I was ill-inclined toward Nabonidus, having accepted the ancient propaganda against him. With a whole lot more learning under my cap, Nabonidus has become admirable and even dear to me. Ultimately, his story (only part of which appears here) strikes me as a classic tragedy. Historically, he was the king of Babylonia whom Cyrus defeated. But I'm getting ahead of myself. The historical Nabonidus relevant for this book was indeed a person of the Babylonian court, son the intriguing Adad-guppi, probably husband of Nitocris (fascinating in her own right), and the father of Belshazzar. Nabonidus had a reputation for obsession with tradition -- the things and ways of the past. He also seems to have been a bit of an autodidact, not having had the benefit of a formal education, perhaps, or the patina of scholarship that scholars from Babylon's long-standing families had.

Incidentally, the tradition of the king's own daughter serving the moon god's high priestess, specifically in Ur was an innovation of Sargon's that lasted for another 500 years. We even know the name of the daughter who served: Enheduanna. We still have several of the hymns that she is said to have composed herself, written "in excellent Sumerian -- revealing her as the first known literary figure; even her portrait has survived." She is shown on a limestone plaque that archaeologist Leonard Woolley discovered at Ur.

The biblical book of Daniel, set during the period of the Babylonian exile but dating from centuries later, occasionally conflates or switches Nebuchadnezzar and Nabonidus. (Notice "switches" not "confuses," because it could have been intentional.) The Bible is a great resource for information about the ancient world, including the history of the ancient Near East. But it does not report things exactly as they happened, and we mistreat its narratives when we expect them to report facts like modern journalists should do. This does not make the Bible "wrong," but rather our reading of it. And we miss what may be of most interest and value in the biblical texts by requiring them to conform to our expectations. Stepping off my soapbox... The biblical book of Daniel portrays Nebuchadnezzar as enduring a period of madness from which God heals him. That's too delicious to ignore.

Many scholars, myself included, believe that the decade that *Nabonidus* (Babylonia's king at the time) spent apart from Babylon lies behind that story, at least in part. In Book #1, I nod to the fact that the Bible chooses to tell the crazy-guy story as Nebuchadnezzar's madness. There certainly was plenty about Nebuchadnezzar that could justify such a representation in the eyes of the people responsible for Daniel-the-Book's final form.

That Belshazzar is sometimes wrongly called Nebuchadnezzar's son makes more sense if they were indeed related. I make the historical Nitocris the mother of Belshazzar (and so Belshazzar is grandson of Nebuchadnezzar). This is not historical but not impossible, either. Contrary to popular (Bible-based) belief, Belshazzar was never the king of Babylonia. He did however, perform kingly duties (and I suspect would have been delighted to be confused as king for real) when his father Nabonidus, then king of Babylonia, was absent from Babylon for those ten years mentioned above.

The conflict between Nabonidus and his son Belshazzar concerning the Babylonian pantheon was real and leads directly into the events of Book #4. As for Croesus, there's a good bit of information widely available about him, and this narrative doesn't stray far from that.

Kara is fictitious; slavery in the ancient world is not. It *is* complicated, though. (Try this on: slaves could themselves own slaves.) People regardless of race or creed could become enslaved in the event of war. And the conditions of their servitude ranged from torturous brutality to virtual autonomy. (A great resource for understanding slavery in Babylonia is Muhammed A. Dandamaev's *Slavery in Babylonia*, translated by Victoria A. Powell.) Finally, whatever the status and conditions of a slave, the basic denial of personal liberty would have been, then as now, dehumanizing and unacceptable to those who experienced it (demonstrated not least by the historical Bariki-ili, who had a reputation for running away).

The Jews. Next to Amytis, my favorite part of this whole story. Some background in super-brief: The nation of Israel, which gained international attention during Solomon's reign in the tenth century B.C.E. when the temple in Jerusalem was built, fractured into two after Solomon's death. The northern kingdom, confusingly also called Israel, was defeated by the Assyrians toward the end of the eighth century B.C.E. Many of those Israelites were removed to places within the Median empire, hence my reference to Jews in the capital, Ecbatana.

Judah, the former Israel's southern kingdom, with its capital of Jerusalem endured. But it was subject to the vicissitudes of politics to the east. Ultimately Babylonia's rise made Judah a vassal state. In 597 B.C.E., Nebuchadnezzar took issue with Judah's Egyptian alliance, laid siege to Jerusalem, and removed Judah's king of only three months, Jehoiachin/Coniah (who appears in Book #1). He also took from among Jerusalem's best and brightest, including the prophet Ezekiel, and took them to Babylon. Ten years later (587 B.C.E.), Judah's effort to rebel was met with devastating punishment. Nebuchadnezzar's Babylonian troops, including the historical [Igliss] utterly defeated the nation, destroyed the Jerusalem temple, brutalized its king, and took another wave of people to Babylon. It is possible that the "suffering servant" of Isa 52:13-53:12 was composed with Jehoiachin/Coniah in mind.

I think that the single most important event in the Bible's development is the Babylonian exile. It's important in two ways: for how it affected the theology and literature already circulating, and because it served as the catalyst to assemble and collect as well as compose what would become biblical texts. There was no "Bible" before this time. For all intents and purposes, there was no Judaism either. That is, the religion recognizable to us today as Judaism largely grew out of the land-less, temple-less condition of exile. It was a painful and a fruitful time.

Among many biblical texts, some of which I cite in the novel, the biblical story of the Tower of Babel was probably written or informed by Jews living in Babylon who had occasion to observe the many and grand building projects undertaken by Nebuchadnezzar. One of those projects was a huge and seemingly endless renovation of the temple of Marduk in the center of the city. People from many different nations, no doubt speaking diverse languages, worked in Nebuchadnezzar's Babylon. (Hence the biblical story's "confusion of tongues" and what Jews saw as an arrogant effort to reach the heavens.) Nebuchadnezzar's policy concerning conquered peoples was to take advantage of their skills and learning, putting such to use wherever they served him best.

It cannot be understated – the enduring effect of efforts to make sense of the chaos and destruction of Babylonian control and the nature of God and God's relationship to people that the exile generated among the intelligent, devout, and literate Jews taken into Babylon. Those efforts and the diversity of their answers permeate the Hebrew Bible and shaped a multi-faceted theology that many centuries later could (not necessarily but by interpretation) identify a Jew, Jesus, as the redeeming incarnation of a fiercely loyal and loving God.

I have tried to show a little of that here. Judean exiles, whom I call simply (and not quite accurately) Jews, permeated Babylonian society. We know of Bariki-ili, the slave desperate for freedom; and we know that Ezekiel exercised a liberty to preach and gather with Jewish elders in Babylonian exile. We know that a community of Jews lived and worked at literary pursuits in a district of the town of Nippur; and we know that many of the exiles from Judah and their descendants ultimately adopted and integrated into Babylonian society.

The Babylonian pantheon was multi-faceted, with gods and goddesses gathering in Babylon once a year from their respective cities in the biggest annual festival, the Akitu. I chose to use the archaic Sumerian name "Nanna-Suen" for the moon god of Harran/Ur rather than the Akkadian "Sin" lest English readers misunderstand the name as some modern moral judgment. The gods and goddesses so named in the novel and many more besides were part of a complex pantheon. The practice of reading divine messages in animal organs is real, as is the anxiety around an eclipse of the moon and the practice of beating copper kettle-drums to keep the bad at bay. The prayers I cite are based on extant documents of the time, and the biblical texts (not yet biblical of course) may have circulated or been composed under circumstances such as I depict.

A few miscellaneous notes: description of the furniture, clothing, and architecture reflects archaeological and scholarly research as much as possible. Media was known for its war horses, which were an international sensation, the product of careful breeding and what some called the magical grass on which they fed. The fields of Media grew exquisitely nutritious alfalfa. The alkaline lake is real, and so are the stone chimney formations that visitors to Anatolia can still see.

Earlier versions of these novels include footnotes citing sources, yet more information, and sometimes my own thinking about what I was learning, mainly to help myself remember what led me to make the narrative decisions I did. I've had illusions of making those footnotes available to readers. But they're terribly unwieldy (in the hundreds), and the research keeps coming. Likewise, any bibliography would number in the hundreds, probably over a thousand. Yikes. So, I include here only those sources (hopefully all) from which I have drawn direct quotes. It feels incomplete. But then, such is life.

ACKNOWLEDGMENTS

I'm guessing that any project that spans at least a decade from inception to completion represents the support, goodwill, and contributions of all kinds from more people than a book's "Acknowledgments" can cover, no matter its author's efforts to be exhaustive. That's certainly true here. My apologies to those I've missed! Thank you.

And thank you, each and every named below. I've had illusions of providing detail to describe the nature of the contributions each person or group (libraries! my students! professional organizations!). But like my bailing on providing an exhaustive list of specific sources and an exhaustive Author's Note, I'm sorry to provide only the barest list here. Its notice – meager – is inverse to my gratitude – great. Thank you.

Finally, a special thanks to my dad, Richard Swenson, and my (late) mom, L. Cecile Swenson whose support of my work has been so unqualified that I've had the luxury of taking it for granted. And to my husband, Craig L. Slingluff, Jr., a huge thanks for being so ceaseless a cheerleader of this project. I'm not sure I ever would have sent these books out into the world without your unflagging enthusiasm for the saga and the needling to publish it, such as only a person sharing one's life, day in and day out, can do.

Thank you! Richard Abate, Khooshe Aiken, Lindsay Allen, Hanadi Al-Samman, Gigi Amateau, American Academy of Religion, American Schools of Oriental Research, Willis Barnstone, Bennington Book Club, Biographers International Organization, Bodleian Libraries of Oxford University, Christiana Brenin,

Laura Browder, Ellen Brown, McKenna Brown, Theo Calderara, Bethany Carlson, Jamsheed Choksy, Susann Cokal, Meredith Cole, Jonathan Coleman, Michael Cordell, Rob Crawford, Cville Women Writers, Stephanie Dalley, Cliff Edwards, Robin Farmer, Louise Finger, Greg Fontana, Jeannie Fontana, Donna Freitas, Shirley French, Kathleen Gacek, Brad Graff, Martien Halvorson-Taylor, Kate Hamilton, Sandy Hausman, Stacy Hawkins, Paul Hilding, Stephani Hilding, Historical Novel Society, Doug Hoffman, Denise Honeycutt, Kate Hunter, Molly Ill, James River Writers, Eric Jarrard, Gretchen Kainz, Andrew King, Dean King, Chris Park, Eva-Marie King, Amelie Kuhrt, John Kutsko, (late) "Boots" Mead, Meg Medina, Manny Mendez, Alex Nagel, Jen Pearson, Stephanie Pearson, The Porches (Trudy Hale), Debby Prum, Ginny Pye, Emilie Raymond, Dianna Rostad, Charles Shields, Guadalupe Shields, Society of Biblical Literature, Maya Smart, Patty Smith, Jack Spiro, Devon Sproule, Beth Stefanik, Matthew Stolper, Jon Swenson Tellekson, Linnea Swenson Tellekson, Deb Swenson, Nigel Tallis, Sandra Treadway, University of Virginia library, Rachel Unkefer, Virginia Commonwealth University library, Virginia (Foundation for the) Humanities, Virginia Commonwealth University library, Claire Wachtel, Pat Watkins, Jon Waybright, Anne Westrick, Vera Wilde, Mark Wood, Women's International Study Center, Writer House, and Irene Ziegler.

MAP

This is a map of the Median Empire, Egypt, Lydian Empire and
Neo-Babylonian Empire in the 6th century BC (1024 px; there
are other sizes available).

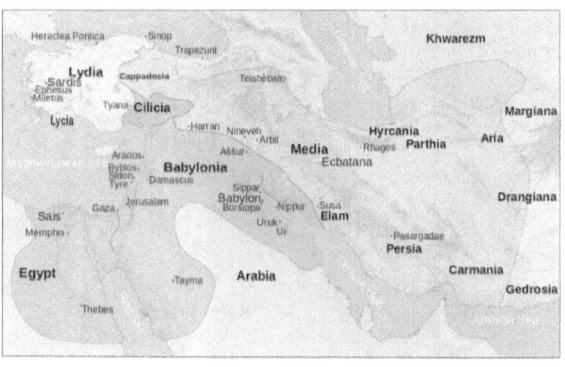

Date: 30 April 2013.

Source: File:Median Empire-hu.svg

ETOPO1 topographic data from NGDC (http://www.ngdc.
noaa.gov/mgg/global/global.html).

Author: Original: User:Szajci; English: User:WillemBK

(page URL) https://commons.wikimedia.org/wiki/File:Medi an_Empire-en.svg

(file   URL)   https://upload.wikimedia.org/wikipedia/ commons/b/bd/Median_Empire-en.svg

Attribution: Original: User:SzajciEnglish: User:WillemBK, CC BY-SA   3.0   <https://creativecommons.org/licenses/by-sa/3.0>, via Wikimedia Commons

ABOUT THE AUTHOR

Kristin Swenson, Ph.D. writes across genres. Tenured professor of religious studies with speciality in the history and literature of ancient Israel (Hebrew Bible), she is passionate about the natural world and loves a good story. All the better if a story connects the disparate threads of women and lesser known persons with what history we have. In addition to her writing, Swenson has developed an eco-grief practice to help people continue to advocate for the wild with equanimity and joy. She also maintains a website celebrating (and advising for) the eco-friendly kitchen. Swenson lives and works in Charlottesville Virginia and Duluth, Minnesota.

ALSO BY KRISTIN SWENSON

FICTION

In the Kitchen with Gracie May (PGB)

Let It Out at the Seams (PGB)

Genie of Pasargad (a Babylon/Persia novel; PGB)

Beat the Kettledrum (a Babylon/Persia novel; PGB)

A Falcon Takes Flight (a Babylon/Persia novel; PGB)

Howl of the Golden Jackal (a Babylon/Persia novel; PGB)

NONFICTION

A Most Peculiar Book: The Inherent Strangeness of the Bible (Oxford University)

God of Earth: Discovering a Radically Ecological Christianity (Westminster John Knox)

Bible Babel: Making Sense of the Most Talked About Book of All Time (Harper)

Living through Pain: Psalms and the Search for Wholeness (Baylor University)

What is Religious Studies?: A Journey of Inquiry (with Esther R. Nelson, Kendall Hunt)

POETRY

Haiku 365 at www.kristinswenson.com